Dear Jane,
I hope you enjoy my
little book. Please remember,
not <u>all</u> of it is true!
Much love,
Paul xx

A Brief Eternity

PAUL BEAUMONT

First Published in Great Britain 2013 by Dangerous Little Books

Cover image © istockphoto.com/teekid

For My Parents

Acknowledgements

I would like to thank the best-selling author, Elizabeth Kay, for her thoughtful feedback and incisive comments throughout the process of writing this book. I could not have hoped for a better writing mentor. The book began as a short story assignment at the culmination of a creative writing course with the Open College of the Arts, and I have the play-write Joanna Laurens to thank for helping me so much with the basics during that time.

Along the way I have enjoyed the endless encouragement of my daughter, Alice, who has cheered every semi-colon and much else besides. My special thanks goes to Kim Moore for giving me space to write; to friends who reviewed and commented, especially David Fine, Bob Newman, and John and Annette Byford; and to Jane Beaumont who helped to get me going in the first place.

I am indebted to Lucy McCarraher for proof-reading the manuscript; for CJ Werleman for saying yes; and to Joe Gregory for his enthusiastic expertise in the nuts and bolts of publication.

Praise for *A Brief Eternity*

I have never seen anyone bring Heaven down to earth quite like Paul Beaumont. His writing is like Douglas Adams meets Julian Barnes, with all of the intelligent wit that entails. Beaumont makes the obvious seem like a revelation, bringing his reader from the sublime to the ridiculous and back. Put reading *A Brief Eternity* on your bucket list, before it's too late.

Tim Hawken, award-winning author of the *Hellbound* Trilogy

A Brief Eternity is an impressively deft debut novel by Paul Beaumont. Couching the big "What if…" premise within a light touch writing style and comedic narrative allows him to pose the anomalies of Christianity through a range of likeable and eccentric characters. The author's biblical knowledge and analysis is spun like candyfloss through an engaging, funny and disturbing quest, which raises as many laughs as serious questions. Above all, a great read.

Lucy McCarraher, novelist and author of
How To Write Fiction Without The Fuss

Set in an afterlife which seems appropriate for the deity we have created for ourselves, *A Brief Eternity* takes a few well-aimed swipes at misplaced beliefs. It's a highly original premise, backed up with plenty of insider knowledge of the more unpleasant aspects of the Good Book. Heaven is not what it seems, and neither is Hell, and there are surprises in store as we explore this undiscovered country with Jerry, our bemused and ultimately indignant hero. It seems impossible to have a satisfactory conclusion to a novel set in eternity, but Paul Beaumont brings off an unexpected and convincing ending. Do we really want to live forever, when we look at it objectively?

Elizabeth Kay, best-selling author of *The Divide*

Paul Beaumont's *A Brief Eternity* provides an incredibly unique and interesting view into one of the most debated topics of all time: the afterlife. The story explores various dilemmas and paradoxes associated with the commonly understood concepts of Heaven and Hell, but with a humorous and entertaining slant. *A Brief Eternity* will make readers think, laugh, and then think some more.

David G. McAfee, author of *Mom, Dad, I'm an Atheist: The Guide to Coming Out as a Non-believer*

Funny and always surprising, *A Brief Eternity* is a knowing take on the after-effects of the Apocalypse in a way that I for one have never considered, and I bet you haven't either.

James Ferron-Anderson, author of *The River and The Sea*

Beaumont's novel is an entertaining and insightful parody of religious delusion. Drawing on experiences and teachings he acquired during his twenty-five year experiment with Christian fundamentalism, Beaumont beautifully depicts the absurdity of the religious inspired after-life.

CJ Werleman, author of *God Hates You, Hate Him Back*; and *Jesus Lied*

A brilliantly funny tale of one man's journey into Heaven following the Second Coming and what he finds there. *A Brief Eternity* had me crying with laughter. Paul Beaumont is definitely an author to watch.

Keri Beevis, author of *Dead Letter Day*

An Introduction by Dan Barker

A Brief Eternity is how religio-philosophical fiction should be written, not with the simplistic predictable purposes and banal outcomes of so many devoted authors who try to disguise their preaching as entertainment, but impelling the reader with plot and thought. This book faces the life-and-death issues honestly, not fleeing from uncomfortable questions or papering them over as so many less talented authors do. Paul Beaumont's lucid writing – often hilarious and sometimes heart-stabbing – makes C.S. Lewis seem sophomoric by comparison, even (dare I say) sacrilegious in the true believer's denial of true human value.

I started the book and read it straight through, cover-to-cover in one day. The scene in heaven's Crown Pub is to die for! Literally. And I have never read such a strange and riveting courtroom scene. On the last page of the book, I cried and yelled "Yes!" at such a candid, vulnerable, creative, surprising, courageous and satisfying ending.

To worship or not to worship. That is the question. Whatever the answer, *A Brief Eternity* deserves rapturous praise.
Dan Barker, author of *Godless*

Prologue

The blast of the horn exploded in Jerry's ears without warning. He dropped the phone that had been absorbing his attention and instinctively crouched, bringing his hands up to protect his head. He shut his eyes tight as terror seized his body.

The noise continued. He had no idea where it was coming from; it seemed to emanate from all around him, matching his hammering heart with its pulsating, insistent throb. The unbearable power of the sound overwhelmed Jerry and such was his disorientation that he felt himself to be detached somehow, almost as if he was floating. He forced himself to open his eyes.

He *was* floating.

A strangled, fearful cry forced its way out of his mouth.

Looking down he saw his shiny black phone on the pavement. The casing had shattered and a fragment of plastic lay a few inches from the main body of the device.

As he continued to drift away from the ground like a sluggish hot-air balloon, Jerry looked wildly around at the scene beneath him. The morning rush-hour traffic had abruptly stopped and many people were standing with their hands clasped around their ears to keep out the diabolical noise. Fear was etched into their upturned faces.

Two women, who Jerry guessed to be in their early twenties, clung to each other, their faces crumpled by trauma.

A few feet behind them a bald man in a grey suit and a red tie stared upwards, open-mouthed, like a muted singer frozen mid-song.

A middle-aged woman with candy-floss hair the colour of muddy carrots had simply curled up in the middle of the pavement and, most distressing of all, Jerry spotted a heavily pregnant woman – backed against the concrete wall at the foot of Charing

Cross Bridge – with both hands clutching at her swollen belly as she tried desperately to keep the noise away from her unborn child. Even though by now he was twenty or thirty feet above her, Jerry could clearly see her repeatedly mouthing the words, "Make it stop, make it stop," as tears flowed freely down her imploring face.

At that precise moment, as if in answer to her unheard pleas, the sound did indeed stop, as abruptly as it had started. In its immediate wake a cloying quietness descended on the city, like the haunting hush of an impenetrable fog.

1

At just after eight o'clock on what promised to be a glorious spring day, Jerry hopped on board the Northern line service at East Finchley station to begin his daily commute to central London. He sat down, the doors glided shut and the train pulled away.

A glossy leaflet lay on the vacant seat next to him and Jerry idly picked it up. It was a religious tract, although its content was somewhat unconventional for that genre of publication. A colourful cartoon depicted a mythical red beast with seven heads being ridden by a beautiful young woman with long, raven-black hair, alluring eyes and a body which was, to Jerry's mind, to die for. She was wearing a bikini, cut from purple and scarlet silk, revealing athletic thighs and a magnificent chest which the fully-stretched material was struggling to contain. The leaflet explained that the lady was none other than the Mother of Prostitutes and the Abominations of the Earth, aka, the Whore of Babylon. It went on to say that the Book of Revelation had her committing adultery with all the kings of the earth, getting drunk on the blood of the saints and generally sowing despair and misery amongst all those she encountered. Exactly the kind of behaviour, Jerry thought to himself, that would give harlotry a bad name.

With unwavering theological certainty, the leaflet revealed the message behind the biblical narrative: just as the kings of the earth had been seduced by the Whore, so were the modern day leaders of the world being misled by false religions. The answer was to embrace *true* religion and become a Jehovah's Witness before the impending apocalypse arrived and the chance of salvation was lost forever.

Jerry read a little more, but soon became bored. He wasn't in the mood to be converted – he never was – so he turned his attention to the newspaper he had picked up at the station a little earlier. The paper was still in the process of wringing its hands over the causes of the spontaneous riots that had taken place a couple of weeks ago in an upmarket suburban shopping mall just five miles from Jerry's flat. The event had unsettled the whole area and, for the first time, Jerry had been uneasy walking the streets of the capital, especially after dark. Copycat riots had flared up in other cities and a sense of menace seemed to have crept into the entire country, along with an irrational anticipation that worse was to follow. As Jerry read the paper it started to look to him as if "worse" had already arrived elsewhere in the world. He scanned one story after another that read like a miserable cliché of international news in the twenty-first century: widespread crop failure had re-ignited two brutal civil wars in Central Africa; a calamitous earthquake had left countless dead in Pakistan; and an alarming increase in military tension in the Middle East had, despite the best efforts of the UN, reached nerve-jangling proportions.

Jerry closed his eyes and set his mind to a happier thought: Rachael. He was still thinking about her as he pushed his way up the claustrophobic escalators and back out into the morning sun. Moments later, as he walked down the steps leading away from the Embankment tube station alongside the River Thames, his mobile let him know that a text had arrived. It was from Rachael.

Hey J, my stars say I should expect surprise 2day. U got hot date 4 me? Flashy dinner? Hope so! R xx.

Jerry knew that Rachael placed as much faith in horoscopes as he did, which was precisely none. However, it was clearly necessary to respond to her shameless appeal to be indulged, so he thumbed his own text in reply.

Sure. Table booked for 8. Surprise is, you're paying!

With a smile Jerry pressed Send. It was to be the last thing he ever did on this Earth.

2

It took a while for Jerry to readjust to the relative quietness after the sound of the almighty horn had stopped. When he had done so he was able to detect the anguished strains of weeping and wailing percolating up to reach him in his elevated position. No sooner had he registered these sounds than he heard a woman's contrasting voice crying out joyously, "Yes; yes. Oh Lord, yes."

Jerry twisted round and there she was, not fifteen feet away, arms reaching out above her; her enraptured face a picture of pure orgasmic ecstasy. She pulled at the hair at the top of her head, her pleasure unconstrained, and screamed, "Take me; take me, Lord."

The sight of a smartly-dressed business woman in her early forties apparently climaxing in mid-air at roughly the same height as Big Ben was undoubtedly a thoroughly surreal moment. But even this was immediately surpassed as he looked incredulously around and saw that there were hundreds, maybe even thousands, of other people also slowly ascending into the sky. The landmark high-rise buildings in the background looked like despairing fingers through which the city's inhabitants were slipping, leaving behind the giant tear of the River Thames glinting in the sunshine upon the weeping face of the Earth.

It was at this point that Jerry looked upwards and immediately understood what had been terrifying the onlookers on the ground. "Jesus Christ," he blasphemed, crudely, but appropriately.

A tall, muscular man, dressed in black, was hovering in the sky above, gazing down at the scene below and exuding complete confidence and control. In his right hand he held a slender golden trumpet.

The trumpet.

The shocking sight of a trumpeter standing unsupported in the sky did nothing to lessen Jerry's terror. Neither did the thought that the trumpet might be blown again, as Jerry realised that he was now far too close for his eardrums to withstand another onslaught. Instead, the trumpet remained at peace and its owner looked straight at Jerry who was immediately struck by the beauty and power of the man's eyes. Never had he seen such bright, sapphire blue. Never had he felt so transparent under the gaze of another being. The exchange, which was only momentary, left Jerry feeling heated up somehow; it wasn't entirely comfortable.

But Jerry pretty quickly had something else to worry about. He carried on rising and, as he still didn't know where he was going, he looked up again.

"God Almighty," he muttered, his profanity maintaining a consistently biblical theme.

Another man was now slowly descending on a cumulus cloud. It was difficult to make out any features, so dazzling was the light that appeared to emanate from him. To Jerry, though, the newcomer's appearance seemed at the same time to be both awesome and absurd. Obviously he was real – obviously! – but there was something kitsch here as well, like a scene from a low-budget Hollywood movie about the Second Coming of Christ.

Jerry's mind suddenly cleared and the thought struck him almost with a physical force. "Holy shit, I'm going to Heaven," he exclaimed, although it would perhaps have been more accurate to say that Heaven was coming to him.

In any event, he had no time left to think. The vision in front of him was fading as he entered a cloud. The whiteness of the light increased all about him so that he lost all sense of direction. Unable to comprehend, disoriented and confused, Jerry closed his eyes and prepared, for the first time in his life, to die.

3

Rachael's aspiration to become an actress of international repute had failed to become a reality. This, in spite of the fact that five years earlier, while in her mid-twenties, her portrayal of Stella in Tennessee Williams' *A Streetcar Named Desire* had been described by her local newspaper as "exquisite". Disappointingly, this now appeared to have been the pinnacle of her thespian achievements rather than a stepping-stone to stardom. Following "exquisite", there had been no exciting call from a well-connected agent promising her auditions in the West End. Instead, a few days later, the Regal's artistic director had taken time out from his job as a solicitor to phone and ask Rachael if she'd like to play Buttons in the Christmas pantomime, *Cinderella*. Even Rachael's love of performing had baulked at the thought of yet another re-run of tawdry cross-dressing and tamely choreographed farce, so she had declined and, in so doing, had quietly closed the door on a dream that had accompanied her since childhood.

Subsequently, working in an office had gradually evolved in her mind from being a temporary expedient to becoming a necessary and not unpleasant way of funding her modest standard of living. Most days she rather looked forward to interacting with people she considered to be good friends. Her current role in the finance department of an international publishing company was interesting and her colleagues, with one exception, were a boisterous, knockabout group who generally had a lot of fun together.

Rachael had arrived a few minutes earlier than usual this particular morning and was intent on reading the article that had caught her eye as she was flicking through a magazine on her journey into work. "Ten Ways to Make a Baby" promised to reveal up to nine methods of which she was so far unaware. She had persuaded herself that it was curiosity rather than latent broodiness that had sparked her interest.

She was half-way through reading about a complicated procedure involving lots of needles when her colleague, Fiona, placed a fresh cup of coffee on her desk, without even having been asked.

"Oh thanks, Fi."

"You're welcome," replied Fiona as she hummed her way round to her own desk, opposite to where Rachael sat.

"You sound happy," said Rachael.

"I am," replied Fiona.

"Well don't be," growled Charlotte from behind a partition. "It's annoying."

Fiona raised her eyebrows in Rachael's direction and received a knowing smile in return.

In many ways the two women were complete opposites, Fiona being petite and bone-snappingly thin, with a voice to match, wearing saucer glasses that tended to exaggerate the sense of timidity that pervaded her gentle personality. She was also unusually prim and no matter how quiet and restrained Rachael tried to be in her presence she often felt she was being slightly vulgar and loud; a raucous crow overwhelming the soft warbling of a dainty songbird.

Since Fiona's arrival a year ago, Rachael had felt the need to shield her from the rough-house playfulness of the rest of the group and, as a consequence of her protective instincts, had been rewarded with a somewhat unlikely friendship with the girl who was nearly ten years her junior.

The office currently comprised a dozen women and only two men, and, as could be expected, female perspectives dominated most topics, none more so than the mating game. Several of the older women were married, but the majority of the pack was not and they tended to possess liberal and relaxed attitudes to relationships with the opposite sex. Here again, Fiona was different.

Her fanatical Christian parents had schooled her rigidly in the need for sexual abstinence prior to marriage and, so far, she had been faithfully obeying their teaching. She had been dating Pete, a guy she met at church, for a couple of years and, as far as Rachael knew, the two of them were very happy together in spite, or perhaps because, of the rules of physical non-engagement.

Rachael had gathered from Fiona's regular Monday morning de-briefs on Yesterday In Church that the services were energetic and entertaining. The congregation consisted of families and young professionals with plenty of genuine commitment to their faith. This was rather different from Rachael's own limp religious upbringing. Even her grandmother had eventually stopped attending the relentlessly dull Beth Shalom synagogue located in the spectacularly inappropriately named Easter Gardens. Rabbi Bernstein had tried for years to get the local council to re-name the street and thereby remove an irritating theological juxtaposition, but they had doggedly refused, pointing out that the road and its name were there first. Despite half-hearted claims of anti-Semitism, and even a three-minute feature on local television news, everyone ultimately got bored with the whole argument and the controversy, such as it was, faded away. In much the same way, Rachael's family gradually lost interest in the synagogue as a whole and simply drifted off and left it alone.

Although Rachael didn't mourn the absence of organised religion in her life, she maintained a hold on the family values it had helped to reinforce and she still liked to celebrate the festivals of Hanukkah and Yom Kippur with her parents. This only really amounted to having dinner together, the vestigial religious traditions such as grinding through unintelligible Hebrew prayers having, much to her relief, long since disappeared.

But, whatever the decline of her own faith, Rachael was not about to defect to somebody else's, no matter how enthusiastically endorsed by personal recommendation. So, the first two or three times Fiona had plucked up the courage to ask her to come to church, Rachael had excused herself on the grounds of prior engagements. However, when it had happened once more she decided she needed to be straight with her well-meaning friend. Looking her in the eye she had explained, "Fiona, I'm Jewish."

"Oh, I didn't realise. I'm sorry."

"There's nothing to be sorry about."

"It's just that you don't…"

"Please don't say I don't look Jewish," interrupted Rachael. People often said this about her when they discovered her background and she always found it mildly vexing.

"No. Well, you don't, actually."

"I know. My hair's too blonde and my nose is too small. You may have noticed I cheat with my hair colour." Rachael pinched her nose between her thumb and index finger, and added, "The nose, however, is one hundred per cent natural."

"I'm sorry Rachael, I didn't mean to upset you," Fiona answered meekly. "It doesn't matter to God what you look like or even that you're Jewish. Jesus was Jewish after all, to begin with at any rate. But church is for everyone now; God is for everyone."

"Even for the Jews?"

"Yes, even for them. I mean, for you. It's for all sinners."

The word "sinners" stumbled into the conversation like a pork sausage salesman at a Bar Mitzvah. It hung around for a while not quite knowing what to do with itself until Rachael decided to grab it by the scruff of the neck and ask what it was doing there.

"Sinners? Is that what we Jews are?"

"Everybody is a sinner, Rachael, even Christians. The only difference is that we're forgiven."

"And the rest of us aren't?"

Fiona bit her lower lip and said nothing.

Rachael looked at her nervous friend and a thought crossed her mind. "If I come to your church, would you come to my synagogue?"

"Do you go to synagogue?" replied Fiona, clearly startled.

"Not for the last twenty years, but I'm sure they'd be pleased to see me. What do you think?"

"I'm not sure," murmured Fiona.

An awkward silence ensued until Rachael decided to bring the conversation to a close.

"Fiona, I appreciate you asking me. Honestly. I just don't think I'm ready for it right now, OK?"

"All right, but come sometime soon. It's really important and I'm sure you'll enjoy it."

"I'll think about it."

Since that discussion a few months ago, Rachael had felt no overt pressure from Fiona to comply with her evangelistic ambitions. She had, in fact, largely forgotten about it and certainly wasn't pondering its implications as she took a last gulp of coffee and finished her baby-making article.

"Very interesting," she said, to no-one in particular.

"The coffee or the magazine?" asked Fiona.

"Both, if I'm honest. Here, have a look." Rachael turned the magazine back to the start of the Ten Ways feature and handed it over to Fiona before fishing out a brush from her red leather handbag and dragging it through her thick, shoulder-length hair a few times. She switched on her computer and, while it was warming up, collected the empty coffee mugs and took them back to the small staff kitchen.

On Rachael's return to her seat, Fiona pushed the magazine across the desk towards her.

"That was quick," Rachael said.

"Yes, well, I don't really need any help in that department any more."

"What?" gasped Rachael. "Fiona! Oh my God! Are you...?"

"Yes!"

"Really?"

Fiona nodded rapidly in reply.

Rachael skipped round the desks and embraced the grinning young woman. "I'm so pleased for you," she said excitedly as she squeezed her congratulations into Fiona's meagre frame. Momentarily, Rachael wondered how Pete had managed the necessaries without damaging any of Fiona's vital organs and, suddenly conscious of the new life within, stepped back a pace so that she could look properly at her happy friend.

"Fiona, I'm amazed. Do you have a date?" she asked.

"Not yet. To be honest we're just so thrilled we haven't really come back down to earth."

Before Rachael could suggest that they must have some idea of timescales, Charlotte interrupted in a voice loud enough for the whole office to hear.

"Did I miss something? Is this National Hug-A-Friend Day, or what? And if it is, why is no-one hugging me?"

"Because you don't have any friends, you old trout," volunteered the office veteran, Martin, as he tried to coax a mangled sheet of paper from the tenacious grip of the photocopier. Charlotte gave him the finger but kept her quizzical gaze on Rachael and Fiona.

"Is it OK to tell everybody?" Rachael asked quietly.

"Yes," came the reply, but with sufficient reluctance for Rachael to realise that, even in her moment of triumph, Fiona's diffidence was going to render her mute.

"Would you like me to tell them?" Rachael offered, to which Fiona responded with a grateful, "Yes please."

So Rachael took charge, turned her friend to face the rest of the room, stood behind her and placed her hands on the girl's shoulders.

"Quiet, please. We've got an important announcement to make," she called out confidently. The room quietened, people stopped what they had been doing and looked in their direction. Once she was sure she had everybody's full attention, Rachael continued.

"Great news everyone. Fiona's pregnant!"

Rachael had been a little surprised herself by Fiona's revelation and from the look on their faces most of her colleagues were also somewhat taken aback. But this was as nothing compared to how Fiona herself reacted to Rachael's statement.

"No I'm not!" she squeaked hotly, indignation and hurt immediately flushing her face. "I am not pregnant," she added, almost spitting the denial as she stood up and turned to Rachael before momentarily burying her face in her hands. It was in that instantaneous flurry of her hand movement that Rachael's eye caught the unmistakeable sparkle of eternally-promised love. But by then it was too late; Fiona had pulled away and was running out of the office.

All eyes watched Fiona leave and, as soon as she was out of sight, they turned back to Rachael.

Confused and momentarily dumbstruck, Rachael looked down at the magazine where it lay open on the desk. She picked it up, searching for an explanation, and saw to her consternation that on the page opposite the article she had intended Fiona to read was another entitled, "Finding the Perfect Partner". The penny dropped with a doleful clunk in Rachael's mind.

"She's engaged; not pregnant."

The tension in the room was immediately broken as ribald laughter greeted Rachael's mortified clarification. "Shh, she'll hear you," she said.

"Well don't blame us," countered Charlotte. "Christ, Rachael, what were you thinking? I mean, she's not up the duff, is she?"

"No, of course not. I should have realised. I mean, she and Pete barely snog, never mind…"

"Screw," added Charlotte helpfully.

"Yes, thanks Charlie, screw. Well I've certainly screwed up, that's for sure. How could I have been such a schmuck? I'd better go and find her."

She picked up her handbag and retreated from the scene of her disgrace with one or two of the office staff still sniggering behind her. Following Fiona's earlier exit, she guessed, correctly, that her upset friend would have taken the elevator down the five floors to the ground level. A short time later, Rachael was there too and spotted Fiona just outside the main entrance sitting on a street bench looking down onto her lap at a sodden tissue crushed tightly into her fist.

"Shit," muttered Rachael to herself and pushed her way through the heavy glass door into the bright morning sunshine. She walked slowly over to the bench. Fiona shifted in her seat as she saw Rachael approach and looked away.

Rachael perched on the bench and wondered how to begin. As she searched for the right words she was suddenly overcome with an insane urge to giggle at the absurdity of her earlier gaffe. She forced herself to concentrate on the task in hand and began, a little shakily, "Look, Fiona, I'm really sorry."

"How could you have said that, Rachael?" cut in Fiona abruptly. "You know I couldn't be pregnant. You know Pete and I have promised to keep ourselves for each other until we're married. It's what we believe in."

"Yes, I know," replied Rachael as gently as she could. "I'm afraid I just got hold of the wrong end of the stick."

Fiona said nothing.

"I'm utterly ashamed of myself," continued Rachael. "It was a terrible thing to say; a stupid way to let down a friend."

Fiona took in a deep breath and exhaled slowly. She took off her glasses and squinted into the middle distance. The sunlight glistened on her wet eyelashes.

Conscious that her communication skills were having something of an off day, Rachael decided the best path to reconciliation was by way of physical comfort. She slid along the bench and put an arm around Fiona's shoulder, whereupon the recently betrothed slumped into her embrace and cried some more. It wasn't long before Rachael could feel the dampness of Fiona's tears soaking through her blouse.

"Sometimes I wish I was more like you," Fiona suddenly remarked, sitting up and making momentary eye-contact with Rachael.

"You mean always being able to find just the right words for every occasion?" replied Rachael.

"No, not quite," smiled Fiona wryly. "It's just that you seem so at ease with everyone, and they all like you. I always feel I'm on the outside somehow."

This time it was Rachael's turn to keep quiet.

"I wanted them all to be happy for me."

"Fiona, they *are* happy for you. Why wouldn't they be? If I hadn't messed up they would still be congratulating you now and making a big fuss of you; you know they would."

"Maybe," said Fiona.

Rachael held her friend's left hand and carefully inspected her new ring. "It's beautiful," she said, and Fiona smiled.

A bus hissed its pneumatics as it came to a standstill a little distance away, disgorging another dozen office workers onto the pavement.

"When did he ask you?" Rachael enquired after the bus had pulled away.

"Well, we've been praying about it for ages and both of us felt led that this was the right thing to do; we were just waiting for the Lord's timing. Then, when we were praying together the other evening, Pete really felt the Lord prompting him that the time was right, so he just came straight out and asked me."

"Wow! I guess you were obliged to say yes then, as he had it on such high authority."

"Yes! That's one reason why I love him; he's so in tune with the Holy Spirit."

"That's lovely,'" said Rachael a little weakly. She was pretty sure Hotline to God would not have been included as a requirement for finding the perfect partner in the article she had inadvertently given Fiona earlier.

"Come on, Fi," said Rachael at last. "Let's go back in and let them enjoy your good news. We can't stay out here all morning."

Rachael stood up, adjusted her skirt and waited. But Fiona remained on the bench and, looking up, said, "You go on, I'll join you in a minute. I'm afraid I got very angry earlier and now I just need to pray and get myself right with God."

"Oh, OK. I'll see you back upstairs then," replied Rachael a little nonplussed, not for the first time, by the proximity of Fiona's faith and her ability to access it so effortlessly.

Within a minute or two Rachael was back on the fifth floor, but decided not to go straight back to her desk. Instead she walked over to the large window at the end of the landing where the big rubber plant lived, idling its time away in dusty neglect. She looked across the top of the ancient plane tree outside to the ornate red-brick Edwardian building across the street, and tried to compose her thoughts. Something had been disturbing her ever since Fiona broke her news and, now that she had forced herself to be still for a moment, Rachael was able to recognise it for what it was: envy. It happened every time; whenever a friend announced their engagement or that they were pregnant she couldn't help asking herself why these happy events were occurring to other people and not to her. She despised herself for it, but at the same time couldn't ignore the fact that, along with a real sense of rejoicing in her friends' happiness, she also felt a little anxious that maybe time was starting to pass her by. The more often it happened, the more she worried about ending up alone.

She allowed herself a few more moments of introspection before pulling herself together and reminding herself just how happy she was with Jerry, and how content he seemed with her. If there was one person who could cheer her up it was him: she would postpone the diet for one more day – again – and get him to take her out that evening for an expensive meal. "Life's too damn short," she said to herself while extracting her mobile from her handbag and beginning to compose a text. Remembering her zodiac reading that she had looked at earlier that day, she included a reference to it as a way of winding him up. She smiled as she sent the message and then plunged back in to face the music at last, doing her best to avoid the mischievous looks that came her way. But as soon as she had sat down again, Charlotte glided over and enquired after the bride-to-be.

"Recovering, no thanks to me," Rachael told her.

"The little stick insect doesn't know how lucky she is getting someone to propose to her. I wish it would happen to me."

"It has happened to you. Twice," said Rachael.

"Yeah, I know. A right couple of losers they turned out to be. I mean, I would like it to happen with someone who knew the difference between a wife and a mother."

"Well when that happy day arrives, let's hope that the person who tells all your colleagues manages to communicate that you and Prince Charming are planning to tie the knot rather than suggesting that you are with child."

"Yes. I'll have to make sure I choose someone bright enough to tell the difference, won't I?"

"Very funny, Charlie."

"Actually, you must admit, it was pretty funny when it happened, Rachael."

"Not for Fiona it wasn't."

"Yeah well, I'm sure she'll get over it. I mean, it's not exactly the end of the world, is it?"

4

It wasn't death that met Jerry in the cloud; it was some bloke wearing a fluorescent yellow jacket.

"Just over here to your right if you wouldn't mind, sir. Thank you. God bless."

Jerry followed the crowd-controller's polite instructions. Ahead of him he could see a vast throng moving steadily towards some kind of brightly lit atrium. The adrenalin that had surged through his still-living body had impaired his ability to walk and he proceeded on trembling legs, noticing for the first time that from underneath the cloud that had previously engulfed him a solid floor had appeared. Once the last few tendrils of water vapour had melted away Jerry could see that he was walking on a shining, white marble surface exquisitely lined with soft ochre veins. He had never before seen such a magnificent floor and he felt that it was almost rude to be walking upon it. How, he wondered, had it been constructed up here in the sky without anyone noticing, and what on earth was holding it up?

He progressed slowly towards the hall. A beautiful, flaxen-haired young woman offered him a drink from a tray she was holding. Suddenly aware of his raging thirst, Jerry took one and drank it, feeling the cooling liquid pass down his grateful throat. It tasted wonderful.

"Thank you," he said as he replaced the empty glass on the tray, and received a spell-binding smile in return, before moving on.

Within a few minutes he had arrived at the cavernous hall: New York City's Grand Central Station, but bigger. Much bigger. Jerry entered the plaza, noticing that at both ends of the hall two enormous staircases swept down into the main concourse. It was towards these monumental stairs that people were moving, encouraged on their way by the obliging stewards. One of them directed Jerry towards the steps on the right, which were already packed with people, all of whom were men. Jerry looked behind him to the opposite staircase and observed that this one was crowded with women. A curious sensation flooded through his mind. He felt he was in a prodigious school of fish being corralled in a particular direction through forces beyond its own control or even understanding. He felt he needed his body to possess its own slipperiness so that, like the other silver fish, he could move effortlessly through the swell. He especially didn't want to come into physical contact with the people around him, as if feeling their touch would reveal something hollow in their nature, expose them as being nothing more than animated manikins. Maybe *he'd* turn out to be similarly vacuous. An empty man floating with other empty men in an empty dream-world sky.

At the top of the stairs there were more stewards, more smiles, and more of the "straight ahead; over there; God bless". The long, wide corridor Jerry and the other dummies were walking along looked as though it had come straight out of a brand new airport terminal. The floor was made from the same expensive-looking marble as downstairs; the lighting was clean and clear without being overpowering; and chic orange and lemon trees, planted in terracotta pots and bearing real fruit, were lined up along the edges of the walkways. Doors were set at regular intervals along the walls and men were being selected and shown through them.

Jerry kept walking. As he did so his sheer terror gradually started to subside. He concentrated on taking just one step at a time, not on trying to make sense of what was happening to him. He walked a long way, maybe as far as a mile. He had no reason to stop until, at last, one of the yellow-jackets caught his eye and motioned him and what were now the remnants of the crowd through a doorway.

The last thing Jerry expected to see on the other side of the door was nudity.

Men of all ages, shapes and sizes were getting changed, hanging up their clothes on pegs above wooden benches, just as they would in Jerry's local leisure centre back in Finchley; except of course that the room didn't smell of sweat and Deep Heat and piss.

A diminutive man – Korean, Jerry guessed – appeared and handed him a package of white clothes wrapped in soft plastic. No words passed between them but Jerry understood that he was supposed to exchange his office attire for the new outfit. Everybody else in the room seemed to be in the process of doing the same thing.

He made his way to a bench that ran along one wall of the room. The place he chose for himself was comparatively secluded, half hidden by a row of deserted jackets and shirts and trousers hanging up above a bench parallel to the one he was now sitting on.

Jerry ripped the plastic packaging from his new folded clothes, screwed it up into a ball and placed it underneath his seat. Before getting changed he realised he needed to pee, so he made his way through the room, which was big enough for at least a hundred people although it contained maybe only half of that now, and found the toilets. He relieved himself in a conventional, wall-mounted, porcelain urinal, wondering as he did so where it had been made and where the plumber lived who had installed it. He cleaned his hands and wiped them dry on a warm flannel which smelt of jasmine.

Returning to his seat, Jerry noticed that the changing room was emptying quickly. The dozen excitable men who remained were laughing and chatting together like good friends. They took no notice of Jerry and he changed hurriedly into his new white tee-shirt and tracksuit trousers.

The Korean made another appearance, this time carrying a new pair of white training shoes.

Jerry slipped his feet into them and found that they were a perfect fit. He tied his laces, stood up and removed his wallet from his jacket. There were no pockets in his new trousers and for a moment Jerry stood simply holding his wallet not knowing where to put it. The Korean pointed to a notice on the wall which declared in white text on a dark blue background, *Please leave all valuables in the changing room.* Jerry read it twice, just to be sure. The Korean sensed his uncertainty and reassured him. "Yes, yes. No need to take money with you. No watch either; not needed. Come, you must hurry now."

Jerry reluctantly removed his watch and put it into his jacket, but then fumbled through his wallet, anxious to keep on his person some token of himself and his immediate past. From the inner folds of the wallet he slid out a picture of Rachael and held it for a moment. It was a passport photograph, one from a series she had taken at a booth and that had ended up a spare. She had let Jerry have it, and he had kept it with him ever since, in an old-fashioned way. He smiled at the picture now, removed his shoe and laid the picture inside, hoping that Rachael would appreciate the gallant intent of his concealment and forgive the base treatment of her precious image.

By the time he was ready to go, Jerry discovered that he was the last to leave.

"Number ninety-seven, sir," he was told by another attendant as he left through a door at the opposite end of the room to the one by which he had entered. "Straight up the stairs and turn left. They're all numbered; you can't miss it."

Jerry jogged up the stairs and headed the way he'd been instructed. He walked along a corridor in which a few people were still milling about searching, like him, for the right entrance. From behind some of the doors that he passed he heard bursts of laughter, sometimes applause and occasionally some singing. He hurried towards his designated door.

When he eventually found it, he was amongst the last to enter the two-thousand-seat auditorium with its steeply banked rows of chairs. Light flooded in from the glass dome situated directly above the semi-circular dais at the front of the room and infused the chamber with a dreamy brightness. Once inside, the light chased itself from one reflective surface to another: white walls, white marble floor, white leather seats and the ubiquitous white tee-shirts and tracksuit trousers worn by every man and woman in the effervescent audience.

Jerry looked around for somewhere to sit, and spotted some empty seats in the fourth row from the front. There didn't seem to be many others available so he made his way there, interrupting the animated conversation of the two young women at the very end of the row. They stood up to let him pass and one of them acknowledged his presence with a smile.

Jerry nodded his thanks and sat down, one empty seat on either side separating him from his neighbours.

He stared straight ahead and found an unblinking Jesus returning his gaze from a painted canvas hanging on the wall at the front of the auditorium. The Son of God was pictured from the chest upwards and he too was wearing a white top, although his was emblazoned with a visage of the Sacred Heart: the vital organ depicted encircled by thorns and topped by wispy orange flames.

Jesus himself, adorned with a traditional beard and shoulder length hair, wore the ethereal expression of classic interpretations of holiness.

Jerry closed his eyes and tried to gather his thoughts, but they would not settle. Instead they swarmed like smoked-out bees inside his head, too distressed to return to the hive and its honeycombed familiarity. He tried, but he could make almost no sense of his experiences and had to admit to himself that he didn't know what the hell was going on.

When he opened his eyes again he saw that a middle-aged man was standing on the raised platform getting ready to address the assembly. He had a flabby, over-fed face, and Jerry noticed that a few tufts of hair were bursting out from the neck of his tee-shirt which, like everyone else's, was white.

Sensing that the meeting was about to be called to order, the auditorium had quietened and the few people who had missed the cue were being shushed into silence by their neighbours. The man at the front gripped the two sides of his lectern, waited a few more seconds, then called out in the elongated accent of the southern United States, "I'm Randy!"

Jerry couldn't stop a schoolboy guffaw escaping his throat at the unintended double-entendre, but it was of no consequence as any sound of his own was drowned out as Randy then bellowed, "In the name of our Lord Jesus Christ, welcome to Paradise!"

An almighty cheer greeted this announcement and the audience leapt to its collective feet with the whoosh of a suddenly-ignited inferno. There was clapping and cheering, hugging and kissing, and a huge outburst of whooping and hollering. The crowd remained alight for a full five minutes and even Jerry, caught up in the tension-breaking emotion of the moment, stood up and applauded self-consciously.

Shining with excitement, the young woman who had smiled at him earlier took a step nearer and embraced him. After a quick squeeze she moved away slightly but still held onto his arms. Her bright eyes locked onto Jerry's and she blurted out, "Isn't he wonderful?"

"Oh yes," Jerry replied, with as much conviction as he could muster. He was immediately aware that he had failed to mirror the girl's level of enthusiasm, so he quickly added, by way of distraction, "He's American, isn't he?"

"American? Why do you say that?"

"Well, he sounds like it."

The girl gave him an odd look and put a little distance between them.

"I'm talking about Jesus."

"Oh, him!" laughed Jerry, as he realised his faux pas. "I think he was Israeli, wasn't he?"

But the girl did not answer. She had turned away and was already locked in her next embrace.

"Or was he from Palestine?" Jerry said to himself, and sat down once more to wait for the commotion to subside.

When the quietness returned it had a fizzy quality to it, like static electricity, and was short lived. The speaker pointed to the large canvas behind him and called out, "It's because of him and his grace that y'all are here."

Bedlam erupted once more and this time, mingled with the cheering, Jerry could make out cries of, "Hallelujah!" and "Thank you, Jesus."

"Well now, if y'all would like to settle down," said Randy eventually, struggling to make himself heard over the noise, "I got some things I need to tell you." He waited a few moments longer and then added, "As I'm sure most of you folks know, what's just taken place here is what we call the Rapture."

More cheers and whistling, plus a loud "Praise the Lord".

"I know; quieten down now, if you can. There'll be plenty of time for expressing all your gratitude later on."

A warm hum of laughter rolled around the auditorium, although Jerry, for one, didn't get the joke.

"As I was saying," continued Randy, "the Rapture is what's happened and the Lord has brought all you mighty fine folks home. Y'all didn't even have to die like the rest of us; He just came and took you as you were and brought you straight to Paradise. Praise his holy name!"

"Praise God. Thank you, Jesus!" responded a number of enthusiasts.

"So is our God full of grace or is he full of grace?"

Judging by the loud chorus of "Amen" most people affirmed Randy's rhetorical question that grace is indeed what God was full of.

"Now many of us, and I don't mind admitting that I was one of them, was expecting that before the Rapture could happen a right old battle was gonna start down there in Israel and them Middle Eastern countries, just as it is prophesied in Ezekiel, chapter thirty-eight. So I guess you could say we were mighty surprised when the Lord Jesus decided he was gonna come back anyway, even though the Jews hadn't all returned to Israel like it says in the following chapter in Ezekiel; or that they'd not seen the light and got themselves converted as Paul says they will in Romans chapter eleven. I suppose we just weren't reading them passages quite right. But anyhow, our wonderful Saviour did say when he was on the Earth that he would return like a thief in the night. And folks, let me ask you a question here: what's the one thing we know about a thief who comes in the night?"

No-one answered.

Jerry could feel himself cringe with the Sunday school simplicity of the bluff American's enquiry. He leaned forward and made a basket with his fingers for his head and stared at the floor, hoping that someone would put the suffering silence out of its misery.

"Yessir," Randy called, pointing to a gangly, red-headed youth near the front.

"You don't know exactly when he's going to come," the young man volunteered.

"Amen! The brother there's got that right. The Lord himself said he was gonna come and surprise us, and he sure did that. But he gave plenty of warning, too. It says right in the Gospel of Matthew, chapter twenty-four that there will be famines, earth-quakes, wars and rumours of wars, and that those things will be a sign that the end is near. Now you just had a belly-full of all such things on Earth, so no-one can say that they hadn't been told."

The Bible reference resonated with the memory of what Jerry had read in his newspaper that very morning. When he had seen those gloomy stories of human suffering he had not detected in them a coded message for mankind, or thought that the dismal events they described presaged the greater cataclysm that had subsequently overtaken the world. Neither had the JW propaganda that he'd stumbled across made him seriously consider the possibility of apocalypse, even though it had been explicitly mentioned. He wondered what else he had been missing, and how unprepared he now was for all that was to come.

And what, indeed, was to come? Was he really going to be conscious – alive – for all eternity? Was that really credible? Could anything last forever? He had to conclude that it was starting to look that way. Either that, or he was having a bloody weird dream.

The audience was suddenly cheering again. Randy, having talked himself to a standstill, had finished his welcome speech. This long overdue cessation had not yet brought proceedings to an end, however; even as Randy was leaving the podium, his place had been taken by a new, serious-looking man.

The difference between Randy and his replacement could hardly have been greater. Eschewing the safety of the lectern, the newcomer stood tall and upright at the front of the stage, fixing his audience with piercing blue eyes. His straight blond hair was swept back from his sharp face and he was dressed entirely in black, with clothes that looked tailored to exactly fit his powerful body. He was the epitome of cool authority.

"I am Nathaniel, an angel of the Lord," he said in a voice as rich and deep as the Earth itself.

Not even Jerry baulked at the suggestion that they were being addressed by someone who thought he was an angel. Absence of wings notwithstanding, no-one was about to argue that this being was exactly what he claimed to be.

Nathaniel stood very still, held his unclenched hands at his side and shut his eyes. His broad chest lifted and fell slowly as he breathed deeply, purposefully. He appeared to be listening, although if that was indeed the case it could not have been to anything inside the auditorium. The room had become densely silent, and all eyes were on the angel.

He nodded his head briefly, then opened his eyes once more. Soberly, he scanned the room, not speaking until, so it seemed, he had looked into the face of every person present.

"It is a serious business to serve and worship the living God. He has chosen you to this end and you will not let him down.

"You know that it is written, *In my Father's house there are many rooms. I am going there to prepare a place for you.* Today that prophecy has been fulfilled and soon, very soon now, you will be taken to those prepared places. This is an act of divine grace, a privilege that as sinful people you do not deserve."

Nathaniel took another long, slow look at all the sinners arrayed in front of him. They stared back at him, transfixed.

"Worship is what you were created for and Heaven is the place where you will be the person God intended you to be, praising him for all eternity. As his word has taught you, here there is no more death or mourning or crying or pain."

At the mention of pain and crying a picture flashed into Jerry's mind. It was the pregnant woman he had seen at Charing Cross Bridge at the start of his Rapture odyssey. Her agony was forcing itself into Jerry's consciousness and wouldn't let him go. What had become of her? Had someone rushed to her aid as soon as that diabolical trumpet had stopped? Had she been lifted into the sky as well and, if so, would that not have added even more to her terror?

27

And what had happened to her unborn infant; she had looked as if the pregnancy was very close to being full term.

Jerry had stopped looking at Nathaniel while he contemplated the unfortunate woman's fate. He was crouching forward, elbows on his knees, examining his thumbs, thinking.

Nathaniel, meanwhile, had stopped talking. He was watching.

Jerry's mind was too busy to notice the silence and he continued ruminating while the audience held its breath.

The realisation that something had changed appeared in Jerry's mind like a well-mannered butler politely clearing his throat in his employer's presence to let him know that dinner was served. He sat up abruptly, looked straight ahead and was met in return by Nathaniel's weapons-grade stare.

"What's the matter, Jerry?"

"Nothing," Jerry replied in a cracked and startled voice.

"I can see that you are worried. There is no room for anxiety here; tell me what's troubling you."

It was clear that Nathaniel was not the sort of angel to take *nothing* for an answer, and Jerry knew a response was required.

"Well, yes, there is something," he managed to say.

Nathaniel encouraged him to continue with a raised eyebrow and a slight inclination of his head.

"When I was floating here," Jerry said, and stopped for a moment as the impossibility of what he had just said registered afresh. "When I was still quite near the ground I saw a pregnant woman in a lot of distress. She was frightened that the dreadful noise from that trumpet was hurting her baby and she wanted it to stop."

Nathaniel continued to look but did not speak.

"I remember how terrified she looked. I was thinking about her just now and was wondering what would have happened to her. Will she be OK, do you think?"

Nathaniel took a while to answer.

"Jerry, do you know the words of the Lord in Mark's Gospel, chapter thirteen, verse seventeen?"

"No," replied Jerry, feeling the anger rising within him as his ignorance was exposed for all to see.

"Then let me enlighten you. The Lord himself, when he lived among you and foretold his return said, "*How dreadful it will be in those days for pregnant women.*" Those days, Jerry, are now these days. They are today."

Jerry's first reaction was that this was a rubbish answer. His second was that he should let it be and keep his mouth shut. But he didn't.

"Will she be alright then, or not?"

Now both of Nathaniel's eyebrows were raised in response to Jerry's persistence.

"Only, I wouldn't want her or her baby to come to any harm; that just wouldn't seem fair."

Jerry and the angel held one another's gaze for a few seconds.

"I think we can trust that the Lord will treat her fairly, don't you, Jerry?"

Jerry noted the hardening of Nathaniel's face and, for a crazy instant, wondered if the angel was about to inflict some terrible curse on him. He told himself that it was only witches that did bad shit like that; the angels were the good guys. Everyone knew that – didn't they?

5

Earlier that day Jerry had arrived in Heaven without the inconvenience of actually having to die first. Now he was sitting alone on a crowded bus reflecting on the fact that he had managed, within an hour of his arrival, to antagonise an angel, something he had not knowingly achieved in all his previous thirty-five years of existence. It didn't seem possible that there was a much worse way to make a first impression than by being singled out from a crowd of two thousand novices by a senior figure and being publicly humiliated.

But it wasn't just the heat of embarrassment that had reddened Jerry's cheeks and troubled his mind, it was the incongruity of Nathaniel's response. After all, Jerry had asked his question because he had been worried about the pregnant lady. Even now, the memory of her anguish caused him discomfort and the tension of the reminder made him clamp his hands together. To his own mind, his concern had been justified and Nathaniel's answer inadequate. He tried to recall it now: something about it being a dreadful day for pregnant women. It was almost like they were being singled out for something especially unpleasant. As if waddling around with the weight of responsibility in your lower abdomen and the fear of labour in the back of your mind wasn't more than enough unpleasantness to be going on with.

The silver-grey bus was driving on the left-hand side of the road, Jerry noticed, just like back home, where he wanted to be. Fighting against a surge of self-pity he looked out of the window at a scene of unsurpassable beauty. A savannah stretched away from the road, with grasses fondled by the wind revealing a dozen different shades of soft yellow hues. Individual baobab trees, with their curiously disproportionate magnificence, were scattered across the plains. In the middle-distance were forests of trees that

Jerry didn't recognise and behind them, further away still, great mountains stood solid and triumphant and shamelessly glorious.

Jerry gazed at the mountains and wondered how they had got there. Had there been a smashing together of heavenly tectonic plates tearing subterranean rocks from their beds and thrusting them agonisingly skywards over countless aeons of time? Or had they, like everything he could see here, spontaneously burst into existence, thereby breaking virtually all of the known laws of physics, and probably most of the unknown ones as well? Had there been the flourishing of a divine wand, or the speaking of a divine word and, suddenly, there was the kingdom of Heaven all dressed up and ready to party? Otherwise how had something so big, so solid, been able to float around in the stratosphere undetected, defying gravity? Why hadn't an aeroplane bumped into it, or a satellite? Still, it couldn't be missed now, that was for sure.

The madness of the situation was in danger of overwhelming his mind, yet nobody else seemed in the least bit worried. A calm had descended on his fellow passengers and they looked as if they were happy to accept what was happening to them without the need to question or understand. Jerry realised that, at least for now, he needed to do something similar. There would be plenty of time for questions and answers later, so he folded his arms around his chest and concentrated on something else: the bus. It hummed quietly and drove smoothly. Jerry surmised that it must be powered by electricity, or the celestial equivalent, and allowed himself to take pleasure in the eco-friendly technology. But, his absorbing distraction didn't last long; the people in the bus had started to sing:

"Jeeeeeeesus, oh Jeeeeeeesus.

"Jeeeeeeesus, we love you, Lord.

"Thank you, thank you, Jeeeeeeesus.

"Oh Jeeeeeeesus, we praise you, Lord."

The sugary-sweet melody glooped into Jerry's ears and he sank an inch or two down into his seat. In contrast, many of his fellow travellers raised their arms and gently waved their hands, fingers splayed, in time with the rhythm of the chorus.

The next verse poured its viscous sentimental syrup into the bus, with only minor changes to the lyrics. Love became glorify and praise became bless, but otherwise the words were the same, and Jeeeeeeesus wrapped his everlasting arms around the singers and the song.

By the time the third verse had meandered into the indistinguishable fourth Jerry could sense that emotions among his fellow travellers were starting to run high.

Across the aisle from him a young man clenched his fist in a gesture of triumph, as if he'd just successfully played an outrageously difficult tennis shot. Nodding his head and, apparently, on the verge of tears he looked towards Jerry who quickly turned away lest his own perplexed look marked him out as even more of an outsider than must have been apparent already.

How were these people able to get off on such mawkish mush; and would he ever be doing the same? Jerry's disquiet deepened with these unhappy thoughts and he once again sought comfort in the view outside.

The scenery was changing. Single-storey, whitewashed buildings had appeared beside the road. They were simple constructions, with a door in the centre and a window either side, as might be expected for a storage shed or an animal shelter.

There were people, too, dressed in grey versions of the same clothes worn by Jerry and everyone else. They were mostly hanging around the little sheds, not doing very much, some staring at the bus as it hurtled by, others just sitting quietly, vacantly even.

Oddly, it was only people that Jerry saw. The animals for which the shelters were intended were nowhere to be seen. Not a single one. Jerry was resisting the obvious conclusion that the buildings were in fact peoples' houses rather than pig sties.

Sometimes there would be a break in the rows of sheds and the grasslands would reappear, but not for long. After a while, the buildings joined in an unbroken chain next to the highway, and spread away from it too, until it became apparent that the road was carving through an enormous, flat urban sprawl.

During the long hours that Jerry had spent on Earth not contemplating the quality of social housing in Heaven, he had never imagined that the property would be quite as bleak as this, or that there would be so much of it. Jerry, who was occasionally embarrassed by his own lamentable sense of direction, wondered how anybody could ever find their way to and from their own particular hutch amongst the massed array of almost identical little homes.

It was a long time before the architecture began to change. Modest two-storey houses started to appear, slowly at first, then in more abundance, until they had completely replaced the sheds and dominated the terrain. Trees and parks softened the vista and Jerry was given the impression that some of the more affluent suburbs of his own city had taken root and replicated themselves on a spectacularly massive scale to provide a comfortable habitat for an unimaginably large populace.

At one point they came to an area of much larger properties, followed soon after by grand mansions sitting on lush verdant lawns which swept down to the road. Jerry saw one colossal house, more of a palace really, with colonnades in front and two shining bronze lions sneering imperiously down their noble noses at anyone impertinent enough to look in their direction. As Jerry's mother was fond of saying, *having wealth is not the same thing as having class.*

Still the bus ploughed on, and the cityscape shifted again, encompassing endless streets of terraced housing punctuated by the occasional high-rise tower block.

They had been travelling for many hours. His fellow passengers had quietened down long ago and many had snoozed the journey away, as if riding a bus through Heaven's suburbia was an everyday event for which it wasn't worth staying awake.

Eventually the bus slowed down and turned off the main highway. Thirty minutes later, after navigating its way through a maze of criss-crossing roads, it pulled up in front of a large utilitarian-looking block of flats, five stories high and broader than it was tall. In spite of its plain appearance, the building evoked a spontaneous round of applause from the newly-awakened passengers, plus a few whistles and, predictably, plenty of cries of "Thank you, Jesus," and "Amen, Lord!"

Everyone disembarked and stood around to take in their new surroundings, enjoying the freshness of the outside air and the gentleness of the warm light. Oddly, Jerry thought to himself, the light seemed no different now to how it had been when they had begun their journey all those hours ago. If they had started in the morning it should now be early evening, but it didn't feel like that, somehow. It was as if time had simply stood still. Jerry looked up into the sky to try to get some sense of what position the sun might be occupying, but he couldn't grasp where it was. In fact, the sun didn't appear to be there at all, in much the same way that it isn't there at night. But this, self-evidently, was daytime.

A middle-aged man approached Jerry wearing the same uniform – white tee-shirt and trousers – and said in an East End accent, "Hello Jerry."

"Hello," replied Jerry.

"My name's Bob."

It was one of those déjà vu moments for Jerry. He just knew that the man's name would be Bob.

"You just come up from my old manor, ain't you?"

"You mean London?"

"That's the place. What's the weather like down there?"

"It's been fine. Today started off quite nice, although I left in something of a hurry so I don't know how it turned out."

Bob chuckled. "Yeah, caught us all a bit on the hop that did. Still, the unpredictable weather's one thing you're not gonna miss. Glorious sunshine everyday here."

"Yes, I was wondering about that," replied Jerry. "I was trying to see where the sun is, but it appears to be missing."

Bob smiled amiably, almost mischievously.

"Blimey, you're a sharp one. Usually takes people months to work out there's no sun. I can see I'm going to have to be on me toes with you."

"So why isn't it dark?" asked Jerry.

"It's never dark in Heaven, Jerry. There is no night. All our light comes from God Almighty himself. It tells us in The Book of Revelation, although I forget where exactly – it's near the end I think – so it shouldn't come as a surprise really. But I've even had men of the cloth up here who've not known that. Who'd have thought it, eh?"

Who indeed, wondered Jerry to himself, unsure whether Bob was marvelling at the ignorance of the clergy or at God's ability to replace the light from Earth's nearest star with his own omnipresent luminescence.

The two men started to move towards the plain apartment block, following the rest of the passengers from the bus plus a number of others who, like Bob, had come out to welcome them.

Six steps led up to the entrance and, above the front door, picked out in concrete relief, *Messiah Mansions* welcomed its residents.

Inside the door the Mansions' air was heavy with the smell of fresh paint.

"You're up here," said Bob, and took Jerry up two flights of stairs and down an echoing corridor.

"This is yours," he said and pushed open the door to room 212. "What do you think?"

"It's nice," said Jerry after taking a moment to look round. "Very nice. Thanks."

The room was spacious and comfortable, much like a suite in a three-star hotel. It had a desk, a small armchair, a coffee table, a flat screen TV on the wall and, somewhat incongruously given the ample size of the room, a single rather than a double bed. There was a large en-suite bathroom with a separate bath and shower, clean towels, toiletries and a white towel robe.

"Good. Good," said Bob, who seemed genuinely pleased. "I'm glad you like it."

"So, is this where I'll be living, Bob?" Jerry asked hesitantly.

"Well, yeah. It's very nice though, Jerry, isn't it? You said you liked it."

"But I mean, for always?" replied Jerry, suspecting that even such a well-presented room might begin to lose its appeal after a thousand years or so.

"Oh, you might be able to get a move somewhere else later, I suppose, if you really want to. It doesn't happen very often though. But you know what they say, nothing lasts forever."

"It turns out they're wrong about that though, aren't they, Bob?"

"I suppose they are," replied Bob softly.

The two of them looked at one another in silence for a moment, each registering the vastness of the time-span that lay ahead of them, and the impossibility of grasping what it would hold.

"You heard of Woody Allen, Jerry? asked Bob.

"Sure."

"Someone told me that he'd said that eternity is a very long time, especially towards the end."

Jerry smiled and said, "That's a good line."

"It is, but he got it the wrong way round. It's especially long at the start. You'll get used to it, son. This is a great place to be, and a whole lot better than the alternative, you can be sure about that."

"Why, what is…"

"It's been a long day. Better get some rest. I'll pick you up in the morning and show you what's what."

"But I thought you said there was no night here," said Jerry.

"I did, and there isn't, but we do get tired and need to sleep. We talk about waking up in the morning, just like we used to back on Earth, although it's really just a figure of speech, I suppose."

Jerry said nothing.

"It's time to sleep," continued Bob. "You must be knackered."

Jerry followed Bob to the door and closed it after him, resting his forehead against the flat wooden surface and looking down to where he might have expected a security lock to be found. There was none; the absence troubled him momentarily, until he reflected that he possessed nothing of his own that could be stolen, never mind that burglary would probably not rank highly as a favourite career of the inhabitants of Paradise.

He turned back into the room and surveyed what was apparently going to be his home for at least the next trillion years, maybe less if he got fed up with it. He walked across the varnished wooden floor to the desk, sat down and opened the top drawer. It contained a leather folder, embossed with the pious bearded face of Jesus underneath the prosaic title, *A New Arrival's Guide to Heaven*.

Jerry flipped it open.

The first page contained a welcome letter from Peter somebody or other congratulating the reader on their choice of residence.

Beyond the letter were sheets and sheets of information concerning religiously-themed amusement parks. *Victory* recreated the key battles won by the Chosen People as they cleansed the Promised Land of those tribes who were no longer going to be allowed to live there; *Sodom and Gomorrah* was an X-rated park that looked at the lives and premature deaths of the not-so-good people of those infamous towns; *Exodus* offered its astonishingly patient customers a forty-year stay in an authentic wilderness (manna and tents included); and *Flooded* featured a mighty deluge which, although a scaled-down version of the original, nevertheless left the punters who visited it in no doubt as to the awesome display of lethal power to which God had once treated the hapless inhabitants of planet Earth. A giant enamelled rainbow was stretched across the entrance to *Flooded* bearing the slogan "Never Again", an odd way to encourage visitors to return perhaps, albeit a reference – as a helpful footnote in the literature explained – to the biblical promise of a floodless future embodied in the seven-coloured arch.

After many pages of golf courses and other leisure facilities, Jerry came across an advertisement for Paradise Zoo, featuring an unlikely photograph of a fully-grown wolf grazing on some grass right next to a perfectly edible, but as yet uneaten lamb which seemed oblivious to the danger posed by the close proximity of its natural predator. The zoo possessed a wide collection of species, some of which had been extinct on Earth for thousands of years, and which had been gathered together to celebrate God's magnificent creation and thereby stimulate people to worship and glorify him still more.

Jerry closed the folder and searched the remaining drawers of the desk, all of which were empty with the exception of one containing a Gideon's Bible. He lifted it out and placed it on the desktop. He couldn't remember the last time he'd looked inside a Bible. He pushed the corner of the book with his index finger and watched his nail whiten as he exerted downward pressure. Three or four times he repeated this action, reluctant to probe inside.

As recently as that very morning he would have considered it extremely improbable that he would have been contemplating reading this ancient book. Now he felt that it might hold the key to him being able to understand what was happening to him and how he might be able to make sense of his life. So, after a few more moments of wavering he turned it over and opened it at the back. One of the few facts that he did know about the Bible was that it began with the book of Genesis and finished with Revelation. Bob had said that the lack of sunshine in Heaven was described at the end of the last book, so he started skimming through the final page or two. It didn't take long to find the reference.

Revelation chapter twenty-one, verse twenty-three: *The city does not need the sun or the moon to shine on it, for the glory of God gives it light, and the Lamb is its lamp.* Then a little further on, *there will be no night there.*

So Bob had been right, Jerry concluded as he ended his first ever Bible study, and not just about the lack of night. As Bob had told him, tiredness was a reality in Heaven and he now felt suddenly exhausted. He briefly visited his bathroom and then slipped into bed.

With a soft mechanical rattle a single blind was lowered outside Jerry's window. Although he hadn't instructed it in any way he was glad of its presence as it shut out much of God's glory and dimmed the light in the room.

The images of the day thrashing inside Jerry's head were less easy to subdue, but eventually they too subsided and he was finally overtaken by blessed, heavenly sleep.

6

Seated around the mahogany boardroom table, the six men, all wearing identical black business suits, stared at him with piercing blue eyes. Jerry sensed their impatience and, looking back down at his computer, searched again for the missing file. The names of the folders in the directory appeared on the left hand side of the screen, not in English but in hexadecimal code. He must have created them that way for extra security, but now he couldn't get his mind to translate them back into something comprehensible. Worse still, the right hand side, where the folder content should have been displayed, remained blank. Heavy with the effort, his index finger tapped the down arrow and the cursor scrolled from one folder to the next. But the result was always the same: tap, tap, tap; blank, blank, blank.

"It's here somewhere," he called out, his voice trembling like a little girl's.

All the men laughed: rude, caustic laughs.

"Shut up, you bastards," he shouted, this time in his normal adult male voice. It emboldened him.

"Anyway, what do you know about it? You've no right to laugh at me. You don't know anything.

"It must be here. Just give me a minute."

But his screen was now completely blank, and Jerry began to cry.

After a few moments of acute embarrassment, he heard one of the men clear his throat.

The cough came again a few seconds later, followed by a voice saying in a mid-west American accent, "Good morning, sir."

The man and his colleagues, the table and computer all disappeared and were replaced by the freshly unfamiliar room in which Jerry had fallen asleep. Jerry's relief at the truncation of his nightmare was tempered by the realisation that a man he didn't know was standing next to his bed and calling him sir. He was also more than a little perplexed to realise that, although the dream he had been having was indeed just a dream, the other unreal experience, the one where he floated off to a new life in the sky-world, still seemed to be true. It might have been easier if it had been the other way around. At least in his real dream all that had gone missing was his dignity and a hard drive full of files, whereas in the dreamy reality that he was now living he had lost his life's entire frame of reference.

His normal politeness had been temporarily misplaced too, shaken as he was by both his dream and his waking.

"Who on earth are you?"

"I am Worthy."

"Worthy of what?" said Jerry.

"I am called Worthy; it's my name."

Somehow Jerry had known the man was going to say that. "That's… unusual," he said.

"It's a Mormon name."

"Oh, you're a Mormon," said Jerry, feeling that he was now foolishly pointing out the obvious.

"Not any longer," said Worthy, a little guardedly. "I was raised in the Church of Jesus Christ of Latter-day Saints. I'm from Utah, you see, and most everyone in my neighbourhood was of the same faith. We used to feel sorry for all those people who thought differently. It was only when I died and came here that I realised – " as he said this there was a slight catch in his voice – "that what I had been taught and believed all my life had been mistaken."

Jerry thought that the man must have died quite young. He looked to be about the same age as Jerry himself; his dark hair had yet to start greying and his features, although unremarkable, were youthful still.

"I'm sorry," said Jerry. "As far as religion's concerned I didn't exactly nail it myself. I guess the important thing is that we're both here now, although, to be honest, I'm not at all sure what you're doing in my room."

"I'm your servant, sir."

"My what?"

"Your servant."

Jerry didn't know what to say.

"I'll keep your room tidy for you, clean the bathroom, and bring you a fresh set of clothes every day. I'll be looking after all your needs."

At this point, Worthy gestured at the pack of plastic-wrapped clothing in his arms and laid it down on the desk.

"Thank you, Worthy. All that sounds very nice, but I'm sure I don't need a servant. I mean, I can look after myself."

"I'm sure you can, sir, but I am here to serve you; it'll be my pleasure."

"Well, I can't say I enjoy housework any more than the next man, but having a servant is a bit anachronistic, isn't it?"

"Not at all," replied Worthy. "It's a thoroughly biblical concept, as I'm sure you know."

"Do I? Is it?" Jerry said, flustered once more by a reference to the contents of a book about which he was so ill-informed. "If you're sure it's OK with you," he added feebly, trying to avoid exposing his ignorance to his newly acquired servant.

"Sure thing. There are far worse things than being a servant in the kingdom of Heaven, after all. I'll let you get ready, sir. If there's anything you need me to do just leave a note on the desk or press this bell here." Worthy pointed to a small chrome plate on the wall above the desk. The word *Service* was etched into it in red letters above the push-button in its centre.

Jerry nodded and then remembered the absence of writing materials in the desk. "I don't have anything to write with," he said.

"I'll drop something off when I next come by," Worthy assured him.

"Thank you."

"You're welcome. You have yourself a great day, sir."

"You too."

Once Worthy had left the room Jerry muttered warily to himself, "Christ, first I go to Heaven, then I get a servant. Things are looking up."

Jerry set about getting ready for the day as best he could. It wasn't easy trying to anticipate what his first day in Heaven would be like, if indeed he could call it a day, given that it would be a period of continual brightness following, and indeed preceding, a never-ending continuum of sunless light. With a struggle Jerry forced himself to abandon such bewildering thoughts and concentrated instead on shaving off his stubble and on the comforting warmth of the shower.

Even so, it was difficult to keep his curiosity in check. Having had the ground taken quite literally from under his feet, Jerry found that he was questioning almost every detail of his new environment. Where was the disposable razor made? What would happen to it once he was finished with it? Was the water going down the plughole in a clockwise or anti-clockwise direction? And later, after he'd finished his shower, how would he find a decent dentist?

This improbable final question came to him when he heard the clink of metal amalgam hitting the sink as he spat out a mouthful of toothpaste froth. Jerry had always been an enthusiastic brusher but his high-energy approach to cleaning his molars now seemed to have got the better of him as he had dislodged his one and only filling and sent it clattering into the basin.

He tried with the tip of his tongue to locate the hole in the tooth, but was unable to do so. The mirror was all steamed up so he cleaned the surface with a towel and peered inside his open mouth. Wherever the hole was it was doing a good job of hiding itself and, if it weren't for the small lump of grey metal that he now tossed into the bin, Jerry could have been persuaded that the filling had been a figment of his imagination. However, in Jerry's mind evidence was evidence and he knew that a trip to the dentist would be required.

His conclusion released yet another flurry of imponderables whirling through his mind. Would he need to pay for his treatment? How would he earn money? Would his job be interesting? How can *anything* be interesting if you do it for all eternity?

He badly needed to stop philosophising and to start focussing instead on the mundane needs of the moment. He picked up the bag of clothes that Worthy had left for him. They were exact replicas of those he had been given the day before. He changed into them, folded yesterday's items and placed them inside the plastic wrapping. He didn't want to make too much work for his butler.

He looked at his wrist, where he normally wore his watch, and felt a moment of sadness at its absence. Then he sat on the edge of the bed to put on his shoes. Rachael looked up at him from inside one of his trainers, her picture still clear in spite of the hours it had been forced to endure in close proximity to the underside of his foot. He took out the photograph and held it in the palm of his hand, wondering when he would be able to see her again. Soon, he hoped, perhaps even today. They had so much to discuss. He worried about how terrified she would have been during the Rapture experience. She was scared of heights and once had stubbornly refused to accompany him on the London Eye because of her fear. He had tried to cajole her into riding the enormous wheel with him and she was close to tears before he realised he had pushed her too far; a miscalculation for which he had to apologise with meek words and a creamy hot chocolate at a South Bank café.

Since the last time he had seen her she would have, like him, discovered that God's existence was as real as the marshmallows she had insisted on having with her drink on that strained morning. As far as he knew, Rachael's religious upbringing had been as passive as his and had left only the mildest of legacies. She had told him, on the only occasion he could recall discussing the topic with her, that she had hated having to go to the special Jewish assembly at school while almost everyone else attended the compulsory Christian one in the main hall. Now that she was in Heaven she would finally be getting her wish and would be able to attend the Christian assembly with everyone else after all; the mother of all Christian assemblies, to be precise.

Jerry, for some intuitive reason, didn't want Worthy or anyone else to see his photograph of Rachael, so he looked around for somewhere to hide it. The Bible seemed the perfect place. Opening it in the middle, he placed Rachael's picture into the book of Ecclesiastes, directly under a text which read, *But the dead know nothing.*

"That can't be right," said Jerry to himself. Even though his biblical knowledge was paltry, his most recent experience had taught him that the dead were indeed very much alive and well, and that they knew plenty.

There was a knock on the door. Jerry snapped the Bible shut and put it back in the drawer.

"Come in," he called.

"Ah, morning," said Bob as he let himself in. "You ready to go?"

"Sure."

They left together, Jerry fretting once more at the absence of any means of locking his door.

"Shall I just close it?" he asked Bob.

"Yeah. It'll be all right. This ain't London, Jerry"

"No, I guess not. Where are we going?"

"We'll get some breakfast, then we'll have church, and then I'll take you to see someone."

"Who?"

"You'll see."

"Someone I know?"

"You know her very well, yes, but I'm not answering any more questions; you'll just have to wait."

The prospect of seeing Rachael so soon acted as significant compensation for the fact that Jerry was going to have to sit through a church service. Of course he knew that going to church would be an inevitable consequence of being in Heaven, and he was dreading it. Even the occasional wedding service that he had attended in the past had left him unmoved, the obvious enjoyment of sharing the couple's happiness aside. To him all the ritual, the genuflecting, the praying and singing had seemed – *had seemed* – like a silly game of Let's Pretend. Fortunately perhaps, he had no more time to dwell on the prospect as he found himself in a noisy dining hall. Evidently the residents of Messiah Mansions ate communally and, judging from the expressions of delight all around, joyfully.

"What do you fancy, Jerry?" asked Bob. "Toast, porridge, eggs?"

"I'd like some bacon sandwiches, please," Jerry replied, realising that twenty-four hours without food had left him famished.

"Sorry, son, vegetarian only."

"Really?"

"Yes, really." Bob turned to face Jerry directly and said with some firmness, "There's no death in Heaven, Jerry, so we can't eat meat."

"Oh, I didn't realise. I suppose it's obvious if you think about it," said Jerry, even though he hadn't thought about it, and nor would it have been obvious if he had. After all, everybody knew that plants are living organisms too, even if they do occupy a different branch of the Tree of Life to their distant animal relatives. It was hardly the plants' fault that the pressures of natural selection had not required them to grow legs on which they could run away, thereby consigning them to the role of sitting ducks in the food chain even, it seemed, in Paradise.

"That's OK," replied Bob, adding, "You weren't to know. I miss the old morning fry-up myself sometimes, but I can't complain, the vegetarian is very good."

The self-service dining hall was brightly lit. It had the feel of a student cafeteria about it, an atmosphere that was enhanced by the youthfulness of most of the clientele. Jerry and Bob helped themselves to a bowl of porridge each and collected a pot of tea from a counter. The long tables in the canteen were almost fully occupied and it was a while before they managed to find two empty seats where they could sit opposite one another.

Jerry watched as Bob bowed his head and mouthed a few noise-less words to himself before pouring tea for them both. The end of the spout of the white china teapot was chipped and a brown stain ran down the underside of its curved swan-neck.

Bob and Jerry were perched on the end of a table next to a couple who greeted them warmly once they had settled.

"Hi Bob, hi Jerry," they said in unison without needing any intro-duction. Bob returned the greeting calling them Roberto and Maria. Jerry was once again conscious of a palpable sense of déjà vu: he had known what their names would be even before Bob had spoken.

"I didn't know you two would be gracing us with your presence today," said Bob.

"Sometimes we like to get out of the big house and come and eat with the proletariat," said the stockily-built Roberto, with a wink in Jerry's direction. He then addressed the newcomer directly, his voice betraying what Jerry thought might be a Spanish accent or something similar.

"So, did you come up in the Rapture yesterday, Jerry?"

"Yes, I did."

"That must have been some experience, huh, to actually be met in the air by the Lord himself?"

"Well, it was quite unlike anything else I've ever experienced, that's for sure."

"I bet," laughed Roberto.

"Were you scared, Jerry? I think I would have been," said Maria, her eyes as dark and shiny as her curly hair.

"I was, yes. And very confused; I just didn't know what was happening."

Maria gave a sympathetic look but Roberto laughed again. "The clues were there though. Earthquakes, wars, all the signs of the End Times," he insisted, parroting the speaker who had so underwhelmed Jerry the previous day.

"So I've heard, but there have always been natural disasters and conflicts, since time immemorial," objected Jerry, and immediately thought better of having done so.

Roberto stiffened, held his fork just above his plate and responded evenly, "There were signs, Jerry. People should have known."

Jerry returned to his porridge and the four of them ate in silence for a while.

Uncomfortable with the slight sense of discord he had unwittingly created, Jerry struck up conversation again. "How long have you guys been here," he asked.

"Probably about thirty years for me; and Maria was called home by the Lord about five years after I had died."

"Seriously?" said Jerry. Neither of them looked as if they were older than their early thirties; they must have died as infants.

"What happened to you? In real life. Back on Earth, I mean."

"What happened?"

"Yes. How did you die, if that's not an indelicate question?" asked Jerry, thinking that it probably was.

"I had a heart attack; Maria just passed away in her sleep, like old people do," replied Roberto.

"Old people? But Maria, you look younger than me!"

"That's very sweet of you Jerry, but I can assure you I was a very old lady once."

Jerry looked incredulously at Maria and Roberto, and then across to Bob, searching for an explanation.

It was Roberto who enlightened him. "The thing is, Jerry, in Heaven you become the person that God really designed you to be. Whatever is your full potential, that is what you reach. People look as God wants them to look and for most people they look their very best when they are young. Thanks be to God."

"But Bob doesn't look so young," observed Jerry, bringing a wry smile from Bob and a chuckle from Roberto.

"Sorry, I didn't intend to be rude," said Jerry.

"It's all right, I understand. I look middle-aged because, I guess, the Lord thinks that I am best this way."

"You guess?"

"Yeah, I assume so. I haven't actually got round to asking him."

"Could you ask him?" enquired Jerry, astonished that a mere mortal (he realised he should have thought, mere *immortal*) might have access to the creator of the universe to ask a question of such inconsequence.

"Probably, but there's not much point. He's decided what's best for me and I have to live with it."

"And you're OK with that?"

"How could any of us be unhappy with what the Lord decides, Jerry? He knows better than we do what we need and what's good for us," said Maria.

"Well, I suppose if you put it that way," replied Jerry, sounding and feeling unconvinced.

Jerry had completed his breakfast before Roberto spoke to him again. "What were you doing when you heard the trumpet call, Jerry?"

"Oh, you mean the Rapture thing?"

"Yes, the Rapture *thing*," replied Roberto, making inverted commas in the air with two fingers from each hand as he delivered the word, *thing*.

"I was just on my way to work."

"And what work was that?"

"I'm a software engineer," explained Jerry, although from the look on Roberto's face it hadn't been much of an explanation. "I specialise in IT security," he added, trying to be helpful, but obviously not succeeding. He offered the dumbed-down version: "Computers," he said.

"Ah, computers. They were a bit after my time. I never needed them in my line of work."

"Which was what?" asked Jerry.

"Missionary. Both Maria and I had the privilege of serving the Lord in our beloved Brazil for over forty years. The Lord did a mighty work there, bringing many, many people from the superstition and darkness of Rome into the glorious light and freedom of our Lord Jesus."

Jerry couldn't think of anything intelligent to say. Not only had he never met a missionary before, he was out of his depth on the distinction between Catholicism and the other brands of Christianity. So he changed the subject.

"Your English is excellent," he said. It was a genuine compliment but no sooner had he said it than both Roberto and Maria erupted in laughter.

"As good as our Portuguese," replied Roberto, a response which drew even more laughter from Maria and a broad smile from Bob.

"What did I say?" asked Jerry.

"Nothing, it doesn't matter," replied Roberto unhelpfully. "Listen, it was a blessing meeting you, Jerry. We have to go now. We'll see you around. Goodbye."

"Bye."

Roberto and Maria picked up their trays and left. As they walked away Jerry heard Roberto say to Maria, "You sink my eenlgeesh eez good, eh?" which earned him a playful dig in the ribs.

"Why was that funny?" Jerry asked Bob, now that they were alone once more.

"Jerry, the world and his wife are here, right?"

"Right."

"They come from all countries, all ages, and they speak all languages. How are we all going to understand each other?"

"Learn English?" suggested Jerry. "It's spoken by a lot of people already. Roberto and Maria seem to have mastered it."

Bob looked straight at Jerry and said, "They were speaking Portuguese. They probably can speak a bit of English, just like you may know one or two words of Dago, but that ain't what they were speaking."

"Bob, I heard them speak English. So did you."

"You're right, we did."

Jerry sighed and turned away. For the first time he noticed a large wooden cross hanging above the entrance to the canteen. Above the cross were painted the words, *For God so loved the world that He gave His only Son*. Underneath it *John 3:16* validated the quote with the chapter and verse reference.

"How well do you know your Acts, Jerry?"

"My acts of what?"

"Not your acts of anything. The Book of Acts. It's in the New Testament, right after the Gospels," said Bob. "In the second chapter is a story of the coming of the Holy Ghost on the disciples. The people who were there at the time heard a great wind and saw tongues of fire appear on the disciples' heads. Now the disciples started to preach the good news of Jesus to the whole crowd who'd come from all over the place and spoke all sorts of different languages. And a miracle took place." Here Bob leaned forward towards Jerry and lowered his voice. "Everyone heard what was being said in their own language."

Bob sat back in his chair once more and slapped the palm of his hand triumphantly on the table. "Imagine that! It was like one of those international conferences where the speaker gets translated while he's talking and everyone hears him through their headphones in their own language. Except it's the Holy Ghost what was translating everything all at once, not some army of translators with fancy gadgets and what-not. And that's what's happening here, all the time: a constant miracle by the Holy Ghost."

"That's amazing," said Jerry, genuinely impressed. "It's like the Babel fish."

"The what?"

"Douglas Adams' book – *The Hitch-hiker's Guide to the Galaxy*. There's a fish that lives in the ears of everyone in the universe and it translates all the alien languages into the mother tongue of its host. It's called the Babel fish."

"There's no need to take the piss, Jerry. I'm speaking about a real miracle, not some made up story about a bloody talking fish."

"Oh, sorry," said Jerry, a little stung by Bob's reaction.

"No, you're alright. There's a lot to get used to in the beginning. I didn't mean to snap."

"That's a pretty cool trick though, all that translation."

"It's a miracle, not a trick."

"Miracle, yes," Jerry corrected himself, and then added after a few moments' thought, "The accent stays, though. I heard Roberto and Maria speaking English but they had Portuguese, I mean Brazilian, accents."

"Yes, I don't know why it happens that way. It might be to allow their own personality to come through in what they're saying, so that you know it's really them speaking."

"Yes, that makes sense."

"It's just enough to get us along. It don't have to be perfect."

"*Doesn't* have to be perfect," teased Jerry.

"Yeah, that's what I said."

Jerry let it pass. If the Holy Ghost wasn't going to auto-correct Bob's grammar then Jerry himself wasn't about to start. He ruminated on this extraordinary phenomenon for a while and then another thought struck him.

"What about written words, Bob? You see those words above the cross?" here Jerry pointed to the wooden cross on the wall, "Is everybody reading those in their own language?"

"Yes."

"So what you see and hear depends on where you're from, what language you speak."

"Don't it always?"

"Yes, very philosophical Bob, but I mean that somehow the pattern of light that has entered my retina is changed so that my brain thinks the letters look like they form English words, and they'll be altered in a different way for a Frenchman so that he'll read French words, even though we're both actually looking at exactly the same image, which may not be either English or French."

"I don't know how it works Jerry; I just know that it does."

"And the light must get modified when people are talking as well," continued Jerry excitedly. "When Roberta and Maria were here it really looked as if they were speaking English; their speech didn't appear to be dubbed, like it would be in a foreign film. The synchronisation between the way their mouths moved and what I heard was perfect. It looked and sounded English, even though they were actually speaking Portuguese. This really is incredible!"

"Yeah well, I just accept it. Trying to understand how it works ain't something I've ever tried to get my teeth into."

"Oh, teeth, yes, that reminds me," said Jerry, pulling himself away from the fascinating topic of simultaneous audio-visual translation. "My filling came out this morning; do you know a good dentist I could use?"

Bob nodded, stood up and looked around the canteen. He spotted the person he was looking for at a nearby table and called out to him, "Jesus! Hey, Jesus!"

Jerry was horrified. "Don't trouble *him*, Bob! Can't we just get an ordinary dentist? I'm not sure I'm ready to meet Jesus just yet."

"It's no bother," insisted Bob who had now succeeded in attracting Jesus' attention and was beckoning him over with one hand and pointing into his own mouth with the index finger of the other in a caricature of dental practice.

A swarthy man appeared beside their table. Lacking long hair, a beard and halo, he did not look like the person Jerry had been expecting.

"This is Jesus Xavier," said Bob. "He's from Spain."

"Thank God for that," said Jerry, rising to his feet to greet the visitor. "Are you a dentist?"

"No, he's not," replied Bob on the Spaniard's behalf. "Jesus and I met earlier this morning and we had a little chat. Show Jerry what you showed me then, Jesus,"

The non-divine, non-dentist held out his hand, in the palm of which rested a dozen fillings, two of which were gold. He opened his mouth wide and pointed inside. "Oook, oh eee-ings," he said, a phrase which was beyond even the power of the Holy Ghost to translate into comprehensible English.

"No fillings," he repeated. "No fillings in my teeth."

"No," said Jerry. "They're in your hand. I can see that."

"I don't need them any more. You see, my teeth are perfect. No use for fillings. Praise God!" So saying he gave Jerry a huge bear-hug and returned to the friends he had been eating with.

"His teeth have been healed," explained Bob. "Just like yours. It's part of being a citizen of the kingdom of Heaven: no imperfections, not even inside your mouth."

"No wonder I couldn't find the hole."

"Have a look around you," continued Bob. "You see anyone wearing glasses?"

"No, now you come to mention it I don't."

"Everyone has perfect eyesight here. Perfect teeth; perfect

bodies. No ageing, no deterioration, no aches and pains. Welcome to a land free from suffering, son."

Jerry was lost for words.

"Let's go and give thanks and worship, shall we?" suggested Bob and, for the first time in his life, Jerry felt that maybe that wouldn't be such a pointless exercise after all.

7

At the back of Messiah Mansions lay a beautifully kept lawn running the whole length of the building and extending some two hundred metres away from it. The lawn was edged with Cyprus trees and contained in its centre an enormous oak. In places, rhododendron bushes ostentatiously displayed their scarlet blooms, providing a stylish counter-balance to the pervading green. People were grouped in circles of ten or so, chatting, praying or singing. This was not the kind of church gathering Jerry had been expecting. There was no grey stone building for one thing, nor pews, nor stained glass windows, nor graveyards, nor grotesques leering down from on high.

"We're pretty informal," explained Bob, as if anticipating Jerry's unspoken question. "There's no building, as you can see. The book of Revelation says that God himself is the only temple in Heaven, so we just meet outside. You'll soon get the hang of things; this is your mob over here."

Bob started to lead the way towards one of the nearest groups and, as they walked over the springy, close-cropped turf, Jerry said, "Bob, something odd seems to be happening whenever I meet people here."

"You know their names, even though you ain't never seen them before."

"Yes, exactly," said Jerry.

"It's a gift from God."

"Like the fillings and other peoples' languages?"

"You what?"

"Like not having fillings and not needing to learn anyone else's language. You don't need to think about other peoples' names; you already know them."

"Got it in one. You don't need to think about anything much up here, Jerry. No worries; no stress. Lovely!"

"Really? I enjoy thinking. I've spent a lot of my life thinking, trying to understand how things work. What will we do if we don't need to think?"

"Worship. We're here to worship, remember, not to think. Come on, let's get to it."

The circle of white-clothed bodies sensed their arrival and a few shuffled outwards to make space for the two of them. They were welcomed by name and responded with similar familiarity.

A small Malaysian woman called Lela stepped forward and said, smilingly, "Are you staying with us, Bob?"

"No, just settling Jerry in," replied Bob.

"Ah, that's good then," said Lela, clasping her hands together and laughing exaggeratedly.

"I'll catch you later," Bob said to Jerry, briefly clutching his forearm with one hand and patting him lightly on the back with the other before exiting the group entirely.

Grinning manically, Lela continued, "Praise the Lord for this glorious day!"

"Amen," the others chorused enthusiastically.

"Jerry, Catherine, Solomon," continued Lela, "We are so delighted to welcome you as children of the Rapture."

A spontaneous round of applause broke out and the three newcomers acknowledged the easy heroism of the moment, Jerry awkwardly so.

"Let each of us thank the Lord, in our own way, for his goodness to us," said Lela, whereupon some knelt on the grass, others bowed their heads, and two or three stood with their arms outstretched and heads thrown back, faces bathed in the warming light. Jerry, ignorant of the protocol, adopted a compromise position, hands resting on the front of his thighs, bending over as though he were talking to a small child, but unsure what to do next. The others closed their eyes and babbled away happily.

Once he realised that no-one was paying him any attention

Jerry straightened up and placed his right hand over his face like a giant five-legged spider. He hoped that in this guise he would give the impression of someone earnestly engaged in prayer while actually being able to surreptitiously see what was going on all around him. He half-turned away from his own circle and spotted Bob in another group a short distance away. Any hope that Jerry had that his impromptu concealment would keep him from being recognised was dispelled when Bob looked in his direction and gave him a friendly thumbs-up sign. Jerry waved back with his free hand, but allowed the spider to remain clinging to his face. Despite the realisation that he probably looked like a bit of an imbecile, he decided to bluff it out, continuing to rotate slowly round, taking in the panorama beyond the fuzzy columns of his out-of-focus fingers. He picked out his first angel near one of the rhododendron bushes. The guy was dressed in the same dark clothing as Nathaniel, and looked strong and athletic like him too. He seemed to be listening, intently. Now that he had spotted the angel, Jerry realised that he had seen a couple of them in the canteen, standing away from the diners, and there were a few more here too, dotted around the edges of the field.

Jerry had turned three quarters of a circle when his neighbour's face came into view.

"You OK, Jerry?"

"Oh sure," replied Jerry, quickly pulling his hand away from his face and turning to look at the group, who were all watching him expectantly.

"Welcome back, Jerry," said Lela, much to everyone's amusement. "I was just saying how I thought you would like to give us your testimony and tell us about how you first met Jesus."

Jerry did his best to quickly recover his composure.

"Um, well the truth is, I haven't really met him yet. I thought I was going to see him this morning, but he turned out to be Spanish and not the dentist after all. He was just another Jesus.

Bob had spoken to him earlier and then he got him to show me his fillings, but they weren't in his teeth any more because he doesn't need them now, and neither do I. I mean I don't need my own fillings, obviously, or his, come to that. Ha! I might be losing you a bit here, so going back to your question, I'm pretty sure Bob might have met the proper Jesus, you know, the famous one. I haven't yet had the chance, though, as I only came yesterday and I expect he's been busy."

There was an uncertain silence which was broken a few moments later by Lela, whose resilient smile remained, in spite of Jerry's chaotic verbal ramble. "I meant when you met him on Earth; when you were a sinner and he saved your soul."

In truth, Jerry didn't really know what was meant by his soul. When he had come across the concept as a child his imagination had conjured up a picture of a translucent balloon located somewhere in his tummy. His teenage years had barely developed the image at all and he had last seen it abandoned on the cusp of adulthood as a soft ectoplasm egg, about the size of a rugby ball, minding its own business and humming quietly to itself.

"Saved my soul?" repeated Jerry limply. The screen had gone blank for real this time "It was…" he hesitated. He thought he saw a flicker, but it had gone before he could grasp it.

"It was such a long time ago," he muttered at last.

"Oh, it can be difficult when we come to know Jesus as children," said Lela straight away. "I myself was saved when I was only three years old. When I was growing up and listening to other peoples' testimonies – how they had done drugs or been prostitutes or thieves before Jesus rescued them – I would be quite jealous! I would wish that I had an exciting story to tell, but the Lord knew best and he got hold of me before I could do any mischief."

People in the group laughed.

"I can assure you I was never a prostitute or a thief, although as for the drugs…!" said Jerry, chuckling and trying to exploit the humorous mood, but nobody else laughed. Instead, Solomon said, "Hey Jerry, weren't you the guy who argued with Nathaniel in the welcome meeting?"

"I'm not sure we argued exactly."

At six foot, four inches, Solomon was even taller than Jerry, and more broad-shouldered too. He had untidy, mousey hair and his grey eyes seemed slightly too far apart on his wide face. He looked across at Jerry and said, "You wouldn't have had a problem with the pregnant woman if you'd known your Bible. Jesus said that it would be dreadful…"

"Yes, *dreadful for pregnant women*," interrupted Jerry. "I heard what Nathaniel said at the time, thank you. I also know that I had seen a woman suffering."

Solomon shook his head and opened his mouth to speak again.

"I'll give mine," interjected Catherine, the short, blond member of the Rapture trio with large brown eyes and a small mouth. "If Jerry doesn't want to share his testimony right now, I'll tell you mine."

"Thank you, Catherine dear," said Lela, as relieved as anyone to escape the embarrassment of a potential squabble amongst their team. "Another time, Jerry," she offered as consolation.

Not bloody likely, thought Jerry to himself.

"I can walk again," said Catherine. "I couldn't before, but just from yesterday I can. It's all I've ever wanted, and the Lord's made it possible."

Her eyes shone as she looked up into the faces of the group whose attention she now absolutely commanded.

"When I was six years old I was playing a game of chase with my older sister, Caroline. We lived in a really quiet area; there was hardly ever any traffic. Caroline ran across the road and I went after her but at that particular moment there was a guy driving his sports car, going way too fast. I don't know what he was doing there, if perhaps he'd got lost or something, but in any case he swerved to miss Caroline and…" Catherine's voice wavered and she looked at the ground momentarily. With her right hand she pushed her hair back into place behind her ear.

"I don't remember, actually, you know, being hit. I broke eighteen bones in my body, and fractured my skull and my spine. It was a miracle I wasn't dead – that's what the doctors said. I was in a coma for three weeks so our church organised an all-night prayer vigil for me. Hundreds of people came and a few days after that meeting I woke up."

"Praise God," shouted Solomon.

"Jesus heals," called another.

"Yes, yes, it was another miracle, that's for sure," said Catherine. "But my legs were useless. I had to have dozens of operations over the next few years, but I never walked again. Poor Caroline felt so guilty about it all. I think in some ways it was worse for her than it was for me. She once told me that every time she saw me in my wheelchair she hated herself for what she'd done. She really went off the rails as a teenager; kicked over the traces completely."

Catherine's words seemed to droop to the ground like the branches of a heavily laden fruit tree.

"Jesus became my best friend. Whenever I felt sorry for myself, you know, for being disabled, I would talk to him and feel his presence comforting me. I always believed I would be able to walk again one day; I knew that's what Jesus wanted for me. Then yesterday, when I was sitting in my wheelchair in the garden, he came for me. As I was coming up I looked down at my chair and I knew I would never need it again. When my feet touched the ground here in Heaven I… I could walk. It's… amazing."

Catherine buried her head in her hands and turned to Lela who wrapped her arms around her and held her tight. Most of the others gathered closely around and tried to embrace the pair of them.

Jerry, never a particular fan of group hugs, but moved by

Catherine's story nevertheless, stayed uneasily on the fringes. The cuddling lasted for a minute or two before the group untangled itself and returned to their positions in the circle.

"Thank you, everyone," said Catherine. She felt underneath her eyes with the tips of her fingers, which she then inspected. "I'm not crying. I thought I would be."

"You can't cry here," Solomon informed her. "Revelation twenty-one says, *God will wipe away our tears. No more death or mourning or crying or pain, for the old order of things has passed away.* Nathaniel reminded some of us of that verse just yesterday," he added, pointedly looking across at Jerry as he did so.

Several people nodded in agreement and one murmured, "That's right: no more tears."

"I'll give my testimony now," said Solomon, straining like a pitbull on a leash. But before he could get going, Jerry cut across him.

"Your sister must be relieved, Catherine."

"What?" replied the young woman, unsure of Jerry's meaning.

"Caroline. No more guilt; now that you're walking again she must be as relieved as you are. Has she seen you yet?"

"No. I don't know where she is."

"Well, it's a big place, but sooner or later you'll get together, I'm sure. Maybe Bob knows how to find her; you could ask him."

"You heard what she said," butted in Solomon. "Her sister fell away, so maybe she's not…"

A burst of laughter and a round of applause came from a nearby group, distracting Jerry and his colleagues.

"Solomon," said Lela, "we'd love to hear your testimony. Please continue."

Delighted to be set free Solomon barked and snapped his way into his story, biting with relish into his favourite subject. Jerry didn't listen. He couldn't be sure but it had felt as if Lela had deliberately prevented him from asking any more questions about Caroline's whereabouts. A nasty little Dark Thought was troubling him; an idea that he didn't want to entertain, so he forced himself instead to mull on what Catherine had told them about her experience. He realised that he would never have described a crippling near-death road accident as being miraculous. If God had been at work that day, surely a more economical miracle would have been to delay the driver by thirty seconds so that the accident wouldn't have happened in the first place. And, if her survival had indeed been an answer to prayer, why didn't God go the whole hog and heal her paralysis?

Jerry's scepticism was challenging him and yet, he couldn't deny, here was Catherine walking as perfectly as everyone else.

He looked across at the young zealot who was now speaking incomprehensible gobbledegook which, so he claimed, was a manifestation of the gift of tongues, an angelic language known only to the angels and, apparently, to Solomon himself. The fact that no-one else could interpret what he was saying made Jerry think it was a gift of limited use, a bit like being the only one on the planet to own a telephone. Oddly, the Holy Ghost was not translating Solomon's utterances and Jerry wondered what the word for *deluded* was in Solomon's angel-tongue, but decided not to ask.

Two of the group had sat down by now and Jerry decided to do likewise as Solomon continued to hold sway. Jerry stretched his arms out behind him and lent back onto their support. He kneaded the grass with his hands, feeling the compact earth push up under his fingernails. The lawn was in superb shape and he wondered whose job it was to cut it and to keep the weeds at bay. Perhaps its pristine condition was the result of yet more miraculous intervention: the Holy Ghost moonlighting from his main job of translator to the masses by doing a bit of gardening on the side.

Jerry let an involuntary snigger leave his mouth at the thought, a noise which drew an unfriendly glance from Solomon as it happened to coincide with his closing remarks.

"Way to go, Solomon," somebody said.

"You're the man, Sol," said Jerry, punching the air with his fist in a show of mollifying solidarity.

"Bless you, Solomon," added Lela, before asking them all to stand up. "Let us praise our Saviour and our Lord. Now is the time to ask the Holy Spirit to pour out his blessing upon us." She closed her eyes and held hands with her immediate neighbours, whereupon the whole group did the same. "Come, Holy Spirit, fill us with your power that our worship may be pleasing to him," she said, and started to sing a chorus not unlike those that had been sung in the bus the previous day. Jerry felt his toes curl as he anticipated the embarrassing sentimentality of it all.

But what happened next wasn't embarrassing; it was astonishing. A thick, opulent warmth seeped into his body and, despite having his eyes closed, he knew that the light around him was intensifying, seeming to penetrate deep within him so that he too became a source of radiance, multiplying the brightness still further to almost painful levels. He felt himself becoming free of all physical constraints. An energy surged through him; a power; a wind. He was flying. Colours exploded in his head and the song being sung by Lela and Catherine and Solomon and his new brothers and sisters – people who he now loved with an unquenchable love – Oh, God! How he loved them – became the most beautiful, triumphant, glorious song he had ever heard. He felt himself transported to a place of perfect wonder; beyond the confines of his own mind; beyond anything he had ever imagined. This was the moment of orgasm, held, suspended, elevated. He felt pure, cleansed and full of goodness. This was happiness; this was joy – beyond joy even: this was ecstasy, incomparable and complete. This was love, poured onto him in a relentless stream of molten gold. This was Jerry as he was meant to be: utterly fulfilled and at one with God.

Jerry raised his arms and sang his heart out with the rest of them, utterly overwhelmed by his Saviour. Jerry and Jesus: one heart, one mind, one spirit.

After an hour or so of this unadulterated bliss, the singing quietened and the light gradually dimmed to its normal level. Jerry sat on the grass and let the tingling after-burn of contentment run through his veins. His body could not have sustained much more of the intensity he had just enjoyed and, judging from the look on the faces of Catherine and Solomon, neither could theirs. The rest of the group began to talk among themselves and smiled knowingly at the newcomers, no doubt recalling the choking thrill of their first heavenly worship experiences.

Jerry had no energy for conversation, amiable or otherwise. He lay on his back, clasped his hands behind his head and looked up at the cloudless sky. This, he told himself, was indeed Paradise.

8

A couple of kicks on the soles of his feet woke Jerry up.

"You planning on sleeping all day, son?"

"Oh, hi, Bob. Sorry, must have dozed off," he replied as he sat up and looked around the near-deserted field.

"Where is everyone?"

"Got things to do, most likely, people to see. And so do we – have you forgotten?"

Rachael!

"Christ! I had. Are we going now?"

"Yep. Are you feeling peckish? We can pick up a sarnie on the way."

"OK."

Their walk took them through a little copse where the bluebells created an illusion of a thin blue mist hovering just above the ground. The air was cool and sweet with their scent, and very still.

"Enjoy yourself this morning?" asked Bob, breaking the silence that had accompanied the two men since they set out together.

"It was…" Jerry searched for the right word, "…overwhelming."

Bob smiled.

"I had no idea it would be so powerful, or that it would make me feel so wonderfully happy."

"Yeah, worship can do that to you."

Preoccupied with their own thoughts, neither spoke again until they emerged from the wood into a public park, the beauty of which made Jerry beam with delight. The scene evoked simple childhood pleasures with its array of cherry trees in voluptuous blossom, each one standing in the centre of a layer of pink petals with which it had carpeted the grass underneath its branches. A fragile, self-absorbed fountain played in the middle of a pond, ⁓ending sparkling ripples across the surface of the water.

Perfect though the milieu appeared, Jerry's subconscious told him there was something missing. He scanned the people strolling across the grass, resting under trees, or kneeling together in prayer. These open manifestations of religiosity were still quite shocking to Jerry, but that wasn't the only element of the environment that seemed peculiar. Suddenly it came to him: there were no children. There were no fathers lying on their backs holding giggling toddlers at arms' length above them; no groups of youngsters charging around the bushes lost in glorious battle; no mothers comforting the little ones who had fallen in the skirmish or whose tears were shed in frustration at their inability to make their own quiet voices heard above the undemocratic clamour of their older siblings. There wasn't even a playground: no swings; no slides; no giant spider climbing-frame with grinning mouth and unblinking eyes.

"Bob, where are the children?"

"They're grown up."

"What, all of them?"

"Yes."

"Even the ones who came yesterday?"

"Yes."

They had stopped by a drinking fountain which was topped by a white dove carved from alabaster. Bob pressed a small brass button on the side of the supporting stone pedestal and a jet of water squirted from the dove's open beak. Notwithstanding the impression of colourless vomit that this created, Bob slurped a few refreshing mouthfuls down his throat. After drying his lips on the back of his hands, he continued.

"Remember, when you're in Heaven you become as God made you to be. None of us was meant to be a child all our lives, was we? So, when kiddies come here they have to grow up straight away."

"Doesn't it hurt, being transformed immediately from children to adults?"

"No, why should it?"

"Well, all that stretching of bones and expanding flesh."

"Nothing hurts in Heaven Jerry, I've already told you that."

Jerry thought about this bizarre revelation. "What about all their childhood memories, and their schooling? How do they know anything?"

"They don't need memories. All our memories of what we did on Earth fade away eventually anyway. And they learn all they need to know while they're here: all about God and Jesus and all things like that."

Bob could see that Jerry was unconvinced so he continued. "There's no better place to learn than Heaven – no corrupt ideas, no anxieties, everything perfect."

"If that's the case, why did God bother with our lives on imperfect Earth at all? Why not just start everybody off here and be done with it?"

"You gotta be born first, you daft Wally; there's no children born up here."

Bob said this with a QED finality that seemed to conclude the debate, until a consequential thought occurred to Jerry.

"The contraception must be very effective, then. Does the Pope approve? The Popes, I should say."

"As a matter of fact, it's the only type of birth control the Popes do approve of," replied Bob softly.

"I thought they were completely against it in whatever form."

Bob's silent assent carried a leaden conclusion back to Jerry's mind where it fell like a shot stag in a glen.

"You don't mean abstinence, do you?" asked Jerry, unable to conceal his incredulity.

"Of course that's what I mean."

"There's no sex in Heaven?"

"That's right."

"You've got to be fucking joking."

"No joking; no fucking."

Jerry looked around him. Many of the people in the park looked young, fit and nubile. He couldn't believe they would not be having sex. He couldn't believe *he* would not be having sex.

"I don't believe you," he said.

"Look Jerry, sex was invented for procrastination."

"I think you mean procreation," corrected Jerry.

"Yeah, that's the one. But we don't need to do that any more. All the people who are ever going to live have already been born."

"I thought we had sex so that we could have a damn good time, as well as securing the future of the species," Jerry said sulkily.

"We have a damn good time here, with Jesus."

"You can't have sex with the Son of God – that just has to be against the rules!"

"Be careful how you speak of him, Jerry. Besides, have you forgotten already how you felt this morning during worship?"

"No I haven't. That was amazing, but even so…"

"Even so, nothing. We used to have sex to make children and to feel good. Now we don't need any children and worshipping God feels fantastic, much better than sex."

Jerry didn't like to admit that this final point was certainly true. He stood looking down at his feet, one hand on his hip, the other gripping the throat of the white drinking fountain dove. He wanted to strangle the bloody thing.

"How can they stop you?" he asked, imagining that some kind of sex police would be needed to enforce the forbearance of such a quintessential human activity.

"You'll find you just don't feel the need."

Jerry scoffed. Although he had not been focusing on the matter unduly, having had more than enough distraction to occupy his mind since the previous day, he was not expecting his imminent reunion with soft, warm Rachael to necessarily be celibate. A memory of a risqué after-hours encounter with his lover in her office flashed into his mind. Anyone could have seen the two of them, if they'd happened to be working late, which was unlikely, but not impossible. The boss, a cleaner, that straight-laced colleague of hers… He'd never met anyone before with even the slightest of exhibitionist streaks, and it had added an intensity he had never expected. And surely now, even if they were able to keep their hands off each other for the time being, their need for intimacy, to say nothing of the physiology of their bodies, would lead inexorably to intercourse.

"And if I do feel the need?" he asked.

"You don't want to get caught in a room alone with a woman, my lad. It's the quickest way to get some unwelcome attention from the angels. From what I've heard you've already had some of that so you'll know what I'm talking about."

Jerry understood immediately, but he hadn't quite exhausted his line of questioning.

"Are you married, Bob?"

"I used to be."

"Oh, I'm sorry. What happened, if you don't mind me asking?"

"We died. Me first, then the missus. Forty-seven years we'd been together."

"Ah yes, 'til death do us part and all that. But your wife's here, so are you back together now?"

"No, we're not. No-one is married in Heaven. Jesus himself told us it would be like this when the Jews tried a trick question on him. They invented some story about a woman whose husband died, so she married his brother and then he died too. This supposedly went on until she'd got through seven brothers in all. I dunno, she must have been a rubbish cook or something. But anyway, the Jews wanted to know who she'd be married to in Heaven seeing as she'd had all seven of them as husbands on Earth. Well, Jesus wasn't gonna be fooled by that. "None of 'em," he says, "because there ain't no marriage in Heaven." So we all knew we wouldn't have husbands and wives up here.

"I still see Brenda most days, mind, and we have a chat and a bit of a laugh. She always looks terrific; always puts a smile on my face, my girl," he added wistfully.

"So even married people don't have sex any more?"

"That's right. And as you know, sex was never allowed outside of marriage, so that covers everyone."

"So I suppose there's no chance of you and me going behind the bushes for a quick shag then?"

"Bugger off, Jerry."

"That's precisely what I was suggesting," laughed Jerry. But his attempt at injecting some comedy into their dismal conversation didn't seem to have worked. Perhaps he had misjudged Bob's sense of humour, as the older man's face was now registering some concern, as if Jerry's throwaway line had been a genuine proposition instead of an attempt at a crude, somewhat inappropriate joke.

"Hold up," Bob muttered, looking over Jerry's shoulder and then starting to walk purposefully in that direction. "You better wait here."

The angel was about ten yards away. Jerry didn't know how long he had been there, just that he must have arrived sometime during his conversation with Bob. As soon as Bob was standing in front of him, the angel gestured with his head towards Jerry. His body language conveyed a degree of grumpiness and Bob was soon in animated conversation with him, although Jerry couldn't hear what either of them was saying.

After a few minutes Bob returned. "Let's go," he said and carried on walking, forcing Jerry to move briskly in order to catch up and fall in step beside him.

"What did he want?" Jerry asked.

"To make sure you weren't being serious."

"About what?" asked Jerry, but Bob made no reply. "You mean about you and me behind the bushes?"

"Yes, that – exactly."

"Well I wasn't; you're not my type."

"Cut it out, Jerry." Bob stopped walking, grabbed Jerry's arm and, moving very close said quietly, "Those guys have no sense of humour, son, but they do have bloody good hearing."

"Sounds like a dangerous combination."

"You could say that." Bob remained in a conspiratorial attitude when he added, "I'm telling you my friend, don't get yourself a reputation." When he had waited long enough to be satisfied that the warning had registered, he let go of Jerry's arm and walked out of the park.

Some twenty minutes later they arrived at a short parade of cafes, whose clientele spilled out onto the golden pavement, eating and drinking. On first impressions Jerry thought that this was a scene that, with the exception of the precious metal constitution of the sidewalk, could have been lifted from any number of contemporary cities in what, until very recently, would have been called the developed world. But then he began to notice other differences too, particularly the absences, as he had done earlier with the lack of children in the park. Litter for one thing. There were no discarded food wrappers or drink cartons. Handbags too: none of the women seemed to have one. Nor were there any mobile phones. Jerry couldn't remember the last time he'd seen a crowd of people where nobody was using a phone to hold a conversation, or to tap out a message, or to search the internet. It made him wonder what kind of slow, inefficient and unconnected life Heaven was going to provide for him and his fellow man. Not that saving time would be necessary any longer; the preciousness of the commodity – the very characteristic that had driven mankind to find increasingly ingenious ways of squeezing more and more out of it – had collapsed under the aching reality of eternal life. What value the instantaneous, he realised, when all the time in the world was available?

Jerry was sitting at a round coffee-table whose marble top was inlaid with coloured glass in the shape of a cross, waiting for Bob to return from the crowded cafe with their lunch. He heard snippets of conversation as people passed by.

"Hank and I were always Rapture-ready, but, oh my, it still took us a moment or two to figure out that this was *really* it when we heard the trumpet!"

Some people would catch his eye as they walked nearby and would occasionally say hello, using his name more often than not, and he would reply in kind. Gradually he felt himself buoyed up by their friendliness and warmed by the radiant heat of God, so that he was able to relax and turn his thoughts once more towards Rachael. It was while he was gliding towards this state of contented anticipation that Jerry witnessed his first death in the afterlife.

Monica had been walking on the other side of the road when she heard someone call her name. With a squeal of recognition she started to run across the road at exactly the moment that a bus had powered silently into the same space. The screech of tyres signalled the driver's attempt to avoid the inevitable, but the vehicle's momentum was too great and it hammered into her, sending her into a paradoxically elegant summersault through the air. She landed fifty yards from the point of impact, her broken body hitting the road with the chillingly frank thump reserved for the collision of lifeless meat with solid ground.

Everybody laughed.

That is, nearly everybody. Some cheered, one or two screamed and a few, like Jerry, were struck dumb.

Monica herself was helped to her feet by one of the ubiquitous black-clad angels to whom she appeared to be apologising profusely. She then came and joined her friends on the side of the road, close enough for Jerry to hear her excited chatter in an American accent.

"Oh, you guys! Did you see that? Crazy! I just haven't got used to those buses driving on the wrong side of the road and you just don't hear them either. That's the second time it's happened to me – it's so embarrassing!"

Monica and her pals moved away and Jerry thought he was going to be sick. He didn't throw up, of course, because there is no suffering in Heaven, as he'd been told earlier and as Monica had just so ably demonstrated. Nevertheless, the sight of her being so violently assaulted had shocked him deeply.

As he gripped the curved metal arms of his chair, he realised he was trembling. He closed his eyes, only to see in his mind's eye a terrible replay of Monica's death-flight. He imagined he heard again the derisory laughter of her friends and wondered what kind of desensitising process had led to these people viewing catastrophe as harmless entertainment. Except that it hadn't been a real catastrophe: Monica had been miraculously protected; even her white clothing had remained un-marked from its searing encounter with the surface of the road.

Road traffic accidents were becoming an unlikely theme of Jerry's first full day in Heaven. He recalled the tragic story from this morning's worship session and reflected how welcome the kind of supernatural intervention that he had just witnessed would have been to Catherine, back in the day. If God could provide instant healing so effortlessly in Heaven, why had it not been possible on Earth? Lord knows, there had been opportunity enough.

Jerry's mind was teetering on the edge of a vortex into which unanswered questions were streaming, their words and question marks colliding and tangling as they were pulled into the blackness below.

"Goat's cheese or brie?"

"What?"

"The panini," replied Bob, holding up one in each hand. "Goats cheese with roasted peppers, or brie with spinach and cranberry jelly?"

Jerry's thought processes were still all over the place and the mention of cheese set him off on a curious track, wondering how that particular food was manufactured here, in Heaven. He was fairly sure cheese-making involved bacteria and, if that was the case, he asked himself if God's provision of an eternity without death had been extended to these faceless, microscopic organisms. Then another thought occurred to him: was the *no sex outside marriage* rule null and void if you performed the act simply by splitting yourself in two?

"Well?" demanded Bob. "Which one?"

Jerry replied dully, "Neither thanks. I'm not hungry."

"You look a bit peeky. You seen a ghost?"

Jerry gave Bob an ironic look. "Isn't that what we all are?"

"Nah. Ghosts don't eat nothing. We're solid all right. Now, you sure you don't want one of these?"

"I'm sure, but you go ahead. I'll pay for my share, though, of course," added Jerry, feeling for where his pocket should have been safely harbouring his wallet, but finding neither.

"Really?" said Bob through a mouthful of melted brie. "You ain't got no money, have you, son?"

"No. I was going to ask you about that."

"Don't worry about it; it's all on the house. Everything's free; we don't pay for nothing. You name it – food, drink, clothes, houses – it's all gratis."

While Bob munched his way through both their lunches, Jerry tried to take in the fact that he wouldn't ever have to earn his keep again. Naturally enough it sounded wonderful, but his sorely tested emotions were having a hard time being flung between happiness and melancholy and, with his mind also stumbling about, bumping into one implausibility after another, he found he was unable to celebrate this latest piece of good news. Instead, he returned to the disturbing events of a few minutes earlier.

"Did you see that accident, Bob?"

"Uh-uh," mumbled Bob, shaking his head while he wrenched off a mouthful of toasted sandwich, leaving a string of cheese momentarily connecting his lips to the remainder of the panini in his hand.

"Heard it, though, and saw her laughing about it afterwards," he added a few chomps and a swallow later.

"I thought you'd said there was no pain in Heaven."

"There isn't. She wasn't hurt, was she?"

"Maybe not, but it looked horrendous."

"It happens all the time," said Bob. "People don't hear the buses coming, walk straight out without looking and, you know, wham! The angels sort it out, though; they even lay hands on the bus so the dents come out from where it hit the dopey so-and-so."

"It was very distressing to see."

"First time, maybe, but you'll get used to it."

"But being distressed is a kind of suffering, isn't it, Bob?"

"Not compared to being walloped by a bloody bus it ain't."

A waiter dressed all in grey came and put two glasses of iced water on their table. Bob sipped from one, wiped his mouth with a napkin and looked carefully at Jerry, who was staring into the distance.

"What's troubling you, son?"

"Trouble," replied Jerry, quickly. "Trouble is what's troubling me. You say there's no suffering or death here but I've just seen someone catapulted across the road; her friends thought it was a huge joke, but I'm left traumatised by watching it all, and that counts as suffering as far as I'm concerned. And then there's all the bacteria in the cheese factory, living and breeding and dying like there's no tomorrow, unless of course they're being kept alive by some special miracle. Are they, Bob? Is that another miracle – keeping micro-organisms alive so that we can all have a nice bit of cheese?" Bob didn't answer. "And you're stuffing your face with a pepper," Jerry continued in a voice which was growing louder.

"That's a fruit, you know, which means the pepper plant's having sex and that's just fine, although it's not fine for people; oh no, no human offspring in Heaven because you can't fucking well fuck any more. And yesterday – just yesterday – I had no idea this fucking place even existed, let alone the fact I would never be able to eat a bacon sandwich ever again, or get my leg over. Ever. I mean, for fucking ever."

Jerry sat back in his chair and folded his arms, glaring at the astonished on-lookers who had been close enough to hear his rant. Bob said nothing, although Jerry thought he detected a slight hand movement, as if his companion was waving someone away. After a while, Jerry's heart rate returned to normal and his breathing relaxed.

Bob leaned forward and said quietly, "It's only natural to be confused at first."

Jerry made no comment. Bob waited a while longer before asking, "Do you play golf?"

"Is that question supposed to lessen my confusion?"

"A friend of mine used to be a Canon in the C of E; worked in my neck of the woods. He's a great one for answering difficult questions, you know, straightening people out and that."

"Is that what I need: to be straightened out?"

"We all need help from time to time, son. A round of golf with Canon John and you'll be right as rain."

"I've only played a few times. I'm not much good."

"You will be; don't you worry about that."

Bob took a large swig of water, stood up and said, "Come on, we've got a visit to make."

Jerry slowly got to his feet. He had never needed to see Rachael more desperately than at that very moment. He set off with Bob to be reunited with his love, at last.

9

Jerry had first met Rachael at a mutual friend's Guy Fawkes party. It had been a dank night of unrelenting drizzle, about as unsuitable an evening for fireworks as it is possible to imagine. Good manners and an emotional attachment to pyrotechnics had forced the guests outside into the tiny garden to watch fifteen minutes of *place in soft earth* phutting and *launch from vertical pipe* rocket-propelled whooshing.

The display had suffered a serious setback when an over-enthusiastic catherine wheel had freed itself from the fence post to which it had been ineffectively nailed, and leapt amongst the party-goers like a Jack Russell on heat.

Everybody bar John, the host, had retreated laughing to the safety of the kitchen, excited by their mild brush with danger and pleased to be dry and beyond the reach of any more out-of-control fireworks. John himself, however, had been determined to get his money's worth from his bumper pack and had stayed outside to finish the show. He'd lit the two remaining roman candles, one of which had immediately fallen over and scorched a couple of feet of trampled grass; he'd then launched the final rocket which exploded somewhere over his neighbour's roof, completely out of sight from all the guests.

Bowing low to acknowledge the ironic cheers coming from inside his kitchen, John had spotted the unruly catherine wheel lying spent and blackened at his feet. He'd picked it up, gathered the remains of the other exhausted fireworks and then succumbed to a moment of madness, breaking one of the cardinal rules of firework displays: he'd chucked the lot onto his smouldering bonfire whereupon they all exploded and set fire to his garden shed.

Seeing that there was now much more fun to be had outside than in, the visitors had rushed back out to the garden. Expert firefighters one and all, they had thrown a mixture of wine, beer, fruit juice and cheesecake onto the shed which eventually proved too much for the flames. They'd petered out, leaving a curious aroma of burnt wood and singed biscuit to meld with the cordite lingering in the smoky air.

By the end of the evening everybody had agreed that this was the best firework party they had ever been to and that John was to be sure to make it an annual event. More importantly, as far as Jerry was concerned, he had spent thirty minutes talking with Rachael, during which they had swapped contact details and established the relevant fundamentals: no current girlfriend for him, no boyfriend for her; they had liked each other and, in all probability, neither was an axe-murderer. They'd started dating a few days later and had never looked back.

Jerry smiled at the memory as the two men walked together. It took them half an hour to reach their destination: a pretty Victorian terraced house in a quiet street lined with eucalyptus trees. Jerry knew instantly that this was exactly the kind of place Rachael would have wanted – full of character and, back in London, completely out of her financial reach.

"I'll leave you to it," said Bob, and he was gone before Jerry had thought to ask him how he would be able to find his way back unaccompanied when he had finished his visit. What did cross his mind, however, was Bob's earlier admonishment about not being caught in a room alone with a woman. Strange that the older man seemed to have forgotten all about it; maybe he simply thought that Jerry would behave himself now that he was a citizen of the heavenly realm. Jerry himself was not so sure, but there was only going to be one way to find out.

He pushed against the little black wrought-iron gate and it opened noiselessly. The perfectly symmetrical path leading to the front door was tiled in red, with black and white diamond tiles along its edges. A low box-hedge separated the path from the dustily warm, tiny, front garden, in the middle of which stood a stone urn filled with daffodils. The sight of Rachael's favourite flowers made Jerry realise that he had arrived empty-handed. For a moment he thought about swiping the daffodils from the pot and presenting them to her, but he knew that his quick-witted woman would not be fooled by such tokenism. Besides, fresh-cut flowers don't last forever. Except, oh God, maybe they did in Heaven! Jerry rang the doorbell before his mind could get tipped over again.

The bell made a conventional *ding-dong* sound which seemed slightly incongruous to Jerry. He might have expected the Hallelujah Chorus rather than the simple two-tone chime beloved of the semis in the Acacia Avenues scattered throughout the English suburbs.

He guessed that Rachael's door – all solid wood and leaded stained glass – would be unlocked, but he wanted to be invited into her house rather than to assume a right of entry. He was also enjoying the intense and delicious sense of anticipation as he looked down at his shoes and heard the sound of hers advancing towards him down the hallway.

"Darling!"

Jerry, who had, naturally enough, always recognised that his mother had a certain beauty, was nevertheless astonished by the sight of the woman who now stood in front of him.

"You look amazing," he said at last. His compliment was followed by a period, it seemed like a long period, during which the two of them simply stood staring at each other. Jerry eventually asked, "Can you believe this is really happening to us?"

"I can't believe my own son hasn't given me a hug yet."

Jerry stepped across the threshold and embraced his mother, allowing some of the guilt of disappointment to be squeezed out of him.

"Come and sit down," she said and led him into a small sitting room large enough for two very comfortable armchairs and a low wooden table, but not much more.

Jerry did as he was told. His mind was a bit scrambled up as a result of Rachael being his mum; that is to say, his mum living in Rachael's house; or rather, the house he thought was going to be Rachael's but was, as was now clear, his mother's. No wonder Bob had been happy to leave him at the garden gate.

Jerry noticed that his mother looked as she had done in photographs from his early childhood. It had been stupid of him to have been so wrong-footed earlier, even if he had been expecting to see his lover open the door. Most people he had seen so far had been young adults, and only that very morning Roberto had told him to expect exactly that to be the case.

"Mum, did you ever really think that you would be in Heaven one day?" he asked.

"I always believed there would be something, yes. Now I'm here I must admit it's not exactly what I imagined, but I'm not complaining. This house is lovely and my friend Gill has moved in just around the corner."

"What about the Rapture? You can't have been expecting that, surely?"

"No, I wasn't, and I was very frightened, of course. But everybody's been very friendly and kind."

"Everyone's been very religious too, at least the ones I've met have been."

"Jerry, you are funny. What did you expect?"

"I didn't expect anybody or anything to be here at all! The idea that Heaven was a real place, especially one somewhere up in the sky, seemed so implausible and childish that I don't suppose I ever gave it much thought. I certainly didn't have any religious faith, and I didn't think you did either."

"I was brought up to go to church," replied his mother, with a defensive edge to her voice. "Even if I didn't go very often when I got older, I'd always say a prayer for you every night before I went to sleep."

"Thanks, Mum; I didn't know you still did that."

"I've been doing it all your life. Perhaps it did some good, after all."

"Yes, perhaps it did," Jerry conceded, "but the other people here all seem to have been missionaries, or at the very least regular church-goers. They're all real fanatics, not simply people with a passing interest in religion. I've never even had that."

"Actually, Jeremy, that's not quite true."

"It isn't? Why do you say that?"

"Make us a cup of tea and I'll tell you the little I remember."

While his mother visited her bathroom, Jerry went to the kitchen to make the tea. He filled the kettle and connected the power lead to the socket using the disappointingly flimsy American-style plug. He waited for the water to boil. He thought that in Heaven there might be quite a lot of waiting, eventually, and that maybe that wasn't going to be such a bad thing as at least waiting could be seen as an activity of sorts, maybe even a purpose, albeit a fairly low grade one.

Jerry dropped a tea-bag into the pot and poured in the water as soon as it had boiled. In a land where the miraculous was commonplace it still needed a tea-bag and a pot to make a decent cuppa, he reflected.

He gripped the tea-pot by its handle and picked it up, cradling its belly as he did so in the palm of his hand. It wasn't hot, or at least, not as hot as he thought it should be. He put it down and picked up the kettle again. He poured some water from the kettle into the sink and saw the steam rising from it immediately. On an experimental impulse he shoved the back of his left hand into the path of the near-boiling water. He felt a pleasant tingling sensation, but no pain.

His mother's shocked voice called out. "Jeremy, what are you doing? You'll burn yourself."

"No, it's all right, Mum, look."

He showed her his hand. There was no reddening of the skin or any other evidence that it had just been exposed to scalding water.

"It doesn't hurt. It's impossible for anything to hurt you in Heaven. When I was on my way here I saw a girl hit by a bus. It sent her flying and she just got up and walked away, completely unharmed."

"How dreadful – that she was run over, I mean."

"As I said, you can't get hurt here. Not much call for all your nursing skills, I'm afraid."

Jerry regretted his words as soon as he had spoken them. His mother had loved her job; she was a natural carer and the idea that there would be nobody that would need her help – nobody at all, ever – had obviously not yet occurred to her. He quickly changed the subject.

"Come on, Mum, you were going to tell me about my religious epiphany."

"Let's go and sit in the back this time, it's a nicer view." They went and sat down in another small room, which his mother rather grandly described as the conservatory. It looked out over a modest garden enclosed on all three sides by cheap, wooden fencing.

"You remember our holiday in Frinton?" resumed his mother.

"Frinton? Was that the one just before…?"

"Just before your father left us, yes."

"I don't think I do recall much about it, no."

"I'm not surprised, what with everything that happened afterwards and, in any event, you could only have been about eight or nine at the time. Frinton's a funny little place on the Essex coast, not far from Clacton-on-Sea. It's terribly old fashioned and fusty. It didn't even have a pub when we were there and they used to close the railway crossing gates on the main road into town at midnight, so if you'd been out drinking somewhere else you couldn't get back in."

"It sounds a riot."

"We chose to go there because we were given the accommodation for virtually nothing. We only had my meagre wage coming in and we stayed in a dismal bungalow that belonged to a friend of your father. I spent the whole of the first day cleaning the place so that we wouldn't catch some dreadful infection. I couldn't get rid of the whiff of dampness everywhere, even though it was a lovely hot summer that year."

His mother shuddered at the memory, reached for the floral-patterned, bone china teacup and took a comforting sip.

"Your father would go out walking on his own for hours, and you and I went to the beach. You found some friends to play with and I sat on my own wondering how I would cope as a single parent."

Jerry felt an echo of his childhood confusion and glimpsed once more a vulnerability in his young-again mother who seemed to be on the verge of tears; a moment of impossible sadness in the kingdom of eternal bliss.

"You coped just fine, Mum, more than fine," he said, reaching out and taking his mother's hand for a moment.

"Thank you, darling, that's sweet of you to say so. Now, where were we?"

"On the beach."

"Oh yes. There was some kind of church group there running a holiday club for children and you went along to it every morning. It was very kind of them to give up their holidays to look after other people's children."

"I do remember something now. We used to sing songs and play games. I think there were Bible stories too."

"Well, whatever you got up to it certainly made an impression on you because at the end of the week you announced you had decided to become a Christian."

"Seriously? I certainly don't remember that. I must have had too much sun. What did you and Dad say?"

"Your dad thought you'd been brainwashed by the Moonies, but I wasn't too worried. I always knew you were a sensible boy who would work things out for himself, and I thought going to church might be good for you."

"I don't recall ever attending church though."

"No, you didn't. You lost your enthusiasm for it as soon as we came back and you were away from the group."

"A holiday romance."

"Something like that."

The two of them looked out of the window. Purple-headed tulips in full bloom crowded the flower borders on both sides of a lawn copiously sprinkled with miniature white daisies. Sweet perfumes like those from an English summer drifted into the conservatory.

"So my religious phase didn't last long?" said Jerry after trying and failing to recall any further details from that distant period of his life.

"No, but you're here now, and that's all that matters."

"Of course. Where else would I be?" Jerry's Dark Thought stirred in the recesses of his mind. "Everybody must be here somewhere," he said, as much to himself as to his mother. "Including Dad."

Jerry's father had left the family home all those years ago for the second oldest reason in the world. Subsequently, in spite of the unsettling presence of his father's boyfriends, Jerry had managed to establish a decent friendship with his dad, and his parents had constructed a workable relationship between themselves too, albeit one which was burdened with a lingering regret.

"I suppose so," was all that his mother could manage in reply.

The doorbell rang, preventing Jerry from exploring the potentially painful topic any further.

"That'll be my friend Gill. Could you let her in while I clear away the tea things?"

Jerry did as he had been asked and opened the door.

"Hello, My Friend Gill," he said, addressing the disturbingly young and not unattractive woman he recognised as being his mother's long-standing chum.

"Jerry! Yes, I rather hope we are friends as we have known each other for such a long time. I am your mother's oldest friend after all."

Jerry let My Friend Gill into the house and closed the door behind her.

"I say, this has been a bit of a shock, hasn't it? I'd just cleared up the breakfast things when that dreadful racket started. It scared the living daylights out of me. And then there was all that flying through the air; I can't stand heights, you know – never could. What a carry on."

"Nice weather, though, don't you think?" asked Jerry.

"Oh lovely, yes. Can't complain about that. Let's hope it lasts, eh? They do say it's well set. I don't care for these outfits though; white never was my colour and there's no shape to these tee-shirts at all. Ah, Judith, how are you, my dear? I was just telling Jerry what a fright we've all had."

Not for the first time, Jerry wondered uncharitably how someone as intelligent as his mother could bear the company of such a miserable old bat – young bat – as My Friend Gill. He made his excuses, hugged his mother once more, promised to return soon, and left.

On exiting the front garden he turned right instead of left and was soon completely lost. He walked for well over an hour, becoming disoriented both geographically and mentally.

"You should probably be heading back home now, Jerry."

The angel had appeared so suddenly that Jerry had almost walked straight into him. He can't have been paying attention to where he was going. Either that or the angel had just materialised out of thin air, which was ridiculous.

"That's what I'm trying to do. I live in a block of flats called Messiah Mansions…"

"I know where you live," interrupted the angel. He pointed along the road to a celestial colleague a quarter of a mile away and told Jerry to head towards him and get his next set of instructions when he arrived there. Jerry thanked the angel and had walked a few paces when he stopped and turned around.

"You said I should be going back home. Why?"

"Because it's time."

It seemed churlish to start a quarrel. He had been intending to go back to his room anyway, if only he'd been able to find the way, but to be told to do so rankled with him. He thought for a moment about arguing the point and asserting his right of free choice, but the truth was he was absolutely knackered and, remembering Bob's warning about getting a reputation, decided that discretion was the better part of valour.

He turned again and walked away. Using the angels as a breadcrumb trail, he eventually found his way to the Mansions. In spite of his hunger he skipped dinner. He was in no mood for any more wide-eyed chat with his God-struck neighbours. He felt out of joint and he needed to try to find a positive resting place where his over-worked mind could allow him to sleep, so he went straight to bed and reflected on the transformation in his circumstances.

He was in Paradise. He would live a pain-free existence for all eternity. He would never have to work again. All his physical needs would be freely provided. He would worship God and, in so doing, experience a spiritual fulfilment beyond anything he had ever known or even imagined. And it would never rain.

And yet, he had an uneasy feeling that maybe Heaven might not be all that it was cracked up to be. There had been moments of unhappiness today: he had seen it in his mother's reminiscing; felt it in the shock of Monica's death-flight; even sensed it in the grumpy angel's irritation with him in the park. And that bloody Solomon was really getting on his tits!

There was more, too: there was his Dark Thought. Jerry knew that he could not silence it forever and, sure enough, it found its voice at last and whispered its diabolical question through the tightly stretched membrane of his denial: *what if there is Another Place?*

10

Rachael listened to Jerry's words once again. She drew a little comfort from hearing his voice, even though she knew beforehand exactly what he would be saying. The recorded message ended and she sighed into the mouthpiece, "Jerry hi, it's me, Rachael. I'm very worried that I haven't heard from you, but I'm still hoping for the best. Please call me when you can. *If* you can."

How long had it been now? At least a week. The absence of natural light made it difficult to tell. Rachael looked at her reflection in the window as the rain outside ran down its surface like teardrops. She had lost weight. Normally she would have been pleased, but pleasure was an emotion that had been suspended for the foreseeable future.

The image of another pale face was thrown back from the window, appearing next to Rachael's own. It belonged to the witch.

"Still no word?"

"No."

"I am sorry," said the witch, gently touching Rachael's elbow.

"I don't suppose you could cast a spell and magic him up for me, could you?"

"I'm afraid my powers in that respect have been very much exaggerated. I could conjure up some tea for you, though, if you give me a few minutes."

Not for the first time, Rachael was momentarily overwhelmed by the barely credible change in her circumstances – in *everybody's* circumstances. She didn't think she would ever be able to understand how, according to what she had been told, it had been possible for both Heaven and Hell to have existed all along, undetected, in some other, mysterious dimensions. Even though this supposed explanation was consistent with some of the more esoteric speculations of modern physics, Rachael had reckoned that physicists, of all people, really ought to know better than to try to string people along with outlandish absurdities that were quite clearly contrary to common sense. And yet, there was no denying, what had once been the Earth had been consumed by Hell itself and, consequently, a reported sixty billion people now inhabited the tired, old planet. Most of these people had died a long time ago, of course, but since the Day of Judgement had called time on the first phase of their afterlives they now had to muddle along with all those who had not died in the conventional sense but who had, like them, failed Heaven's entrance exam. Living space was at an all-time premium.

The demons, some of whom had many years' experience of working in the housing departments of local councils, had risen to the challenge and pretty much everybody who wanted a roof over their head had been able to get one. Large swathes of re-cently-vacated housing had become immediately available throughout the USA's Bible-belt and, in many other regional Christian clusters. In addition, vast numbers of dwellings had simply emerged out of the ground, along with many of their previous owners. Overall, though, demand outstripped supply and a certain amount of sharing of accommodation had become inevitable.

Rachael considered that she had been lucky, her eternal con-demnation to Hades notwithstanding. If she was going to have to share her flat with a witch, she imagined she could do a lot worse than Beatrix, who knew how things worked in Hell: how to stay on the right side of the demons, and how to make the most of limited resources. She was also multi-lingual, which was something of a godsend, so to speak, having mastered most of the English language from the fifteenth century onwards, as well as picking up a working knowledge of the more popular demonic tongues.

The two women had found common ground almost as soon as they had met, in that neither conformed to the other's stereotype. "You don't look like a Jew," Beatrix had commented on learning of Rachael's ancestry. "And, you don't look like a witch," Rachael had responded. It was true. In fact, Beatrix was remarkably well-preserved for a woman with over half a millennium under her belt. Her thick, ginger hair was long and well groomed and although her face was lined it still retained some of the elasticity of youth. She had told Rachael that far from being the result of a magical poultice, the true explanation of her relatively youthful looks was to be found elsewhere. She had died young – tragically so – and in Hades the ageing process is a lot slower than it is on Earth. Essentially, everyone starts off with something like a replica of the body they die with and they age very gradually as time goes on. The ageing curve is asymptotic to death's unerring constant; people become older, without ever getting old enough to die. The witch had said that most people considered this to be the very definition of eternal punishment.

Those who had died old, or very many thousands of years ago, now looked decrepit beyond belief, existing in mere wisps of cadaverous bodies, tugged along the streets by the wind like broken kites, begging for sweet oblivion, providing a constant reminder of the inescapable fate awaiting all who existed in this wretched place.

The sound of an old English madrigal drifted in from the kitchen. It was one that Beatrix was fond of singing, rooted as it was in memories of happier times and, God knows, she had had precious few of those.

Orphaned at twelve years of age she had been forced to live on her wits, alone, on the edge of a community which was suspicious and fearful of the bad luck that had affected her family. Her inherited pagan traditions didn't help, although the herbalist practice that came with it did, so much so that she was sought out secretly by some for remedies to ailments that the priests and other quacks were unable to heal. Nevertheless, the modest successes of her treatments and the all-too-clandestine gratitude of her clients were not enough to save her when her trial began; quite the opposite, in fact.

The case against her rested on the crucial evidence of the presence of her *familiar* near the dead body of a sow that had been struck down in the night by a mystery illness. There could be no doubt that the cat was indeed Beatrix herself as they both had green eyes and they had never been seen together. All that remained to confirm her guilt was to find the Devil's amulets secreted in her body. The priest who conducted the search – in private, for fear of exposing his congregation to Satan's power – had been blessed by God with a manhood tailor-made for the explorative task in hand.

After the rape Beatrix was almost grateful for the death sentence. *You shall not suffer a witch to live* was a biblical ordinance that allowed no wriggle-room for either alternative interpretations or disobedience, and the only person to do any wriggling that day was Beatrix herself, for a full two minutes, on the end of the rope. If she died thinking that providence had handed her the shitty end of the stick in life (or whatever was the equivalent medieval vernacular) she might at least have tried to find comfort in the compensation offered by the holy church, that her earthly punishment would buy her favour in God's sight such that even she, a whore of the Devil, might enter his Paradise. No such luck. Before it was handed to her on the dark side of death, the other end of her particular stick had been dipped into the stinking turd of divinely-determined damnation. Her tortuous dying had carried no truck with God.

On hearing the story for the first time a few days previously, Rachael had felt that the whole female gender had been violated, to say nothing of the desecration of justice.

"How could they possibly have treated you like that?" she had demanded.

"I don't know. I never went near that pig."

"I'm sure you didn't. As for the idea that you could turn yourself into a cat, and back again, it's so preposterous; so ignorant. That bloody priest should have been the one swinging, not you."

"He said he was doing God's work and everyone believed him. I don't think it helped that I had been brought up with a different belief and didn't go to the church like all the others."

"You and me both, Beatrix."

"Yes, I know. But that's why we're here, Rachael, instead of being in Heaven."

Rachael had opened her mouth to speak but had found no words to say. The idea that a person's eternal destiny could depend upon something as fragile, as accidental, as their religious beliefs, most of which were simply inherited from parents, seemed so ludicrous that only the most gullible and naive could possibly entertain it. Somebody like Fiona. Who would have thought that she would have been right all along? Timid Fiona, whose black-rimmed spectacles, abandoned on the bench outside her office block, remained one of the abiding images in Rachael's mind from that terrifying day.

The wind flung a handful of gritty hailstones at the window as Beatrix passed Rachael a mug of tea.

"Thank you. I'm freezing; it's so cold."

"It is always cold," replied Beatrix, gliding out of the room with her own sweet-smelling infusion.

Rachael sat down on the small, pale yellow sofa, as far from the window as she could get, and wrapped herself in a blanket. The newspapers lay in a pile on the coffee table next to her. Astonishingly, they had continued production and had all come out the day after the Rapture. Rachael had bought several titles, each of which had produced large Judgement Day souvenir specials featuring reports of mayhem from around the world, along with learned articles on eschatology from surprised academic theologians, all of whom were rapidly revising their opinions of mainstream biblical scholarship to include a previously unthinkable accommodation of what had been a despised literalist interpretation of much of the New Testament.

Jesus' own promise that, *some who are standing here will not taste death before they see the Son of Man coming in his kingdom* – the failed prophecy that had given rise to the mad myth of the Wandering Jew – along with Saint Paul's expectation of his erstwhile Master's imminent return, were quoted as proof positive that as the Second Coming had not taken place when predicted by the founders of the faith, it clearly wasn't going to happen at all, at least not as a real, physical event. There was considerable pique that the incontrovertible evidence of their own eyes had trumped the brilliance of their hermeneutics, although they were not as cross as the *Daily Mail,* which couldn't quite decide whether to be more furious with the atheists for being wrong or the fundamentalist Christians for being right.

Rachael's phone rang and she crossed the room to pick it up from the window sill. A picture of her mother appeared on the phone.

"Hello, Mum."

"It's your father here, Rachael."

"Oh, hi, Dad."

"I'm using your mother's phone, love. I don't know where mine is; it must be here somewhere but what with all the chaos I don't seem to be able to put my hand on it."

"Call it."

"What?"

"Call your phone. You'll hear it ringing and then you'll know where it is."

"Oh yes, good idea. I'll try that."

To Rachael's dismay she noticed that a small puddle of water had formed on the sill underneath the window. She hurried to the kitchen to get a towel with which to soak up the pooling liquid.

"Terrible business this, Rache."

"I guess you don't mean losing your phone."

"Ha! No, not that. This end of the world shenanigans."

"Dad, there's water coming in through the window frame here. On top of everything else I've got a damned leak now."

"Don't worry, love, I can fix that for you, just as soon as the weather eases up a bit."

"It won't ease up. Beatrix says it never stops raining. And she should know; she's been here for five hundred bloody years." Rachael started to cry. "Come on, love," her father said. "There's enough water around without you adding to it." In spite of her misery Rachael coughed up a half laugh, half sob.

"I'll pop round with a tube of mastic. It'll be right as rain, you'll see. No pun intended!"

"Thanks, Dad."

Rachael pushed the damp towel hard into the corner of the window frame.

"Rachael, I want to ask you something."

"Go on."

"Will you come to the schul with me and your mother?"

"The synagogue? Are you serious?"

"I know it's a long time since we've been, but we need to stick together in times like these. It's our heritage after all."

"But it's wrong."

"Well, we may not have been quite as observant as some others over the years, but even so..."

"No, I don't mean it's wrong to go to the schul; go if you want. I mean the *beliefs* are wrong, you know? It can't have escaped anyone's notice that all of us Jews are here in Hell because we didn't believe in Jesus. Even the Chief Rabbi must be able to see that."

"Ah yes, but you know Jesus himself was a Jew. He came to the Jewish people first, didn't he? That must mean something."

"Yes, it means we blew our chance! All those years waiting for the Messiah and when he finally turned up we crucified him. We're the Christ-killers, remember?"

"Well, that's one way of looking at it."

"Oh come on, Dad, it's the only way. Face the facts."

"But Rachael, religion has got nothing to do with facts. It's about community and tradition; it's what people believe."

"Even if the facts completely contradict that belief?"

"Especially if the facts contradict that belief. Religion is designed to give you hope when the facts give you despair."

"You've changed your tune."

"There are no agnostics in Hell, Rachael. Or atheists for that matter. That is, they are here but they've abandoned their old beliefs."

"Precisely! I've noticed that all those celebrity atheists have gone very quiet. Everyone believes now that the inescapable evidence has rendered disbelief in God impossible."

"Ah, you're right; I know it. Listen to your unbelieving father mumbling on like an old rabbi! The truth is, I don't know what to do. Your mother would like us all to go together. Will you come – for her if not for yourself?"

Rachael carried the sodden towel to the kitchen and wrung out the freezing water in the sink.

"I'll think about it."

"Good girl. You'll need to let me know by tonight, though. I've got three tickets held and I need to tell them if you're not going to use yours."

"Since when did you need to book tickets for the synagogue?"

"Ever since there were more people wanting to get in than there was room to accommodate them. They have eight or nine services on the Shabbat, each an hour long."

"Good God! I had no idea."

"Rabbi Bernstein was telling me that it's like that everywhere."

"You've seen Rabbi Bernstein? I thought he was dead by now."

"He was dead, but you know how it is with the dead Jews." Rachael said nothing. "So the rabbi came over to welcome us and he told us that religion is more popular here and now than it has ever been. It's not just the synagogues, but all the mosques are full to bursting, and the temples. It's only the churches that are empty."

"It's madness," said Rachael as she tossed the towel back onto the wet sill and wrapped the blanket around her shoulders.

"Did you see the documentary on Mohammed last night?"

"No."

"He's the Muslims' holy prophet."

"Dad, I know who Mohammed is."

"Yes, of course you do. Anyway, it was fascinating, in a macabre sort of way. According to the programme, after he died Mohammed went straight to Hell and was mortified to discover how wrong he had been. Naturally he wanted to live an anonymous existence because he was worried that his followers would seek him out and take revenge on him for misleading them. He got away with it for a while, but once the place started to fill up with more and more Islamic martyrs from the Crusades and other holy wars it became increasingly difficult for him. He was too well-known to hide forever and they found him eventually. Then what do you suppose happened?"

"They beat the crap out of him."

"No, the very opposite, at least to begin with. They insisted that Allah was the one true God and that he, Mohammed, was his prophet. Islam was true, according to them, and the fact that they were in Hell was simply Allah's way of testing their faith. Having sacrificed their lives for the cause they weren't about to give up their beliefs and hopes as well, just for the pedantic reason that they hadn't gone straight to Heaven."

"To enjoy their virgins."

"Exactly. To enjoy their virgins. Quite."

"So what did Mohammed have to say to them?"

"He tried to reason with them; told them that the Christian infidels had actually been right after all and that there wouldn't be any Muslims allowed into Heaven, for which he apologised."

"And how did they respond to that?"

"Well, *then* they did beat the crap out of him. Actually, they stoned him for blasphemy to be precise."

"The Muslims stoned Mohammed for blasphemy?"

"Yes. I know it doesn't sound very likely, but that's what happened."

"Even though he's Allah's prophet and the most revered person in all of their culture?"

"Yes, but they got around that by saying that it wasn't really him blaspheming, it was the Devil talking through him. It had happened once before, you see. You've heard of the Satanic Verses?"

"*Dad*, I'm not stupid."

"Sorry love, I know you're not. Well, the Satanic Verses are pagan utterances that he was supposed to have spoken as part of the revelation of the Koran. He referred to a couple of goddesses, apparently, but retracted the statements when the Archangel Gabriel told him off. As far as the Muslims here in Hell were concerned, this latest blasphemy was something similar: the *Satanic Confession* they called it. They vented their collective spleen by stoning him, but their beliefs remained intact because they said it had been the Devil talking again, not Mohammed.

"It was on the telly because this week some of the Ayatollahs who have recently found themselves in Hell along with the rest of us had insisted on meeting Mohammed. He reluctantly agreed, perhaps because he wanted to put an end to it once and for all. But, as you can imagine, they didn't like what he had to say in the slightest. In fact, they stoned the poor sod all over again."

"How many stonings can one guy take?"

"There's no limit, it seems. He's in hospital and it will take him a long time to recover, but they can't kill him. None of us is going to die; you do realise that, don't you, Rachael?"

There was a pause before Rachael said in a quiet voice, "Yes, Dad, I know."

"Hmm, well, not an easy concept to grasp at first. Maybe we'll all learn something useful tonight. You are going to watch, aren't you?"

"I suppose so. I don't really want to, if I'm honest."

"No, I understand."

There was a silence between the two of them which was partially filled by the wind wailing mournfully on their behalf.

Almost without thinking, Rachael blurted out, "I still haven't heard from Jerry."

"Ah."

"I'm really worried that he might be in Heaven."

"I thought you said he was an unbeliever."

"He was. Is. I don't know. His mum was sympathetic to the church and probably had him christened as a baby."

"It takes more than a little ritual to qualify for Heaven. I read in the paper that you have to have *taken a decision for Christ,* or some such thing."

"Then why won't he return my calls? It doesn't make any sense. I know he would call me if he could."

Rachael spoke forcefully, and they both knew why. By way of collusion her father said simply, "I'm sure you're right. You've always had a good nose for these things."

Suddenly Rachael wanted the conversation to be over. "Thanks, Dad. I'll come to the schul with you and Mum tomorrow."

"OK, honey. Thank you. I'll confirm the tickets and we'll see you there. The service starts at ten. Love you. Goodbye."

"I love you too, Dad. Bye."

Rachael slumped back down onto the sofa and tossed the phone onto the cushion beside her, pondering her father's words. Using a demonstrably false religion to generate a sense of hope seemed an unlikely act of mental gymnastics to her; a trick that she couldn't ever imagine being able to pull upon herself. Still, she had been wrong about religion when she knew that God didn't exist, so perhaps she was wrong again, now that she knew that he did.

She would go to the schul with her parents, for their sakes and for hers. Getting out of the flat would do her good; she had to overcome her fear of doing so eventually. Beatrix had told her it was safe outside; the demons made sure of that. These were the same demons who had frightened her on that first day of terror, corralling the crowds back to their homes even as the Earth erupted all around them, disgorging the inhabitants and structures and stench of Hell. Just one look from those demonic blue eyes – eyes which would have demanded a more lingering engagement in any other circumstances – seemed to have sufficient power on their own to control the mob and, if more conventional force had been necessary, the snarling dogs would have been happy to oblige. Even Charlotte had refrained from giving the demons the benefit of her acerbic opinion and had moved along with everyone else in uncharacteristically quiet subservience.

Rachael chewed the anxiety into her fingertips. She considered the possibility of housework but decided against it; things were not yet that desperate. She opted instead for a lukewarm shower, using minimal shampoo and almost no soap. Frugality was to be her new watchword. By the time she had finished and had per-suaded enough water to transfer itself from her body to the musty dampness of the bath-towel, and had then dressed herself in her warmest clothes, it was time for the programme to start.

11

Rachael returned to the lounge, where Beatrix was already settled and had turned on the TV. The witch had mastered the remote control on her first day of sharing the flat; not that she considered this to be a big deal since, as she explained to Rachael, she had always made it her business to get to know new dead people over the centuries and, as they brought with them their fresh ideas and technologies she, along with the rest of the Underworld, had kept up to date with human advances. There were even rumours that Hell enjoyed more sophisticated technology than Heaven itself, although these were as yet unsubstantiated.

The newsreader finished her summary with an update on the prophet's condition. Heavily sedated, peace was indeed upon him at last and he was expected to make a full recovery. Again.

"And now, the eagerly awaited live interview with Beelzebub – the first since the Second Coming. The programme is being transmitted in English from Broadcasting House, here in London, although simultaneous translations are available via the red button."

The applause of the studio audience heralded the start of the show and onto the stage stepped a remarkably calm-looking presenter. He wasn't someone Rachael recognised; maybe he was from an earlier era – Jonathan somebody-or-other – she didn't catch the name.

"My guest tonight hardly needs any introduction. He is popularly known throughout the world by various names – *Satan*, the *Devil*, *Beelzebub*, the *Prince of Darkness*, the *Father of Lies* – names which evoke a sense of evil and wrongdoing and, let's face it, downright unpleasantness. His reputation goes before him to such an extent that if he turned up on your doorstep to take your daughter out on a date, the parents among you might think twice before dreaming of a white wedding or the patter of tiny cloven hooves around the grand-parental abode." (*Definitely from an earlier era*, Rachael mused while the audience laughed nervously.) "But who is the real Being behind the popular conception? Is he really deeply wicked, or just deeply misunderstood? Let's find out shall we? Ladies and gentlemen, please welcome, the Devil!"

The studio was plunged into darkness except for a row of deep red up-lighters which illuminated the back wall behind Jonathan. In the middle of the wall, an arched opening spewed forth dry ice and a chilling vibrato of violin strings scratched out the horror film music that always accompanies the most tense and terrifying scenes. There was movement in the backlit archway. Something was coming and a fearful moan began rising from the audience as the violins reached their screaming climax and the creature burst through the opening.

A camera closed in on its red face as it looked slowly round with unblinking, yellow eyes. Its teeth were bared and the flesh on its face was folded up onto its high cheekbones and onto the bridge of its nose in a snarl of pure venom. It was breathing heavily as the camera slowly panned out, revealing at the top of its forehead two stubby horns.

"You're kidding me," said Rachael. Glancing across to Beatrix she added, "This has got to be a joke, right?"

Looking back at her television screen she saw that the Devil was now gripping the base of his neck with his fingers and pulling at his skin.

"My God, what's he doing?"

The skin was being grotesquely stretched and as he started to writhe and strain it became apparent that he was attempting to pull off his entire face, live on global television. He succeeded and his effort was greeted with a mild gasp and a relieved round of applause.

The Devil ran his hand through his dark, glossy hair and smiled. He was so impossibly handsome that for a second Rachael wondered whether he was wearing another mask to cover up a more ordinary face. Normally she didn't like goatee beards, but his suited him perfectly, giving his face a simultaneously playful and intelligent look. As for his gorgeous demon-blue eyes – *what was it with the blue eyes around here?* – they conveyed a sense of soulful beauty that was as alluring as it was unexpected. Indeed, such was the extent of the de-masking transformation that for an insane moment Rachael felt she might stand on the sofa and yell, "Oh, but he is ravishing!"

"Now you didn't really think I looked like that, did you, darlings?" said the Devil, in a suave English voice, rich and warm. Smiling, he held up the limp mask in his right hand and added, "Such a cliché!"

He was a tall man and in a few long strides he had crossed the stage to where the interviewer stood. Holding him by the shoulders he gave Jonathan a kiss on each cheek and presented him with the mask.

"For me?" the surprised TV host asked.

"Naturally."

"Thank you."

"Don't mention it. To be honest I'm rather frightened of it. Imagine seeing that hideous face looking back at you from the mirror every morning. Ugh! I hope you'll agree that the real me is much more handsome than that ugly brute!"

"Oh yes, yes. Definitely," said Jonathan.

"Jonny, you're such a sweetie," said the Devil as he blew an extravagant kiss towards the interviewer.

Rachael thought to herself that being Lord of the Underworld had at least one very obvious advantage: he was unaffected by the gradual ageing malaise that corroded the human population. Now that she came to think about it, she hadn't seen any wizened old demons either. The supernatural hosts, she hurriedly concluded, obviously lived by a different chemistry to her own species.

Jonathan and the Devil were sitting down and had exchanged a few more pleasantries before the interview proper began.

"First things first. You are known by many different names; which one do you prefer?"

"I answer to them all, but my friends call me Billy."

"Billy?"

"Yes, it's a corruption of Beelzebub and, as you know, corruption is something of a speciality of mine."

The Devil sat back in his chair, pleased with his own joke. The audience enjoyed it too.

"He's got a nice smile," said Rachael.

"Yes," said Beatrix. "He has."

Rachael noticed how immaculately Satan, or Billy, was dressed. His expensive dark shirt and tight jeans were wonderfully set off by his exquisite Italian shoes, giving rise in her mind to her first optimistic thought in an age: *there must be some great shoe shops in Hell!*

"Tell me, er, Billy, were you surprised by the Second Coming?"

"Well of course I was. They never tell us anything much, you know. Although I knew the dear boy would return sometime, I didn't know exactly when that would be. I was actually in the bath when it started. I didn't even get time to do my nails."

"I'm sure that was the least of your worries. Do you have a message for all the billions of newcomers here in Hell?"

The Devil adopted a classic *jazz hands* pose and cried out, "Surprise!" Despite the dubious nature of the joke, laughter filled the studio.

He continued, "First of all I'd like to welcome you by saying how truly sorry I am that you're all here," – more laughter – "but please don't believe everything you may have heard about us before you arrived. In spite of what Hieronymus Bosch may have painted to the contrary, we won't do unspeakable things to your bottoms – not unless you're very naughty that is – and, as you've no doubt already noticed, you won't be spending your time being boiled alive in a lake of fire. The weather isn't very good I'm afraid, but on the upside you won't have to sing those dreary sycophantic hymns that Old Man Yahweh is so obsessively fond of. We all do our best to get along and try to be nice to each other, and if you do the same everybody will be able to have some fun." The Prince of Darkness ended his little speech with a wink to the camera.

"I understand that you plan to make London your new home. Why is that?"

"Oh, darling, I just adore your theatre here. LA was lovely too, don't get me wrong, but I've been there a long time and I feel I need a change. Plus, I get to live in the old Queen's house; a palace fit for an Old Queen – isn't it just perfect?"

Jonathan nodded and smiled.

The Devil continued, "I'm hoping to direct some experimental theatre myself – nothing too grand to begin with. I just have to persuade the powers that be to let me have a go."

"I thought you *were* the power that be."

"How right you are, Jonny. I'll get started straight away, then!" The Devil allowed himself an affected giggle.

"If I may move onto weightier matters," the interviewer went on, "some theologians are saying that the Tribulation will follow the Rapture, meaning that there will be years of terror unleashed on all the inhabitants of Hell. What do you know about that?"

Rachael leaned forward in her seat. This was an answer she wanted to hear.

"It's just playground talk; a load of silly nonsense."

"But it's in the Bible."

"That doesn't make it the gospel truth you know. Besides…"

The Devil hesitated as he allowed the weak laughter to stop and, as he did so, his face took on an altogether gloomier mien. "What difference would a few years of torment make in all eternity? What difference would even a thousand years make? None at all." Billy was speaking quietly now and took a few moments to compose his thoughts. "You have never walked in the cool of the evening with Jesus Christ have you, Jonathan?"

"No."

"Well I have. Such a wonderful boy. To be excluded from his presence for ever and ever is punishment enough. Plagues and pestilence and torment are just a spit in the bucket compared to the loss of his love. His precious love."

Jonathan seemed uncertain how to proceed for a moment as his guest stopped talking and stared at the floor in front of him.

"Many people might be surprised to hear you talking this way. I'm sure most of us would have assumed you and Jesus would be mortal enemies. How would you describe your relationship with him?"

"I loved him. Part of me is still in love with him. How could it be otherwise?" The Devil's voice seemed to catch.

"My God, he's almost crying," said Rachael, reaching across to touch Beatrix on the arm, perhaps to reassure herself that she wasn't the victim of a prank in which the most unlikely declaration of love in the history of the universe was being made.

"Such a time we had together when I took him out to the desert. Just the two of us for forty days and nights. He had such poetry. He was so very sensitive and caring. Whenever we were hungry he would turn a snake into a fish; a stone into bread. Simply a word from him – that's all it took. The same when we were thirsty: he would make water pour from a rock and, as if that wasn't enough, he'd turn the water into the most glorious wine. I never wanted it to end. I worshipped the very ground he trod."

"And how did he feel towards you?"

"I think it's safe to say he found me quite a temptation."

"Did anything… happen?"

"I'm afraid I'm sworn to secrecy on that," replied the Father of Lies, adopting a coy look as he did so. "Let's just say the version you read in the official biography isn't exactly how I remember it.

Not that we would ever have had any peace together, his old man would have seen to that; he never did like me."

"This is God the Father you're talking about, not Joseph the carpenter."

"Of course, you silly goose. The real dad, not the surrogate. The one in whose image all mankind is supposedly made."

"Why do you say *supposedly*?"

The Devil crossed his legs, leaned back in his chair and entwined his fingers on his lap. His face glistened slightly under the studio lights. He adopted the air of a learned professor about to reveal an important truth to an earnest student.

"For the very reason that you ask that question; any question, in fact."

"I'm not following you."

"Not yet, no, but you're curious aren't you? You want to know the answer. You always want to know the answers to questions that you ask, do you not?"

"Of course; it's my job."

"You want to find out the answers to questions even when you're not working. Everybody does. But tell me, what is the one characteristic that our omniscient God cannot have that, with delicious irony, his favourite creatures have in opulent abundance?"

Jonathan didn't answer, but Rachael did, at exactly the same time as Beelzebub himself.

"Curiosity."

"If you already know everything," the Devil continued, "you can't be curious about anything. The Old Man didn't want a great dollop of curiosity added to the mankind recipe at all – he just wanted fawning simpletons – but I can be very persuasive. 'Darling,' I told him, 'you can have Americans for mindless worship, but let everybody else think for themselves!'"

The audience was even more delighted with that joke than the teller himself. Like an old pro he let the laughter die down before going on to say, "I just knew that gag would work well in London but, my loves, you know I don't mean it. Some of my most faithful friends are Americans. Truly. I love the Democrats and they all love me."

"You're saying that imbuing people with curiosity was your idea?" said Jonathan.

"I think I'm claiming some of the credit for that, yes."

"Didn't curiosity kill the cat?"

"Meeeow!" replied the Devil, clawing the air playfully with his fingers.

"But seriously, wasn't it mankind's curiosity – the desire for the knowledge of good and evil – that was the cause of all the trouble, back in the garden of Eden?"

The Devil looked at Jonathan with a wry smile on his face. "My darling boy, you have been doing your homework. The quaint little story of Adam and Eve, with me starring as Mr Snake, the most despicable of all villains. I so loved that costume!"

Again there was laughter, but Jonathan persisted in a serious vein.

"It is the reason why it all went wrong, though, isn't it? It's where our relationship with God was broken and mankind was kicked out of Paradise, metaphorically at least."

"Not just metaphorically, I'm sorry to say."

"And that means…"

"Go on," said the Devil evenly.

"It means he decided to make us with curiosity even though he knew that for billions of us, for the vast majority of people, the consequence would be eternal damnation and endless suffering."

A hush had poured into the studio just as the dry ice had entered it at the start of the show.

"It makes you think, doesn't it?" said Professor Beelzebub.

"It certainly does."

The audience remained silent as the rude heaviness of their entrapment weighed upon them. Then, the Devil, suddenly tired, reached across and laid his hand on Jonathan's knee and whispered,

"Let's just do the best we can, shall we? After all, we have the rest of our lives to live. And thank you for having me on your show."

The screen in Rachael's living room went blank as Beatrix poked the Off button.

"That's not what I expected," said Rachael after she and her companion had gazed at the television for a while.

"You'll get used to him," replied the witch.

Rachael wondered what else she would get used to. She was feeling oddly numb and thought, with characteristic self-criticism, that she ought to be registering a greater sense of shock. *Shocking*, was exactly the word her mother would use. *The Devil himself on television, bold as you like! What were they thinking? Utterly shocking.* As if an appearance on TV was the real outrage, not the fact that he existed in the first place; or that Hell had slipped its mythological moorings and was now firmly located on planet Earth; or that Yahweh had known all along how dreadfully things would turn out, but had allowed it anyway. Everything was shocking. And when everything shocks, nothing does. No wonder she was numb. What source of happiness could possibly be found to redress the balance and restore any sense of well-being? Rachael shuddered as she glimpsed her future: an emaciated soul clinging to the grounded and tattered kite of her fading body.

Beatrix's voice relieved her of her introspection. "You look tired. Shall we go to bed?"

"Yes please. I am tired, and cold. Besides, I'll need all my strength for tomorrow."

"Why, what will you be doing?"

"I'm going to the synagogue: the house where the God of the Chosen People used to live."

"For what reason?"

"Oh, you know. Curiosity."

12

As soon as she saw the bus turn into the top of her road Rachael ran downstairs.

She had loved the high-ceilinged Edwardian house that contained her flat from the moment she had first seen it. Although hers was the smallest of the six apartments within the building, she had happily mortgaged herself almost into penury in order to purchase it, in spite of its tiny size and the fact that the road on which the house stood hosted an almost continual stream of traffic, including the number 107 bus which stopped right outside the shared front door. Her father had warned her that the noise would drive her nuts, and that people on the top deck of the bus would be able to see right into her bedroom. He was wrong about the former but right about the latter, and she got used to both. Early one morning, for reasons she had never quite explored, Rachael decided to indulge the somnolent commuters in a little voyeurism. She was standing by the window wearing just a tee-shirt and slowly started to pull it up to reveal her nakedness. She had stopped just as the swell of her breasts became visible, because it was obvious from the look on his face that one of the passengers was very definitely wide awake! The erotic charge that this wilfully brazen act had given her body astounded Rachael, and she wondered what powerful forces of exhibitionism might be being constrained within her respectable, middle-class frame.

Eroticism, however, was the last thing on her mind this morning; the rain and the smell saw to that. It must be the drains that were the cause of the sulphurous aroma: all that extra shit having to force its way through London's ancient sewers. Quite how the city's infrastructure was going to cope with this mass of humanity and its waste was anybody's guess.

Rachael had scheduled her exit in order to minimise the time she had to spend outside. Just as well, because during the thirty seconds that it took the bus to reach her she almost lost her battle with the wind for ownership of her umbrella. Flustered, she climbed on board the filthy bus and began her westward journey across the northern suburbs.

Everywhere she looked she saw that the once-familiar territory had been transformed by the sudden appearance of thousands of ancient buildings; constructions of such aching decrepitude that they seemed to be held together by sheer will power. It was almost impossible to believe that they really had simply burst upon the scene just a few days ago.

Rachael wiped away a patch of condensation on the inside of the window and peered into the gloom. They were passing a meat-packing factory. Next to its iron-gated entrance, half a dozen market stalls had been set up by traders selling animal entrails and other body parts. Each stall advertised its speciality with the head of its chosen beast stuck on top of a pole. Pigs, sheep, cows and goats stood as blind sentries, refusing to see the funny side. Heavily muffled, grey customers huddled around a brazier, warming their hands like defeated strikers on a picket line waiting to be sent back to work. The demons and their lively dogs watched from a distance.

The bus rumbled on, labouring up a hill at the top of which stood an empty church. On the big wooden doors somebody had painted, using bright pink aerosol spray, a stick-man on a cross. Alongside the crude picture was written the theologically bewildering phrase, *You Fucking Judas, Jesus*. Rachael wryly observed that at least the author had had the grammatical awareness to include a comma.

It took an hour, twice as long as normal, to reach her destination: Easter Road. Rachael got off the bus and battled her way through the rain and the sodden crowds to the synagogue.

She squeezed into the busy, steaming entrance hall, which was smaller than she remembered. The place smelt of damp clothes and body odour. As she stood looking for her parents, a woman asked if she could get past, and Rachael moved aside. The woman thanked her and went by, trailing her two small children in her wake.

Two small children!

Rachael stared after them as their mother led them into a side room – the same one that had been used to teach Rachael and her contemporaries nearly a quarter of a century earlier. Other mothers and their children were making their way into the room as Rachael struggled to process the awful realisation that the presumed innocence of childhood had been an insufficient protection against the implacable justice of the Almighty; the judgement of Jesus.

Fucking Judas!

The thin arms of her own mother embraced her and Rachael felt her stiff, lacquered hair against her cheek. It takes some nerve, Rachael thought admiringly, to refuse to allow the end of the world to get in the way of an appointment with the hairdresser.

"You're not eating," her mother said as soon as she had released her daughter and stepped back to look at her.

"No, not much."

"You must eat, Rachael."

"*You* don't."

"I eat plenty; look at me."

"I am looking; there's nothing of you."

"'I eat. Harold, tell her."

But Harold wasn't listening. Instead, he was gently ruffling the head of a small girl who looked up at him with brown eyes as large and sad as a puppy dog's.

"Why are *they* here?" Rachael asked her father.

"Where else would they be?" he replied, unbuttoning his heavy tweed coat as he did so.

"They could be in Heaven. They've done nothing wrong."

"In the camps they took the children away from their parents, Rachael. You want them to do the same thing here?"

"They took them away to kill them in the camps. If I had a child I would want it to be in Paradise, not in this god-forsaken hole for all eternity."

Rachael had to bite her lip to stop her tears. Her father came and stood very close and hugged her for a long time. "So would I," he whispered eventually, "So would I."

"I couldn't leave you and Mum."

"I know, but a loving father will do anything to give his child the best possible life, even if it brings about his own suffering."

The intimate moment was interrupted when a drooping man put his hand on Rachael's father's shoulder. "Hard times, Harold," he said.

"Simon. Yes, indeed. You remember my daughter, Rachael?"

'Mr Droop' nodded. "Esther," he then said, greeting Rachael's mum in turn.

They showed their tickets to the man on the door and the four of them moved into the main auditorium, Simon and Harold heading to the men's side, Rachael and Esther taking their seats with the women.

Rachael's mind was too cluttered to really focus on the service and she drifted in and out, occasionally resonating with distant memories, sometimes seeing the rituals as if for the first time.

After some singing and praying, the large scrolls containing the Torah were carried around the room and people held out their hands to touch them as they went past. They were taken to the front and unfurled on the large wooden lectern. A man with a widow's peak ran his finger across the scroll until he found what he was looking for. Eagerly he read the passage in fluent Hebrew, excitedly bobbing up and down as he did so. For the benefit of the non-Hebrew speakers, like Rachael – *bad Jewish girl!* – he also translated into English God's words as recorded in the book of Leviticus.

If you will not listen to me and carry out all these commands, and if you reject my decrees and abhor my laws and fail to carry out all my commands and so violate my covenant, then I will do this to you: I will bring upon you sudden terror, wasting diseases and fever that will destroy your sight and drain away your life. I will set my face against you so that you will be defeated by your enemies; those who hate you will rule over you and you will flee even when no-one is pursuing you.

Rachael remembered staring, as a child, at the circular window high up in the front wall. She recalled seeing the sun streaming through the yellow glass and the Star of David sparkling in its centre. She had fancied at the time that God himself had been looking into the synagogue with his blazing eyes to see if they were all being good. Today that same window was dark. God was no longer looking in; he had seen enough and had taken his gaze elsewhere.

If in spite of this you still do not listen to me but continue to be hostile towards me, then in my anger I will be hostile towards you, and I myself will punish you for your sins seven times over. You will eat the flesh of your sons and the flesh of your daughters.

Rachael guessed that her father would be having a hard time visualising having her for dinner in the cannibalistic sense implied by the Scripture, no matter what the circumstances. *A loving father would do anything for his child.* She searched the far side of the room to see if she could locate him and just glimpsed the top of his head beneath his under-utilised kippah. As her eyes swept back she noticed a dumpy man sitting on the end of the row, the other side of the aisle, sweating. He wrote something in a little notebook then smiled and nodded in her direction. Rachael didn't know who he was and looked away.

They will pay for their sins because they rejected my laws and ab-

horred my decrees. Yet in spite of this, I will not reject them or abhor them so as to destroy them completely, breaking my covenant with them. I am the Lord their God. But for their sake I will remember the covenant with their ancestors whom I brought out of Egypt in the sight of the nations to be their God. I am the Lord.

When the reading was finished and the scrolls rolled up, the congregation stood to sing, unaccompanied, in Hebrew. There is no sound more poignant, Rachael thought, than a synagogue full of Jews singing in harmony to the God who has, after all, rejected them.

Rabbi Bernstein began to speak. "We are the people of the covenant. God is faithful and he calls us to confess our sins and the sins of our fathers, so that we might once more enjoy his favour. Moses teaches us this, just as he taught our ancestors. Our hope must be that one day God will hear the cries of his people, see our tears of repentance and, remembering his ancient promise, gather us to himself and surround us with his love. God at peace with his chosen people once more, but this time for all eternity. What a vision!"

Rachael felt herself flush with embarrassment as her perspiring observer stood up and called out, "It's the vision of a blind man!" She hated this kind of scene – it seemed so very impolite – but the rotund man was not going to keep quiet.

"How can you not see? God has abandoned us; there is no re-demption for the Jewish people."

There were a few murmurings of assent from the congregation, but the silver-haired rabbi responded quickly. "You think this is the first time the Jews have been abandoned, huh?" he said. "Come on, Eli, have you forgotten our history so soon? What is to say we cannot overcome our present troubles?"

"Rabbi, these aren't *troubles*, this is judgement. HaShem isn't going to rescue us; he's the one who put us here."

"Then he has the key to let us out."

"Sure, just as soon as he realises what a big mistake he's made."

"God doesn't make mistakes, Eli, you know this."

"No, but people do. Our mistake was to believe the wrong promise, or obey the wrong commands. I don't know exactly how or why but we got it wrong. Why make it worse by pretending he's going to come and rescue us?"

"If you turn your back on God now you will have nothing – an eternity of despair. We cannot abandon hope when hope is all we have."

"That's what they told us in the camps," said a broken-looking old woman who had now also risen to her feet.

"Yes, Mrs Mendel, I know; you have told us this before," said the rabbi, trying to prevent the service from disintegrating into a free-for-all.

But Mrs Mendel had a trump card to play. "My great-aunt was in Treblinka; this is how I know." The grim kudos of a holocaust victim, even by proxy, permeated the room and hushed the restive congregation. "She has told me that they always spoke of hope. Even when their friends disappeared – they all knew what was happening – the rabbis told them the same thing: never give up. In the chamber," her voice was little more than a dry whisper as she took them to the moment of ultimate desecration, "they prayed, covering their heads, just with their hands." Here Mrs Mendel slowly lifted her own hand and placed it flat, on top of her head. "Like this. Then, when it was all over, they found them-selves in Hell. You can imagine how that was for them."

The woman turned around, her watery eyes seeking the faces of her listeners, most of whom found themselves unable to return her stare.

"My great-aunt says that at least all the Nazis did was to kill us. With God there is no end to the punishment."

"If we repent…" Rabbi Bernstein began, but Mrs Mendel held up her hand to halt him.

"No, we are the old, spent wife. God is with his young mistress now. She has his full devotion and he doesn't hear our weeping. We are sagging and wrinkled, and we cannot win him back."

In the moments of silence that followed Esther reached for Rachael's hand and squeezed it.

"Then why are you here, Sarah?" the rabbi asked quietly.

"I am a Jew. It is Shabbat and this is my schul. Where else would I be?"

Poor Rabbi Bernstein, Rachael thought, humiliated in his own synagogue, and Sarah Mendel, trapped in her failed religion. Curiously – and Rachael remembered how it had been curiosity that had been partly responsible for her coming here – she sensed an unaccountable sadness that she hadn't involved herself more thoroughly in the Jewish community before now. How odd that she could retrospectively covet temporal solace in the midst of eternal grief.

As the final hymn filled the building with musical melancholy, Rachael felt herself caught up in the communal sense of betrayal and abandonment. It had been a mistake to come and she got up to leave soon after the singing finished. She managed to get as far as the entrance hall when sweaty Eli, the self-appointed fifth columnist, accosted her.

"Stella! I knew it was you."

"It isn't me. I'm not Stella; you must have me confused with someone else."

"Maybe not now, but you were."

"What?"

"*A Streetcar Named Desire*, at the Regal. You were Stella. When was that, five, six years ago?'

"Yes, that's true. How on earth do you know that?"

"I covered it for the *Echo*. You were very good; stuck in my mind. Very rare to get such an exquisite performance in am-dram."

"*Exquisite?* I remember that word being in the review."

"Are you still acting?"

Rachael looked at Eli as if that was a silly thing to say.

"Sorry, silly thing to say! *Streetcar* was pretty much my last gig. Too many cigarettes and too much booze saw me arrive in here soon afterwards, so I wouldn't know if you'd carried on or not."

"No, I didn't. That play was my last gig too."

"I've always loved the theatre myself, so after I'd settled here I got a job as an agent. It's what I do when I'm not giving the rabbi some stick! Anyway, I know of a role coming up that I think would suit you perfectly."

"Really? Why me?"

"The director's looking for someone fresh, with your kind of build, your kind of face."

Rachael touched her cheek. "My kind of face?"

"Yes. Young; pretty; Jewish, but not too Jewish."

"I'm not sure if I should be flattered by that or not."

"Oh, you should be flattered. Of course, if you're too busy with something else then I can always look elsewhere."

"No, don't do that," said Rachael, far too quickly. In this place of unrelenting nightmares a dream or two might be just what she needed.

Eli took out his notebook, tore out a page and handed it to Rachael. "I've written down the time and place for the auditions. I'll tell them to expect you. My number's there as well; let me know how it goes."

"OK. Thanks. But, wait a minute, what's the play about?"

"They'll explain that when you get there. It sounds very exciting; the director uses a lot of improvisation. I think you'll like it, Rachael."

"You know my name."

"I never forget a name, or a pretty face. Rachael Bennett, the best Stella I ever saw."

Rachael wanted to ask Eli how many different Stellas he had actually seen, but he had turned and, with surprising dexterity, pushed his way through the crowd.

Rachael's parents were talking to some people she didn't know, but eventually made their way over to where she was standing.

"I hope old Eli wasn't pestering you too much," said her father.

"No, he was fine. I'm glad I came, after all."

"You'll come back to eat, then?" said Esther in a way that precluded a negative response. Rachael accepted the invitation and the three of them forced their way outside into the black, freezing rain.

13

Jerry was loving the sensation of rain on his face, even though it wasn't from a real cloud. These water droplets were being sprayed from high above the giant, sunken tank that would act as the stage, but they felt just like the genuine article. This was one of the reasons that he had come: the undimming refulgence of God's glory had made him feel dried out and had created within him a longing for the meteorological variation that had added to the unpredictability of life back in London. Already, some of the details of that existence were beginning to pale, in spite of the fact that he had only been in Heaven – how long? – just a few weeks. The absence of natural darkness made it difficult to tell.

Flooded was part-museum, part theatre. Jerry and Catherine had spent a couple of hours in the life-size reconstruction of the Ark, complete with its stuffed animals and helpful explanations of a day in the life of Noah and his family, most of which consisted of shovelling shit. Made to the exact dimensions specified in the Bible, the museum Ark included only an eighteen inch gap for ventilation under the roof. Even with the use of electric fans the atmosphere inside was stifling, making a two-hour visit the most that anyone could stand. The idea that a real menagerie of this size would be able to survive for a year with such inadequate access to fresh air, in an atmosphere fuelled by incessant animal farting, struck Jerry as implausible in the extreme. Given the explosive levels of methane that would have surely built up, he concluded that the real miracle of the story was that the voyage ended with a gentle landing on Mount Ararat rather than with a bloody big bang.

The Beetle Room had been Jerry's favourite: over three hundred thousand boxes, each labelled and containing a pair of every single ----ies of the little insects, was a sight to behold. Jerry had asked one of the guides how they would have been collected, given that new species were still being discovered on the Earth right up until the Rapture, and that it would take someone nearly a century to collect all of them even if they gathered them at an unlikely rate of ten different species every day. The guide, with a commendable sense of the ridiculous, replied that the animals came to Noah, he didn't have to go and fetch them. Jerry smiled at the thought of the marching, swimming, flying beetles coming from all over the world, no doubt guided by the Holy Ghost, to the safety of their wooden boxes. He had thanked the guide for the innocent explanation and had moved on.

During what Jerry ironically thought of as his leisure time, he had started to read the Bible that had been thoughtfully left for him in his room at Messiah Mansions. He had done this in response to several barbed comments from Solomon who seemed to regard him as unworthy of his place in the kingdom of Heaven, especially given his ignorance of the Holy Scriptures. In a rare convergence of their opinions, Jerry agreed that he knew very little of the Good Book and set out to eradicate his ignorance in this respect.

So far he had managed the first eleven chapters of Genesis, which he had found to be both funny and violent in equal measure, but never credible. This was another reason for his visit to *Flooded*, to see with his own eyes the reconstruction of the fable. That, and the desire for cool, soft rain.

He and Catherine had positioned themselves in front-row seats that guaranteed them a good drenching. Jerry had asked Catherine if she would like to come with him and had been pleased when she had said yes straight away. It wasn't a date – perish the thought – but Jerry was enjoying her company and her enthusiasm for her rejuvenated able-bodied life. He also detected in her, so he thought, some echo of his own anxieties: he fretted about his continued inability to find Rachael, and he knew that she also felt uncomfortable about the on-going absence of her apostate sister, Caroline.

"I loved the aviary," said Catherine. "So many beautiful birds I'd never seen before."

"Yes, and there was only a pair of each type, as far as I could see," replied Jerry.

"There were only two of everything."

"I know, but when I read the story the other day, sometimes it said there were two of every type of bird, and sometimes that there were seven."

"Are you sure? I didn't know that."

"When did you last read it?"

"I can't remember. Ages ago."

"Well, look it up. It's very confusing. There's different numbers depending on whether the animals are clean or unclean as well, although with all that water sloshing around you'd think there'd be more than enough for them all to have a bath."

Catherine gave Jerry a withering look. "It doesn't mean clean like your laundry. Some animals are clean in God's sight and some are unclean."

"How does he decide which is which?"

"I don't know."

"Are birds clean?"

"Some are, yes."

"Fish?"

"Mostly OK I think, although the Jews don't eat shellfish because they're definitely unclean."

"Poor things. The Jews, I mean. Good for the prawns, though. What about fleas?"

"Now you're being silly."

"OK. Dinosaurs – clean or dirty?"

"Oh yes, I was wondering about them. They didn't have any on the Ark in the museum, did they?"

Jerry laughed. "Of course not! They wouldn't fit on board; and even if they had, by the time they had landed all that would be left would be one fat T Rex and bugger all else."

"Not necessarily. Not if they were babies."

"Little cuddly ones that were still being fed on milk?"

"You're being silly again."

Jerry looked carefully at his friend and wiped some rainwater from his forehead. "Catherine, there were no dinosaurs left on Earth by the time man evolved."

"I don't believe in evolution. I'm a Creationist."

Jerry studied Catherine's face for signs of irony. He had never before met an adult naive enough to give credence to an ancient myth penned by unknown authors in an age of deep superstition, over and above one of the best-attested scientific theories of all time.

"Why?" he asked, after some delay.

"Because that's what the Bible teaches."

"You don't think it's just another made-up story like all the other creation legends around the world?"

"Why would God put something in his book that wasn't true, Jerry? Next you'll be saying that the Flood didn't really happen."

"I don't think it did. Of course there have been lots of terrible floods throughout history, but one which covered the entire planet with water and killed every single creature except for those squished into the Ark is just not feasible."

"Then what do you think all this is about?" asked Catherine, gesturing to the tank in front of them where the story would soon be re-told.

"They're just acting out a parable, that's all. It's only a story to warn people to be good and not to fuck about."

Jerry immediately regretted his smart-arse use of the vulgar expletive, which he'd intended as a reference to the sexual promiscuity of the doomed occupants of the antediluvian Earth, but which he realised had offended his companion.

"You're so naive, Jerry," Catherine scolded, in a neat reversal of his own recently-formed opinion of her.

Further quarrelling had to be suspended as a foursome of two men and two women pushed past them to take their seats. The newcomers seemed none too happy at having to sit in the wet zone.

"We would have been able to get decent seats if we'd come straight here instead of going to the zoo," said one of the women.

"Yes, but how was I to know it would be shut when we got there?" replied the man to whom she had addressed the comment.

"I'm just saying, that's all," the woman said. Turning to the other two in the party she asked, "Are you two going to be all right here?"

The two simply looked at each other and shrugged.

"Kids today, Jerry, they don't know they're alive." Alf, the beleaguered man who had initially protested his innocence of the zoo closure, confided in Jerry. He had turned away from the other three adults who Jerry now realised would have been his wife and children back on Earth. "They never bothered with zoos at home, but they insisted they wanted to go to the one here to see the famous wolf and lamb together. But it's because the wolf misbehaved himself that they closed it today."

Jerry suddenly remembered the literature he'd seen on his first day in Heaven. "Oh yes, I've heard about that – Paradise Zoo, isn't it? – where the wolf lives with the lamb? You have to feel sorry for the lamb: not only does it never get to grow up, it has to spend all its time living next to its most notorious predator. What is that all about?"

"It's a prophecy," interjected Catherine. "It comes from Isaiah and it says that in Heaven the wolf and the lamb will live together, and something like a cheetah or a leopard will lie down with a goat, I think. The zoo must be where the prophecy is fulfilled. I think it's wonderful."

"Yeah, well we didn't get to see any of it," said Alf. "It looks like the wolf got a bit bored with his vegetarian diet and sitting right next to him is this fat, juicy lamb and, as you can imagine, nature took its course."

"He ate it?" asked Jerry, trying not to laugh.

"Not quite; according to some people we met as they were coming out, he had it in his mouth and roughed it up a bit. Apparently the angels got there quick as a flash and saved the lamb but it was badly shaken. That's why they closed the zoo: the main attraction is the novelty of seeing the two of them together, but I don't suppose little Larry will feel like going anywhere near those big teeth for a while."

"What else would you expect?" said Jerry. "You can't teach an old dog new tricks: once a carnivore, always a carnivore."

"Not necessarily," said Catherine. "I don't think God designed them to eat other animals. To begin with they must have been herbivores; they only started killing once sin entered the world at the Fall."

"Wolves were vegetarians?" laughed Jerry. "Have you seen their teeth? They do look like they've been made to rip into flesh rather than chew the cud. Our friend T Rex the same. If they were designed, it was with the intent to kill from the word go."

"That would be cruel," said Catherine.

"Yes, but is it less cruel to foist suffering upon their victims as a result of a conversation between a woman and a talking snake?" (As Jerry had actually now read the story of what had supposedly transpired in the Garden of Eden, he was seduced by the power of his little knowledge and therefore emboldened enough to hold an opinion on the subject.)

Catherine took her time to answer. "When God created the world everything was perfect, just like it is in Heaven. But man sinned and corrupted it; that's where suffering and death come from. It was man's fault there was pain in the world, not God's."

"OK, let's say you're right and that all the wolves and lions and sharks ate hay or flowers or seaweed, even though they look well-adapted to running after other animals and eating them instead. And let's assume that not a single fly was accidentally ingested into one of the mouths gobbling up all the grass. (What did spiders eat, by the way? Oh, it doesn't matter.) Parasites lived happily in their hosts without causing so much as a little itch, never mind death, and nobody even sneezed because the common cold virus just minded its own business and lived off fresh air. Everything was perfect, exactly as it is in Paradise now. Then along came sin and the carnivores discovered their teeth and claws – big time – and an orgy of killing and suffering began. What's to stop it happening again? Somebody, somewhere in Heaven, is going to do something wrong and when that happens won't there be suffering and pain again, just like before?"

"No."

"Why not?"

"Because we won't sin."

"What, never? Not in a million years? Not in a million times that?" Jerry felt it would take him a lot less time to transgress, and suspected that he might have done so already.

"I never thought of that," said Alf, who looked like he'd never thought of anything very much.

"Even if we do sin," said Catherine quietly, "He will forgive us and there will be no more pain; none at all, Jerry."

Her last comment sounded more like a plea than a statement of fact. Jerry wanted to ask why God couldn't have behaved so magnanimously the first time round, but he knew he was operating outside the tiny envelope of his theological expertise. He barely understood what it really meant to sin, although he was sure that on everybody's list *don't kill people*, and *be kind to dumb animals* would be two of the key commandments. Besides, he realised that, for the second time since they had arrived, he had probably offended his companion. Who was he, after all, to engage in a pseudo-intellectual debate on suffering with someone who knew more about it from first-hand experience than he ever would? So, he lightly touched Catherine's arm and said, "Yeah, no more pain."

The sudden announcement that in today's programme Noah would be played by himself was greeted with a mighty roar by the eighty thousand spectators. When the noise had died down, Catherine turned to Jerry, a little smugly, and said, "So, you still think it's a fairy story?"

Jerry had no defence. He simply smiled and thought to himself how odd it was that the first famous person he would see since he arrived in Heaven would be someone he had previously thought of as being the central figure in a myth. Given the unlimited amount of time he now had at his disposal, he hoped that he might eventually meet every famous person who had ever lived. Furthermore, it was theoretically possible for him to meet them all an infinite number of times, by which time they might not be famous any more. For now, though, his starting point would be Noah, live at *Flooded*, looking not a day older than the six hundred years the Bible had fancifully set for his age when the deluge had begun. Jerry felt a little sorry for him that God had determined that the old boy should look like the Ancient of Days for ever more, but suspected that no-one would have believed that Noah was who he claimed to be if he appeared young and sprightly. The price some people had to pay for their art!

All the other members of Noah's family were to be played by actors, the announcer informed the crowd. Jerry guessed that the original cast members were pretty fed up with hearing the same sermon by now and had made themselves unavailable for selection, an opinion reinforced when the spectators were told that Noah would only be preaching for thirty minutes today, rather than the one hundred years he had originally spent browbeating the inhabitants of the Earth to try to get them to repent from their wickedness. Clearly, he made up in tenacity for what was obviously lacking in brevity and persuasiveness, Jerry concluded.

"God sees your evil deeds and commands you to repent!" Noah bawled from the top of a rocky island located in the centre of the concrete tank which would house all the entertainment. The tank was the size of a soccer pitch and surrounded on all four sides by the terraced rows of comfortable seats reminiscent of those found in the VIP areas of modern sports stadia. Each seat had its own TV screen and, with a light touch of the finger, it was possible to select any one of a score of camera shots to view the action in close-up, high-definition. That, at least, was the theory; in practice Catherine's screen seemed only to transmit a picture of the part of the stage closest to where they were sitting, and Jerry's remained impassively blank no matter how hard he thumped the console. Perhaps the law that electronics and water made poor bed-fellows was universal after all.

"Turn from your wrong-doing or the Lord will wipe you from the face of the Earth."

The rain was falling more heavily now that Noah had started to preach. Large drainage holes covered with iron grids appeared at regular intervals across the bottom of the tank, but their valves must have been shut as there were already a few inches of water covering the floor.

Twenty or thirty other islands, all slightly lower than Noah's, were scattered throughout the tank. They were populated with small groups of people and animals, all busy with their wickedness. Hilariously, at least from Jerry's perspective, they were all animatronic rather than flesh and blood. The human models moved with those odd little juddering motions so peculiar to elementary robotic mannequins. Three males on the island closest to Jerry and Catherine were grouped together in violent pantomime: one lying on his back being stabbed in the throat while his assailant had his head bashed with a rock held in the trembling grip of the third dummy. The murderous cycle was repeated every minute and its utter clumsiness had Jerry in stitches.

Elsewhere, two other male animatrons embraced and stole the briefest of kisses, mouth to mouth, then glanced around before starting the whole procedure all over again.

"You are an abomination; you do only that which is detestable in my sight, says the Lord."

Families of people on most of the islands were engaged in all the normal family activities – eating, sleeping, mating and killing each other – while groups of animals did much the same. Although he was aware that nobody anywhere near him was finding any of this remotely funny, Jerry found himself laughing uncontrollably at the sheer gaucheness of the performance. Eventually he recovered his composure and asked Catherine why she thought animatrons were being used instead of real people.

"Because it wouldn't be right to ask people to sin," she replied.

"Even if it was just pretend?" asked Jerry. "Besides, apart from the odd fight they don't look like they're misbehaving too badly."

"All that you do is evil," screamed Noah, as if to personally correct Jerry's liberal-minded tolerance. "The Lord is sending a great deluge upon the Earth. Repent or be swept away in his merciless judgement."

Although more melodrama was hardly needed, at that precise moment a bolt of lightning flashed across the stadium followed by an ear-splitting crack of thunder. If ever there was a sign, Jerry thought, that God was not pissing about with his warnings then that was it, especially as the rain now adopted monsoon proportions. However, instead of turning over a new leaf the people simply carried on just as before, slaves to their pre-programmed software code, much like the original human counterparts on which they had been modelled.

Along one side of the tank a causeway led to the bottom of a loading ramp that provided access to the scaled-down Ark. Pairs of robotic animals were now awkwardly shuffling along the causeway towards the ramp. During the Biblical Flood it had allegedly taken seven days to load two of every species onto the Ark (a timescale that had seemed improbably brief to Jerry when he had read it), but as considerably less time was available for *Flooded* only a small sub-set had been selected for salvation during the show. One of the rhinos, on arrival at the ramp, lost its mechanical footing and toppled over onto its back. It lay upside down, its legs stupidly pawing the air, until a number of stagehands managed to heave it back onto its feet. Jerry, once again, was beside himself with laughter, but his amusement didn't last long.

"Vengeance is mine, says the Lord," rang out Noah's triumphant voice in conclusion of his dreadful sermon. And then, *all the springs of the great deep burst forth, and the floodgates of the heavens were opened.*

The drainage holes in the floor disgorged black water at a terrifying speed and rain hammered down from above. In no more than a few minutes a number of the smaller islands were engulfed as the water level rose rapidly. The noise of the cascade and the accompanying thunder was almost overwhelming and Jerry fancied that he could hear, mixed into the cacophony, some screams of genuine fear coming from members of the audience. The churning mass of feverish water continued to rise and the tank was already at least two thirds full. Such was the force of the downpour that it was difficult to see across to the other side, but as far as Jerry could make out all the animals were now miraculously inside the Ark and its door was being steadily pulled shut.

In spite of having secured their own immortality, the terrifying fear of death evoked by the simulated flood was too much for some people in the audience, and a number of them were hurrying from the stadium. Jerry himself wondered if he and Catherine should put some more distance between themselves and the demonic waters.

The bodies of three kangaroos and a zebra swept past them, bounced and buffeted by the currents.

Be kind to dumb animals.

Waves were hitting the top of the tank and water was splashing onto Jerry and Catherine's legs when the rain finally started to relent. Every island was completely submerged and the tethered Ark floated in one corner of the tank, brooding.

Jerry's body was rigid with tension. He had not been anticipating just how much fear the horror of the flood would generate. God knows what it must be like to experience a real one.

Then he saw a body. Face down in the water and completely motionless it looked every inch like a real-life dead person.

Don't kill people.

He glanced at Catherine to see if she had noticed, but she was staring at her TV screen, one hand held to her open mouth. Jerry tried to position himself to see what was troubling her but, as he did so, she sprang out of her seat and jumped into the water. Momentarily astonished, he quickly pulled himself together and was at the side of the tank in a second, hauling her out of the tank.

"What on earth…" he began.

"He looked so real," she interrupted. "I couldn't bear it."

Cradled in her arms was an animatronic baby. Its circuitry had not yet switched off and it was still moving its arms and legs.

"He was floating on his back; he was still alive!" she said, through great sobs of grief. She cried, and cried, and cried, in the New Jerusalem, where there is *no crying or pain, for the old order of things has passed away.*

An angel suddenly materialised beside them, ripped the baby out of Catherine's arms and threw it back into the swirling water, where it was dragged into an eddy and disappeared from view. "It is a sin to oppose God's judgement," he spat into her face and marched off.

"We're leaving," said Jerry, and he gently led Catherine away from the savage scene.

By the time they had reached the cafeteria their clothes had dried out. Sitting down with their coffees in the enormous, sparsely-populated room, they could hear the roar of the crowd in the distance.

"I guess that's the dove coming back with the olive leaf," said Jerry.

Catherine didn't reply. She had said nothing since they had left the show. Jerry waited a few more minutes and then said, "You were very brave jumping into the water."

"To save a robot?" she replied.

"It looked real enough."

The two of them were silent again as they contemplated all that they had seen.

"I never thought about babies dying in the Flood," said Catherine at last. "Why didn't...?" her voice trailed off.

"Why didn't God send an angel to do what you did?" said Jerry.

"Yes. No. Why didn't anyone listen to Noah?"

"Are you kidding? You heard him shouting and hollering at everyone. They probably thought they were better off drowning rather than listening to any more of his awful preaching."

Catherine sipped her coffee and didn't disagree. They could hear a hymn of praise being sung to Jesus in the stadium. The words thanked him for his faithful, loving kindness.

"Catherine," said Jerry, "do you think God really wanted to save those people?"

"Yes, of course. Why wouldn't he?"

"Well, as you said, no-one took any notice of Noah's ranting, but God would have known that beforehand, so why did he adopt a strategy that he knew would fail?"

"There was no-one else to send."

"In that case, why not send a tribe of talking monkeys? That would have got everybody's attention. I'd certainly listen if an ape swung down from the trees and told me to mend my ways. Of course, God would have to make the animals talk."

"God spoke to Balaam through his donkey once, but…"

"There you go, then!"

"They still wouldn't have listened."

"In that case they deserved to drown for complete stupidity. Anyone who won't take any notice of his ass doesn't deserve his place in the gene pool."

"That's unkind. You can't kill people just because they're stupid."

"No, but apparently you can kill them just because they're bad, even the ones that could not possibly have known any better."

A long pause followed. People were starting to come into the cafeteria. The show was obviously over. Catherine covered her face with one hand and reached across the table with the other, which Jerry held tightly. He felt the beautiful softness of her skin and watched as her tears dribbled down her cheeks and splashed onto the table-top. Thinly, she gasped, "He was just a baby."

14

Jerry had hardly seen Catherine in the few days that had passed since their visit to *Flooded*. He would have liked to have talked to her but she seemed to be avoiding him and, although this saddened him more than he cared to admit, he realised she needed to deal with the trauma in her own way. He was having his own struggle to assimilate the knowledge he had gained: God could stand by and watch adults, children and sentient animals die ghastly, choking deaths without so much as lifting a divine finger. Moreover, the Almighty had discharged the murderous waters as an act of unilateral judgement without providing any means of escape for those who, at least in Jerry's view, were completely innocent. Even if the whole story had indeed been a parable, it was difficult to see God emerging from it in a good light.

Jerry was not enjoying the worship quite so much any more. The sensation was still spiritually orgasmic but it felt like making love to an impossibly beautiful woman who remained aloof and unable to connect with him in any deep or meaningful way. He was half-thinking that this must be his fault; after all, everybody else seemed perfectly happy. And he had questions, so many questions piling up in the back of his mind. He knew he needed help and, for this reason, he was travelling to the golf course to meet Bob's friend, Canon John.

He looked out of the windows as the bus passed the palatial properties of the righteous: enormous houses that were now the dwelling places of those who had been especially godly all their earthly lives. Given the paucity of his own religious commitment on Earth, Jerry felt he had been exceptionally lucky to have qualified for the comfort of his single room at Messiah Mansions.

Even so, he was not quite at the bottom of the pile. There was an entire underclass of servants who were employed to keep the wheels of the heavenly infrastructure oiled. Like Jerry's personal butler, Worthy, they all dressed in grey and lived in the shantytown shacks that Jerry had originally mistaken for animal shelters on the outskirts of the city. They were drawn from the Christian cults and sects that had grown up like fungus on the main branches of the church: Mormons, Seventh Day Adventists, Christian Scientists, Jehovah's Witnesses. Although all the members of these peripheral denominations shared a sense of disappointment, not to say astonishment, that they had been rewarded in such a way, they nevertheless got on with their jobs without complaint: serving food, sweeping the streets, cleaning the toilets. The Roman Catholics had been expecting to spend long periods of time in purgatory working off the penalty for their sins and most couldn't cope with the guilt of being given a place in Heaven for free, so, at their own insistence, many of them worked too, alongside their heretical brothers and sisters.

One fact Jerry had failed to establish was the whereabouts of the non-Christians. Solomon had gleefully informed him that they were in Hell, where they deserved to be and, moreover, where all those who hated Christ would choose to be. But Jerry was unconvinced, not least because most people who he had known back home hadn't given Christ a second thought, never mind worked up enough of an opinion about him to actively hate the guy. Needless to say, Solomon had spouted some scriptural reference to justify his view – a quote from Jesus saying that those who were not for him were against him – and then gone on to claim that if there wasn't a Hell then Hitler and all the Muslims would be in Heaven and that just wouldn't be fair, would it? Jerry had given up at that point, certain that an omniscient, all-loving God would be above such nonsense and would act justly. Nevertheless, it was true that so far he had not caught a glimpse of either Hitler or any Muslims and, subsequent to his *Flooded* experience, his confidence that God would be compassionate to all had undoubtedly been dented.

Bob was evasive when Jerry raised these awkward questions with him and he simply referred him to the Canon. Jerry expected that this man of the cloth would be able to allay his fears, not just about the fate of non-believers in general, but about Rachael and his other friends and family in particular, and this is what had kept his panic at bay. Just.

One thing that was beyond doubt, Jerry thought as he began eating his succulent wrap: the food in Heaven was excellent. He had developed a real penchant for goat's cheese, especially after he'd discovered that there was, incredibly, only one goat in Heaven! The fortunate creature lived a happy life, eating whatever took her fancy and providing a few pints of milk every twenty-four hours for the daily miracle. And what a miracle it was: one that made the feeding of the five thousand look feeble by comparison. Through the miraculous intervention of the Holy Ghost, the entire heavenly requirement for goat's cheese was generated from the modest udders of this single lactating animal. Quite why such a system had not been available to the underfed masses that had withered on the pre-Rapture planet in their billions was another of Jerry's queries that Bob had not satisfactorily answered, other than to try to assure him that starvation was caused by the greed of mankind rather than any lack of provision on God's part.

The bus brought him at last to the St Stephen the Martyr golf course and he alighted. It had been a good journey: the passengers hadn't been singing and the bus hadn't run anybody over.

Even from first glance, Jerry knew that the championship-standard *Stephen* would provide him with a challenging afternoon. Walking up the entrance drive, Jerry heard the metallic thwack of a perfectly struck golf ball and turned towards the source of the noise. He saw the white ball bounce along the softly sculpted fairway and roll towards a green so luxuriant that it nearly hurt his eyes to look at it. White sand bunkers, azalea bushes and a sparkling lake completed a scene of thrilling, almost erotic beauty. This was not, Jerry realised, a course on which someone of his inability should be playing.

Canon John greeted him warmly from the clubhouse doorway, where he stood with two full sets of clubs in expensive-looking golf-bags.

"John, I'm not sure I'm up to playing at this level," said Jerry. "Maybe I should go and practise on the driving range before I actually play on the course."

"Nonsense. I've got you a set of clubs already; you'll be fine."

"I'm left-handed," said Jerry.

"That's no excuse, these are left-handed clubs," John replied cheerfully.

"How did you know?"

"Lucky guess!"

"I don't believe you."

"Oh, all right, Bob told me."

"What else did he say?"

"That you had a few questions to ask me. That's why I didn't book any caddies today. I usually take Marcus with me, he's one of the Christadelphian lads who works here, but we'll be more private on our own, provided you don't mind carrying your own clubs."

"I'm happy to carry them; it's using them that will be the problem."

"Really? You're a big tall lad. I would have thought you would have played some sport back on Earth."

"Yes, I was in a cricket team for a few years."

"Batsman or bowler?"

"Batsman – middle order, usually."

"Highest score?"

"Well, I got a hundred once on an easy wicket playing against a mediocre bowling attack."

"Ha! Don't be so modest. If you can hit a moving ball that well you'll have no trouble with these little rascals. They just sit where you put them and wait to be smacked down the fairway. Come on, let's see what *Old Stony's* got to say for himself."

The Canon set off briskly towards the first tee and Jerry had no choice but to follow. "Who's Old Stony?" he asked.

"The golf course," replied the Canon. "It's our little joke, those of us who play here every day. We call it that because of the way that Stephen met his end rather than because of a surfeit of rocks on the fairways, I'm pleased to say." They had reached the tee and the Canon was pulling a fearsome driver out of his bag. Jerry was looking blank. "Stephen was the church's first martyr, Jerry. He was stoned to death – Acts chapter seven. They named the golf course after him."

"Ah," said Jerry. "Nice. To name the golf course after him – obviously. Not the stoning, I expect that stung a bit."

"I daresay," replied Canon John and climbed up onto the flat tee. As soon as he did so, a tinny voice sounded out from a loudspeaker positioned at the top of a nearby speaker-post. "Welcome to St Stephen the Martyr Golf Course on this beautiful day in God's everlasting kingdom," it said with squeaky enthusiasm. "This is hole number one: five hundred and sixty-eight yards long, par five, stroke index sixteen. May your game today bring great praise and glory to his wonderful and holy name!"

"Don't take any notice of that," said the Canon.

"OK," replied Jerry, a little taken aback. "I wasn't sure how playing golf was going to bring praise and glory to God anyway, to be honest."

"I meant you should ignore the information about the hole. It's only actually, let me see…" said the Canon, fishing out a paper scorecard from his back pocket, "…four hundred and thirty-two yards, par four. Nice start: easy as sin."

He was a stocky man with thick dark hair and wild eyebrows.

He loosened up with a couple of practice swings and then brought the full force of his club onto the ball, leaving it in no doubt that it should get as far away as possible, which it duly did, settling in light rough near the edge of the fairway about halfway to the green.

"Good shot," said Jerry, and nervously stepped up to take his turn. He settled over the ball, licked his lips, glanced towards the flag on the distant green, swung and missed.

"You have to do it for Jesus, Jerry, not for yourself," the Canon said, helpfully.

"How do I do that? I don't even know what you mean."

"Just try concentrating on him, that's all."

So he did, hissing Jesus' name through his teeth as the club-head arced down through the air. This time, instead of an empty and humiliating whoosh, Jerry heard a satisfying click. His golf ball soared into the air and landed twenty yards or so beyond the Canon's own ball, ideally positioned for an approach onto the green.

"Christ, what a fluke," said Jerry.

"There for two," replied the Canon, ensuring that Jerry understood they were playing to the rules and that his first air-shot had actually counted.

"Before you tell me what's troubling you," he continued as they walked down the fairway together, "I'd like to find out a little about your Christian life back on Earth."

"Well, my road to Damascus went via the beach at Frinton. It was a dry town back then, so perhaps God was trying to tell me something."

This had become Jerry's standard response whenever anyone asked him about how he became a Christian. It usually raised a smile or two and most people didn't notice that he then skipped the whole of the rest of his life and talked about how much he was enjoying Paradise. It was the best he could do to assimilate himself into the culture, even though he still used the technically correct but formal term *God*, rather than the cringe-worthy soubriquet *The Lord* so favoured by his heavenly compatriots.

"How old were you when you were converted?"

"I was just a kid. To be honest with you, I'd forgotten all about it. My mother told me what had happened when I went to see her here, in Heaven. Apparently there had been some people running a religious holiday club for children; I'd gone along to it and had come back a member of the God Squad."

"What was your church life like after that?"

"Non-existent. I only went to the occasional wedding or funeral. I didn't have any church involvement."

"All this must have come as something of a surprise, then."

"You have no idea! I just expected that when you died that was it. I certainly didn't think Heaven would be real. In fact, that's one of my questions. If it was here all along, why couldn't we see it?"

Canon John had reached his ball and therefore delayed his answer. His iron shot didn't quite have the legs or the direction required and finished short and to the right of the green, leaving an awkward chip and putt for par. Jerry's, in contrast, pitched perfectly and ran to within six feet of the hole. He looked in disbelief at the face of his club, hoping to find some clue there to his unexpected golfing brilliance.

"The best explanation I can give you," resumed the Canon, "is that Heaven existed all the while in a parallel universe, one that you couldn't detect from Earth in any way. When the Rapture came, we burst through into the physical reality that you had been inhabiting and your world was subsumed in ours."

"And all the people who had died before the Rapture, they were already here."

Canon John motioned as if to say something, but kept quiet instead.

"How did you all get here?" asked Jerry. "How did you get from one universe to the other?"

"I can't answer that, I'm afraid. I just know that I arrived here immediately after my death. I'm not enough of a scientist to tell you how it happened, although I do know that modern physics has predicted the existence of parallel universes for some time now. For me, it's enough to know that God took care of it. If you want to understand the mechanics you'll have to find a really good physicist, and that's not going to be easy."

"I'm sure I can get hold of one of them eventually – I've got plenty of time."

"Time won't be the problem; most of them didn't believe that this would be one of the parallel universes anyway," responded the Canon, ambiguously. Before Jerry could ask him what he meant, the churchman was preparing himself for his next shot and couldn't be disturbed. He chipped the ball over a bank that was between him and the green, but it gathered pace on the smooth surface and rolled twenty feet past the pin. Jerry sensed his playing partner's frustration and decided to put further questions on hold.

The Canon two-putted for a bogey five, but Jerry sunk his ball with a single shot. He felt exhilarated: a par score was way beyond his expectations and would have been even better if he hadn't messed up his first shot.

Two holes later and Jerry was still only one shot over par while Canon John had slipped to two over. A fifteen-foot putt on the fourth hole gave him the first birdie of his life while the Canon, who didn't seem to be having quite so much fun, dropped another shot.

Jerry was starting to feel embarrassed and wondered if the Canon suspected him of falsely understating his golfing prowess. "I really don't know how this is happening," he said. "I've hardly ever played before, and it was certainly never like this."

"It's because you are now the golfer that God always wanted you to be."

Jerry laughed. "And what sort of golfer is that?"

"I'd say pretty close to scratch from the way you're playing. You're very blessed; I'm a twelve handicap myself."

The Canon read Jerry's thoughts. "I won't get any better, Jerry, no matter how much I practise, and neither will you. This is what God has ordained for us. Of course, I'd like to be as good as you, but back on Earth I played off twenty or twenty-one, so I'm grateful for the improvement."

"Won't that get a bit boring – playing golf for all eternity and never getting any better?"

The Canon looked at Jerry as if he'd just uttered an offensive profanity. "I certainly hope not!" he said. "Golfing on beautiful courses like this, with no rain or cold, no queues on the tees, is part of what makes Heaven paradise for me."

Jerry hit a three hundred yard drive over a glittering brook onto the edge of a green cradled in a semi-circle of palm trees. It was a heavenly shot, unlike the Canon's which he shanked into the rough a hundred yards short of the hole.

"It feels like cheating, somehow," said Jerry as they set off to play their next shots. "To get to this level, any level, without having to work for it."

"It's a gift, Jerry. You just need to be thankful."

"But why is God interested in how well I play golf? Why would he care what kind of golfer I was, let alone make me a good one?"

"He's interested in every aspect of our lives, and when we do things well it glorifies him."

"Really? Does that apply to everything?"

"Yes, everything that we do is to bring him glory, which is why we have to do it to the best of our abilities. The whole human race is here to worship and glorify him."

The Canon chipped impressively to within a few feet of the hole to give himself a fighting chance of rescuing par, then Jerry recorded his second-ever birdie to go one under for the round.

"Why is it like that?" Jerry asked as he teed up his next drive. He struck the ball well, but it landed in a sand trap which stopped it in its tracks still a hundred yards from the green. He was struggling to articulate an incongruity that had been troubling him since he discovered that God was real and not simply a fictional character from a cleverly marketed children's fantasy. "Why did he need to make an entire species with the sole purpose of worshipping him?"

"Not just humans, Jerry, the whole of creation serves that requirement. Mankind is the pinnacle of God's work, so we have the greatest responsibility."

For the first time, Canon John drove his own tee shot further than Jerry had driven his.

"So God made everything to glorify himself? Doesn't that sound a bit…" Jerry hesitated to find the right word, "…narcissistic?"

"No. More egocentric, I'd say," replied the Canon, to Jerry's surprise.

"And you're OK with that?"

"I think God can do what he likes; he made everything and it's how the universe works best, in submission to him."

"And when people don't submit, then what happens?"

"That's when things start to go wrong."

Jerry had a decent lie in the bunker and a clear view of the green. A regulation pitch shot would get him onto the green with another chance for a birdie, but it didn't happen. It took him two shots to get out of the bunker and another to make the green. He finished the hole one over for the round.

Things were starting to go wrong.

Before he took his next tee shot, the Canon had to apologise once more for the incorrect talking post information. "We'd be better off without them," he said. "Half the time they are completely wrong and to be perfectly frank with you I find the constant religious chatter a little…"

"Annoying?"

"Unnecessary, Jerry. It's not as if we're going to forget who's who and what's what, is it?" So saying, the Canon hit a terrible shot which resulted in the ball scudding along the ground to bury itself in some inhospitable rough less than a hundred yards away. Jerry's own shot was almost as bad.

"Why don't they fix it?" asked Jerry. "It can't be that difficult."

"Oh, something to do with a computer problem, I'm told, and you know what they're like."

"As a matter of fact, I do know a bit about them, yes."

"In that case I'll get you introduced to a friend of mine at St Isidore's. It's where all the computing is done up here, although they don't seem to be very good at it. Maybe you can sort out this little problem for them."

"Certainly. I'll be pleased to help, if I can. Why is it called St Isidore's? It sounds more like a hospital than a technology centre."

"He's the patron saint of computers. Don't ask."

The two men played the next few holes on opposite edges of the respective fairways, so opportunities for conversation were limited. When they came to the thirteenth (*Par five, stroke index fifteen, praise the Lord for his glorious hole*) they were both six over par but seemed to have got their games back under control. Two straight, long drives looked like giving them some decent chatting time, so Jerry took courage in both hands and plunged in.

"John, before the Rapture happened I don't think I really believed in God, and neither did any of my friends. We weren't particularly unusual in that respect; only a tiny proportion of people in England went to church. But here, almost everybody seems to have led very religious lives beforehand, and I'm wondering why I haven't met anyone else like me yet. And where are all the Jews and Muslims and Buddhists, and all the other people who weren't practising Christians?"

Jerry's mouth was dry and he could feel the sweat on the palms of his hands. Simply voicing a question so closely related to his Dark Thought had set his nerves on edge. He felt like a man who had forced himself to ask his wife to confirm her faithfulness to him, hoping that she would, but suspecting, deep in his heart, that… oh, God, surely not that.

Canon John took an unsettlingly long time to reply and, when he did so, it was with a question of his own. "*Shall not the Judge of all the Earth do right?*"

Jerry's stomach lurched. "Meaning what?" he asked fearfully.

"It's a quote, from Genesis. It's what Abraham says to God just before the towns of Sodom and Gomorrah are destroyed with burning sulphur by the Lord. Do you know the story?"

"I've heard of it."

"Well, the point is that God shows himself to be a judge, one who is very intolerant to what the Bible calls unrighteousness. Abraham's question is a rhetorical one: God, being perfect, will judge perfectly. But make no mistake, Jerry, a judge is what he is."

Of course I've not been faithful to you, darling, whatever gave you that impression?

"And those who he finds guilty, what happens to them?"

"We're all guilty. We all deserve eternal punishment: we should all be in Hell, not Heaven."

"But we're *not* in Hell, are we? We're all here; we're all in Heaven!"

"All of us, Jerry?"

"Don't piss about! You know what I mean," shouted Jerry, gripping the golf club so tightly in his hand that his knuckles had turned white and his fingernails were digging painlessly into his hand. The boil of anxiety that had been steadily growing in his mind since he first set foot in this alien world was finally lanced. He could contain its poison no longer and the words came out like vomit: "*Is there a fucking Hell?*"

145

Canon John looked down on the ground, avoiding Jerry's wide-eyed stare. "Yes," he said quietly. "I'm afraid there is."

Slept with your boss? Oh, yes, many times. Your best friend? Naturally! I'm very popular with all your friends; they don't seem to be able to get enough of me!

Jerry could hear his own heavy breathing. "Who's there, John? Who's been sent to Hell, apart from Hitler and the Muslims?"

"Those who didn't accept Christ as their Saviour."

"That's just about everybody, for Christ's sake!" Jerry yelled. "That's Rachael, my dad, my friends. There must be billions of people there."

The Canon said nothing.

"What happens to them in Hell, John? Is it fire and brimstone and torture and all that crap?"

"I've never been, Jerry. The Bible images don't make easy reading, but..."

"But what?"

"You have to trust that God would get it right. You know, *shall not the Judge of all the Earth...*"

"Yes, I heard you. And no, I don't trust him to get it right." Jerry's mind was flooded with *Flooded*. "He let the babies drown. The children. The fucking zebras! That's not justice, that's indiscriminate slaughter."

"You need to calm down, Jerry," said the Canon evenly. "You don't want to attract attention."

Jerry looked around quickly, but couldn't see any angels.

"They don't usually bother us out here, but they'll come very quickly if there's a fuss."

"A *fuss*? Is that what I'm doing, making a fuss? I've just found out that almost everybody I know and care about isn't simply somewhere else in Heaven, but they're in a place of eternal damnation. That bloody imbecile Solomon was right all along! I thought I'd just been put in the wrong location, with the religious nutters, simply because I was coerced into reciting some magic formula I didn't understand when I was a child. How the hell does that qualify me to be here? I had no more belief than Rachael."

"Once your name is in the Book of Life, Jerry, it can't be erased. Rachael is your sister, or girlfriend?"

"My girlfriend."

"What was her religious faith?"

"She had none. Her parents were Jewish but neither she nor they went to the synagogue any more. I think she may have gone as a child but as an adult she was, I don't know, just not interested."

"Hmm, being a non-observant Jew doesn't sound too promising, but you never know."

"I *have* to know. How can I find out where she is?"

"Jerry, you don't have to know. I often get asked this question: people want me to find out if this person or that person is in Heaven. I tell them that sometimes ignorance is bliss. It's better to live with the hope that something might be all right, than with the despair that comes from the certain knowledge that it isn't. And, you know, eventually we forget. You cannot hold onto earthly memories and relationships forever."

"Is that what you've done? Have you just forgotten about all those non-believers you loved? Is that what everybody does?"

"I worked for the church all my life; all my family were religious, apart from a much younger brother, and I hardly knew anyone else who wasn't a believer. The vast majority of Christians only know other Christians, so the problem hardly ever arises."

"Heaven cannot be Heaven for me knowing that people I love are being tortured for all eternity. It cannot be Heaven for anyone who has that knowledge."

"That's why it's better not to know."

"Bullshit. I have to know for certain."

"OK, OK, I'll tell you the little that I know, after we've played our next shots."

The Canon found the middle of the green with a beautifully judged five-iron. Jerry swung madly at his ball, clipped the top of it and watched it hop two feet away. He took a single stride and hit it again. The ball fizzed away in a graceful curve, clattered into a tree and rebounded with a sullen plop into a lazy pond. "Lost ball," he said, irritably.

"The only way to be sure is to look in the Book of Life," said the Canon after completing the hole. "If her name is in there she'll be in Heaven; if not, she won't."

"Where do they keep the book?"

"It's not a physical book, not any more. All the names used to be written in by hand, but a few years ago they started a big project to modernise it and they put everything onto a computer. All the work was done at St Isidore's."

"So I can look it up there?"

"It's not available to the public, Jerry, but someone might be able to help you, especially if you do them a favour. I've never heard of it happening before, though."

Jerry had lost his appetite for golf and simply trudged alongside the Canon as the latter continued his round.

"John," he said, halfway down the sixteenth fairway (*Par four, stroke index five; Jesus, oh Jesus, we love you!*), "did you always believe in God?"

"Yes, I always had a faith."

"So you always knew, or thought you knew, there would be a Heaven and a Hell?"

"When I started in the church as a young man I preached my heart out in order to try to save people from Hell. I was convinced that everything the Bible teaches is true."

The Canon had reached his ball and the two men stopped walking. He pulled out a seven-iron from the bag, but instead of getting ready to take his shot he held the club upside-down, the handle on the ground with both his hands clasped around the striking end. He looked into the distance for a while and then turned his attention to Jerry. "I couldn't keep it up. Christianity, at least the brand that I had been weaned on, makes fantastic promises: Jesus will be your personal friend; he will guide and help you; he will heal the sick and give you anything that you ask in his name. Unfortunately, the reality was very different: in spite of my fervent belief, all I ever really felt was his absence. The only answers to prayer were for trivial things that doubtless would have happened anyway, and he didn't answer those prayers that were really important: marriages failed; the church didn't grow, it shrank; and there were no miraculous healings. As the gap increased between what was supposed to happen and what I was actually experiencing, I searched the Scriptures even more zealously for God, but that just made things worse. The God who is described in the Bible is a terrible Being, one that deserves our fear, but not one that any decent person could possibly worship. His behaviour is despotic – the Flood isn't the half of it – and I eventually concluded that he could command no moral authority by which to judge the human race. I stopped believing in Hell altogether and hoped that God was actually much better than he was portrayed in his biography."

"The Judge of all the Earth shall *not* do right."

"Touché."

"So this was a bit of a surprise to you too, then."

"I still had a remnant of a belief in some kind of spiritual afterlife, but not a physical one like this. It was more of a wish than a solid expectation. Then, soon after I came here, I discovered that Hell is as much a reality as Heaven, and I despaired. That's when I started playing golf every day; to numb out the pain."

"Pain in Paradise?" said Jerry. "So I'm not the only one."

The Canon said nothing.

"Does it work? The golf: does it make you forget?"

"Most of the time. Not so well today."

"I'm sorry about that."

They didn't speak again until they were on the eighteenth hole with its beautiful, tree-lined fairway and wide, flat green nestling inside two sandy bunkers.

"What happens when you worship, John? How do you block out all your despair?"

"I still get some of those wonderful sensations, although they're not as strong as they were when I first arrived. The emotion of worship fades away eventually, especially if you know how nasty God can be."

Jerry remained quiet for a while, swilling around the word *nasty* in his mind. "What will you do about it?" he asked.

"There's nothing I can do. My name is in the Book of Life and I'm not going to volunteer to spend my time in Hades."

Jerry watched the Canon make his final putt before asking, "If I can get into the Book do you want me to see if your brother's name is in it, John?"

The Canon looked long and hard at Jerry before saying quietly, "No thank you, son. It's better that I don't know."

15

Never before had Jerry so longed for e-mail. The Canon had promised he would speak to his contact at St Isidore's, an angel called Uriel, as soon as possible, but this meant taking time out of his busy golfing schedule in order to travel to the office and have the conversation face to face. A whole week had elapsed between Jerry's round of golf and Canon John sending his caddy, Marcus, to tell him that St Isidore's would indeed welcome his help.

"Because it saves time," he had said to Bob when extolling the virtues of instantaneous electronic communication, even though he knew it was a lost cause.

"No need for that, Jerry," had been the predictable reply. "You want to pace yourself a bit better or you'll drive yourself into an early grave." Bob, at least, had found that remark to be very funny. "Besides," he'd continued when he'd stopped laughing, "your friend Solomon tells me that this web malarkey of yours was mostly used for pornography. We don't want none of that filth up here, thank you very much."

"Well, it's true there were some terrible things made possible by the internet, but it also gave the whole world unprecedented access to knowledge and ideas. You could use it to find out almost anything, all by yourself."

"We don't want lots of new ideas and fancy knowledge. We got Jesus; what more do we need?"

Jerry had not answered. What he needed was to know how he could get into St Isidore's and search the Book of Life, and he wanted to know quickly. But *quickly* wasn't on anyone else's agenda so he spent his time impatiently, avoiding people as much as possible by staying in his room, ploughing further into the Bible and watching the telly. By the time he got the answer he was hoping for, he was sick and tired of the banal Christian testimonials and soporific singing being broadcast on virtually every one of the hundreds of television channels.

The one bright moment during his tense week had come when he had met up with Catherine. She had looked pretty, and he had told her so. Her response had been to offer a shy *thank you* and to link arms with him for a brief walk around the worship lawn. He informed her of his plan to look for Rachael's name in the Book of Life and tentatively asked her if he should search for her sister, Caroline, as well. "Yes. Yes, of course," she'd replied hesitantly.

"If I can't find her, you know what that means?" he'd asked, as sensitively as he could.

The look of supressed pain on Catherine's face made it clear that she understood perfectly, and this time she did not answer the question.

The morning of his visit to St Isidore's came at last, and Jerry asked Worthy for directions to the technology centre. His butler was happy to oblige and went on to say that a number of his friends from the Church of Jesus Christ of Latter-day Saints worked there. Genealogies, he explained, had been important in the church's work of baptising dead non-Christians, and a large database had been developed to house the critical information.

"Does it work?" Jerry had asked, suddenly interested.

"Well, of course there's always the chance of duplicate entries and incorrect spellings, but a lot of effort had been put into cleaning it up."

"I meant the baptising, not the database. Can you turn a dead unbeliever into a Christian?"

Worthy looked down to the floor, his enthusiasm punctured. "No. I don't believe that particular temple ordinance was effective."

"Pity, it would have been useful," said Jerry with sincerity.

It was late in what would have been the afternoon in Earth-world by the time he arrived at the drab, single-storey building which housed Heaven's information technology nerve-centre.

"Hello Jerry," said a bored-looking man called Zamaleki, sitting behind a cramped desk in the dusty reception area. "Uriel's expecting you. I'll show you where he is."

They pushed through two sets of double doors into a large room containing about one hundred desks arranged in five columns. A conventional-looking computer sat on top of each of the desks, less than a quarter of which were occupied. "Not many folks left at this time of the day," the receptionist said, looking around at his co-workers. Jerry spotted one man in white, whom he guessed would be a Roman Catholic paying off his self-imposed debt. The others, among whom Worthy's Mormon friends could doubtless be counted, were dressed in their regulation grey.

Half-way down the room, Zamaleki stopped and pointed to a glass-walled office located at the far end. "He's in there," he said, then turned and ambled lethargically back towards the reception.

Service with a smile, thought Jerry as he made his own way towards Uriel.

He knocked politely on the door and immediately Uriel leapt up from his desk and bounded out to greet him. "Jerry, Jerry, Jerry," he said as he flung his arms around his visitor. "I'm so pleased to meet you. Thank you for coming. Canon John tells me you're a *real* software engineer. Is it true, Jerry? Are you properly qualified and everything?"

"Yes, I guess so."

"Oh, praise the Lord!" said the angel, clasping his hands together and closing his eyes affectedly. "Hardly anyone knows anything about computers in Heaven. We're mostly all self-taught and it's so difficult to keep up. Take me – no head for technical things at all. I wouldn't know a byte if it bit me on the nose. Ha! Very creative though – that's what I'm really good at. Not quite sure why they put me in this job; nobody else wanted it, I think. All the angels are hopeless when it comes to technology. Anyway, I said I'd have a go. I thought, well, how hard can it be? Ha! Silly me. Very hard, is the answer, as I found out to my cost. Not to you, though, clever clogs – easy as sin, as our friend John would say, not that I should use that phrase. Naughty Uriel!"

Uriel smacked the back of his own hand in mock admonishment. He then looked at Jerry with a trace of puzzlement in his expression, prompting his visitor to ask, "Is everything OK?"

"I was just wondering, are you Catholic or Orthodox?" said Uriel.

"Neither. C of E, if anything." This was a convenient ruse Jerry had discovered to cover up his lack of familiarity with religious custom and practice. The Church of England was apparently so accommodating in its doctrine and so broad in its taste that nobody seemed surprised by the ecclesiastical ignorance of any person who claimed to have sheltered in its soft and tolerant bosom during their time on Earth.

"We've not had one of those in here before, but we can do with all the help we can get, so welcome aboard!"

Uriel smiled broadly, but seemed unsure of what to do next, so Jerry suggested that he could make a start straight away.

"Oh yes, do. If you have time. It's a bit late in the day, isn't it?"

"The sooner I begin, the sooner it'll be done. Where can I sit?"

"How about over here?" Uriel asked, directing Jerry to a desk directly outside his own office. Unwilling to be overlooked by anyone, especially a management angel, Jerry suggested one in the next row along, in an isolated position. "I'm left-handed," he offered by way of explanation. "Ah, I see," his gullible host responded.

"Do you want me to show you how the system works?" Uriel asked uncertainly.

"I'm sure I can figure it out," Jerry said, to the angel's obvious relief, and he sat down to begin. He felt fear pull at his guts, insisting that he recognise the terrible magnitude of what he could be about to discover. He fought to maintain his composure and for a moment even flirted with Canon John's cowardly stricture that ignorance knows best. He closed his eyes and breathed deeply. Anyone watching would have assumed he was praying. He nearly was.

It was odd to be back in front of a computer, especially one that was some way short of being state-of-the-art. Jerry moved the mouse and the blank screen jumped into life, revealing a seraphic picture of Jesus looking heavenwards: an object lesson in pious wallpaper. A single icon in the shape of a cross was located in the bottom left-hand corner of the screen. Jerry clicked on it and the program directory was revealed. He studied it for a moment, found his way to *Databases* and there it was, filed just one level down: the *Book of Life*.

Two thoughts occurred to him: one was just how fast his heart was beating; the other was that this seemed far too easy. He scanned the list of databases. *Entertainment and Leisure* was surely where he would find the files he had ostensibly come to correct. There was another called *Trials,* which intrigued him but he knew he couldn't afford to be distracted. The *Book of Life* was his target and, without further delay, he moved the cursor into position and double-clicked.

An image of a leather-bound book appeared on the screen and in the centre, to Jerry's dismay, a box which demanded a password. "Shit," he muttered under his breath. Quickly he typed in *Book of Life* but was met with *Incorrect Password*. He tried again, changing the case, running the words together, adding the definite article, but each time he was denied access. *The Saved, The Saints, The Christians,* even the obvious *Password* all met with the same response.

155

"Think, Jerry," he said to himself. He was an expert in IT security, he should be able to solve this. *If only I knew who had created the file* he thought, knowing from experience that many people default to the simplest of passwords, such as their children's names and birthdays, when needing to protect files. But whose file was this? Ultimately of course it was God's, but he didn't have any children. Unless…

Jerry hurriedly typed in the most memorable name of all: Jesus. *Password Incorrect.* "Damn." All lower case: same result. All upper case: same again. What about his birthday? Even Jerry knew that Christmas Day had only a one in three hundred and sixty-five chance of being Jesus' actual day of birth, and he wasn't sure that he was really born in the year nought either, but this was a password candidate, not a history lesson. It had to be worth a try. For partisan reasons he plumped for the European date format rather than the non-sequential US equivalent.

J-e-s-u-s-2-5-1-2-0-0-0-0

Hallelujah! He was in.

The sound of an angelic choir burst from his computer at full volume, followed by an American voice proclaiming loudly, "The *Book of Life*, all praise to God in his holiness."

"Fuck!" Now everybody in the office knew what he'd done. He looked quickly round and to his relief saw that there were now only a dozen people left, and all of those were sitting some distance away. Nobody was looking in his direction. He'd got away with it.

"What are you doing, Jerry?"

"Uriel! Hi! Um, I was just…"

"That's the wrong file. You won't find anything to do with golf courses in there."

"Yes, sorry, my mistake. I should have let you show me where to look after all."

"No, my fault, it was unfair of me to let you struggle on your own. But how did you get it to open? It's got one of those pesky pass-codes on it."

"A password, yes. Not a very difficult one to guess, I'm afraid. You should make it more difficult if you want to keep people out."

"Oh, no fear, I have enough difficulty remembering them all as it is. I keep a list of them written down. Don't tell anyone though, I'm not supposed to do it."

"I promise," said Jerry, touching his heart to show he meant it.

"Thank you. Not that I should need to get into the *Book of Life* any more, I'm pleased to say. The wretched thing has been the bane of my life."

"In what way?"

"Actually, it was all a misunderstanding but, talking to you as a friend, I did get a bit upset at the time."

Jerry wondered how they had become friends already, but realised that having an angel on his side, even such an emotional one, might do him no harm. He got up, wheeled around an additional chair for Uriel to sit on, and asked him what had happened.

"Well, the boys had been working very hard on the Book project and, really, they'd done ever so well. I was so proud of them. Then, one day, they wanted to run a little test to see if they'd written a bit of their code correctly. What's it called when you need the computer to do a thing for you on its own without you having to tell it all the time?"

"A macro? A sub-routine?"

"A sub-routine, yes, that's the one. You *are* an expert, aren't you? I wish I knew all this clever stuff. Anyway, this sub-macro, or whatever, was supposed to close down the whole *Book of Life* at the end of the *End Times* so that no more names could be entered."

"A lock-down."

"Yes, yes, that's what they called it too," Uriel said, excitedly clapping his hands together. "You see, the boys had at last got all the names of the *saved-so-far* in the file and they wanted to make sure it could be shut properly when the time came. Nathaniel wasn't here just then," (Uriel wrinkled up his nose distastefully when he said *Nathaniel*) "so they asked me if they could do the test. I was trying to be helpful and they were very keen to try it, so I said yes."

Uriel stopped for a moment and picked at the side of the desk looking, Jerry thought, as if he was going to cry.

"Anyway, it worked rather too well. The *Book* closed perfectly but then they couldn't open it again."

"They did it live in the database, rather than in a test environment?" asked Jerry, his professional sensitivities offended at such a crass mistake.

"I don't know what they did, but it stayed closed and we all know what happened next."

"What happened next?" asked Jerry, who obviously didn't know.

"Well, as no more names could be entered into the *Book*, Jesus had to return to Earth and call a halt to everything."

"You mean the Rapture?"

"Yes."

Jerry looked steadily at Uriel. "You're telling me that the Second Coming happened because of a software error?"

Uriel fidgeted in his chair. "I'm sure it was going to take place soon anyway, it was just brought forward a little, that's all. Besides, it wouldn't be fair to people who were becoming Christians if their conversions didn't count just because of a problem with the database."

"No, not fair at all," Jerry said ruefully, wondering quite where fairness fitted into the concept of anybody not having their name in the *Book of Life*, Christians or otherwise. Then another thought occurred. "Why couldn't Jesus just fix the problem with a miracle?"

"Miracles are one thing, software problems are something else entirely! And in any case, if everything that went a little bit wrong was put right by God, what kind of life would that give people?"

"A safer one?" suggested Jerry. "Happier?"

Uriel pulled a face. "I don't know about that. Anyway, I told

Nathaniel that it wasn't really my fault, but he was ever so grumpy. You'd think the world had ended. Oh, wait a minute, that is what happened, isn't it?"

Jerry didn't reply. He turned to his computer, closed down the *Book of Life* and opened the file directory once more.

Uriel slid over to his chair. "Let me show you. Here, this one," he said pointing to *Entertainment and Leisure*, but Jerry had spotted something else. "What's *Tribulation?*" he asked, aware that the name was vaguely familiar. "Just a game that some of the guys play," Uriel replied. "I don't like it – too violent for me."

Jerry decided against further interrogation and, within a few seconds, had fired up the appropriate program for St Stephen the Martyr. "Thanks," he said to Uriel and the angel retreated to his office.

With Canon John's paper scorecard in front of him Jerry worked his way through the file correcting the par values and stroke indices where required. He was tempted to edit out some of the religious embellishments that his golfing partner had found so unnecessary, but suspected that might draw unwanted attention. By the time he had completed the task, only he and Uriel remained in the office and it was clear that his time was up. He needed to think quickly.

He pushed back his chair and hurried to Uriel's office. Opening the door just enough to stick his head through, he said, "I've finished that job Uriel, but I've just realised how late it is. Must rush. Let me know if you need some more help sometime." He left immediately and ran towards the exit. Just before he got to the double doors he looked back and saw that Uriel was already closing up his office and momentarily had his back turned to Jerry. Seizing his chance Jerry dived under the nearest desk, crouching down to make himself as small as possible.

He could hear Uriel walking towards him, but he couldn't see him. The angel was praying. "Thank you Jesus for sending Jerry today. He seems such a nice boy, and so clever. Oh, and sorry again for that little mishap with the Book. Oh yes, you're right, I did say I wouldn't mention it any more." He let out a child-like giggle and then started singing a happy little ditty: "Oh praise God in his holiness, praise him in the firmament of his power."

"Good night, Zamaleki. I'm last, you can go home now," he called cheerily to the receptionist as he walked through the grubby foyer. The singing faded as he left the building, "Praise him in his noble acts; praise him in his noble acts, tra-la-la."

Jerry stayed where he was until he heard the main door open and close once more. He waited a further five minutes until he was sure he was alone and then crept out.

He hurried back to the desk he had been using earlier and within moments had turned off the computer's sound system, just to be on the safe side, even though there was no-one else in the building. He opened the Book and quickly found where he needed to enter the relevant data to search for Rachael.

The first fields required her names: Rachael, Esther, Bennett – he was sure she had no other middle names. He entered her date of birth and typed in London, England for her birthplace. Given that place names and country borders had altered so much over the centuries, Jerry wondered how the database would manage the complexity of all those changes. Hopefully there had been somebody in the team of *mostly self-taught* software engineers smart enough to work that out.

There was nothing he could enter in the one remaining field – date of re-birth – but as this information was only required to further narrow the search it was not compulsory. With a mix of fear and excitement, he pressed *Run Query*.

A box appeared on the screen showing a pair of praying hands surrounded by a circle of dots. The dots lit up and faded consecutively in a clockwise direction, giving the impression of marking time.

Jerry knew that searching such an enormous database would take a while, even for a sophisticated system which this appeared not to be, so he forced himself to think of Rachael in order to try to calm down. He pictured her chained in a hellish dungeon and had to fight with his memory to replace those harrowing images from the unproven, ugly present with something more heartening from the past. Finally, her thick, blond hair came to mind, and the way the strands from her long fringe would sometimes drift across her face and partially obscure her grey-green eyes. He remembered the way she would push her hair back over the top of her head and smile as she caught him looking at her freshly-revealed loveliness. She had freckles across the bridge of her nose, which added to her look of enchanting prettiness.

He missed her.

No records exactly matching your search criteria were found. Run new query?

Jerry stared at the candid message on the screen. His eardrums detected his own blood being pumped furiously round his head and the back of his skull twitched in time with his heart-rate. It *couldn't* be true. He must have made a mistake; perhaps there was a different spelling of Esther, or maybe he hadn't remembered her birthday correctly. He was, after all, forgetting so much about his previous life.

He ran another query, this time with a wider set of parameters. He entered Rachael Bennett, born in England in the year and month he knew to be correct, but omitting the exact date. The praying hands reappeared and Jerry wished he could find a means of adding a single entry to the billions already in the database. It didn't seem too much to ask. Indeed, it wasn't too much to ask: the details of twelve Rachael Bennetts appeared in front of him. He only needed one of them to be *his* Rachael.

He thrashed through the details. None of the Rachaels had Esther as a middle name, all had specific re-birth dates and three

161

had died prior to the Rapture. Of the remaining nine, five had been born in London and all but one of these had lived there at the time of Jesus' return. Jerry opened the records of the four most likely candidates and each time found further details of their lives: names of parents and siblings, church denomination, as well as last known address. None of them matched Rachael. In desperation, he checked the details of all twelve of the women, but the outcome didn't change. Rachael Esther Bennett; born of Jewish parents; resident of London; happy, balanced, beautiful girlfriend, was not in the *Book of Life*. She was lost.

"You are not authorised to access this information."

Jerry jumped at the sound of the voice right behind him, banged both his knees hard on the underside of the desk but, of course, felt no pain whatsoever. He had no need to turn around to know the voice's owner, having recognised it immediately from the unpleasant public confrontation he'd had with the angel on the day he'd arrived in Heaven.

Nathaniel lowered his mouth to Jerry's ear and whispered, "What exactly do you think you're doing?"

"I was looking for someone."

"Did Uriel show you how to get into this file?"

"No. He doesn't even know I'm here. I hacked into it myself."

Nathaniel spun Jerry's chair around and looked down fiercely at him. "So, did you find who you were looking for?"

Jerry felt his anger rising. He looked up at Nathaniel and replied, "No, she's not on the list."

"And this has upset you."

"Of course it's bloody upset me. How the hell can it not? My precious friend is being eternally punished and I'm supposed to forget all about it?"

"Actually, you weren't supposed to find out at all, but now that you have, I think you need to show a little more gratitude. A lot more gratitude, in fact."

"Gratitude?" spat out Jerry. "What on earth am I supposed to be grateful for?"

"That you're not there too, with your *precious friend.*" Nathaniel stood up, put his hands on Jerry's shoulders and leaned in very close to his face. "I think it's high time you found out exactly what it is that you've been saved from, don't you?"

Jerry stared back, his whole face burning with contempt.

"I'm going to organise a little educational trip for you tomorrow, Jerry. It'll do you the world of good – you'll see. Bob will tell you all the details after morning worship. Don't be late."

Nathaniel held Jerry's shoulders a few moments longer and looked intensely into his eyes. "I'm watching you; you need to be very, very careful." Then he stood up, allowing Jerry to get out of his chair and announced it was time to be going. Standing beside him, Jerry became even more clearly aware of the angel's strength and athleticism. This was not someone to mess with, let alone provoke into enmity, although quite what he had to fear Jerry didn't know. Certainly not physical pain, and what greater anguish could be imposed beyond that which he was now suffering?

Passing through the lobby area on the way out, Nathaniel thanked Zamaleki and told him that he had done a good job today. "Not as stupid as he looks," he added to Jerry as they left the building.

16

Very much to Jerry's surprise, Bob gave him a Bible to take with him on his educational trip to Hell. Not just any Bible either, but one in which the page centres had been carefully cut away to create a hidden cavity big enough to contain, say, four packets of cigarettes.

"I want you to pick up four packets of cigarettes," Bob explained to the incredulous Jerry. "Hide them in the Bible so that no-one sees them and bring them back. You'll find that when you get to the souvenir shop you'll see a big black lad working there called Joe. He'll have a name-badge on. Tell him I sent you and that you've come to pick up some smokes. He'll take you out the back and give you the fags in exchange for apples. I've put six in here but four should be enough; they seem to like apples from Paradise best of all down there – I think it's their idea of irony." Bob opened a white canvas bag he'd been carrying, showed Jerry the apples at the bottom and carefully laid the Bible on top. "Here, have the bag. You'd better take some water with you as well; it can be bloody hot there and you don't want to get dehydrated. When we get to the handcart we'll pick up a couple of bottles."

"The handcart?"

"Yes. You're going to Hell in a handcart."

"Really?"

"No, of course not; there's a lift, you daft sod." Bob laughed extravagantly at his own joke. He continued for a long time until a coughing fit literally doubled him up and he had to hold onto Jerry for support. "Sorry son," he rasped, wiping the tears from his eyes and eventually regaining control. "Oh dear. Now, where were we?"

"We're going to Hell."

"Oh yes, let's be on our way, then."

"Why should I get you these cigarettes?" Jerry asked as the

two of them set off to the bus stop. The anger he felt as a result of the previous day's events had refined itself into truculence and he wasn't going to give his mentor an easy ride. "It must be against the rules for you to smoke here; I've never seen anyone else doing it."

"They're not for me, or at least not all of them; and you don't need to worry about the rules. Besides, if you do a tidy job for me I can put in a good word for you with Mr Nathaniel. I expect you could do with getting into his good books."

"I don't give a shit about him. If he's got a good book then I certainly wouldn't want to be in it. There's only one book that counts and she's not…" Jerry couldn't bring himself to finish the sentence.

Bob said nothing. Instead, after a few minutes of silence between the two of them, he started to whistle the tune of a popular chorus and, in next to no time, every passenger bar one, was singing and clapping along whilst swaying from side to side in their seats. Jerry felt as if he was in a mobile sit-down disco for the mentally impaired. Perhaps his own marbles were starting to lose themselves too, as he tried to contemplate an eternity wilfully neglecting a miscarriage of justice on an unimaginable scale. He knew it would be beyond him. And now, as if things were not crazy enough, he was being told he had to smuggle contraband cigarettes into Paradise. He closed his eyes and tried to shut out the tortured screams of insanity building inside his head.

He must have succeeded because he was not wrapped in a straightjacket when they arrived an hour or so later at their destination: the Hellevator.

"Who thought of calling it that?" he asked Bob.

"Dunno. Clever though, don't you think? You get in the queue and I'll fetch some water. Still or sparkling?"

"Sparkling, please – to go with the wit."

Jerry saw that there were hundreds of people already lined up ahead of him. He exchanged greetings with those nearest to him and it became clear during their brief conversation that travel on the Hellevator was not restricted to those following angelic orders; anybody could go and Jerry wondered how often he might make this trip to the Underworld.

"I've got you a large bottle each," said Bob when he returned a few minutes later. "They're a bit heavy, but better safe than sorry."

"Is someone else coming?" asked Jerry.

"Thanks, Bob," said Solomon who, having just arrived, reached over Jerry's shoulder to take one of the bottles.

"OK, I've got to dash," said Bob. "Be nice to each other now, the pair of you." He turned and forced his way through the growing mêlée.

"I didn't know you were going to be here," said Jerry, stating the obvious.

"Yeah, well, Nat came round early this morning to ask me to go and see it for myself. He wants me to keep an eye on you at the same time, to make sure you understand it all properly, you know. I said I'd be happy to do that, although it's no trouble really. I wanted to have a look down there anyway, especially as it's all going to kick off real soon."

Solomon was moving his weight from one foot to the other while he said this, as if he was too excited to keep still.

"What's going to kick off?"

"Can't say. Smart name, that." Solomon nodded in the direction of the Hellevator where the pun was depicted in large, red, three-dimensional block capitals above the lift shaft. His springy legs had really got into their stride now and he was practically bouncing on the spot.

"Yes, brilliant. Now, what's going to kick off?"

"I told you, I can't say."

"Don't be a prick; you know you want to tell me."

Solomon stopped jigging and stared at Jerry. "All right, but keep it to yourself, OK?" He looked around and came closer to Jerry, lowering his voice conspiratorially. "It's the Tribulation. They're getting ready for it now. It's only a matter of time, and the time is nearly upon us."

Jerry shook his head. "Solomon, the Tribulation is a bloody computer game. It's not real."

"Oh yeah, like you'd know all about it, wouldn't you? For your information, the Bible says that the Tribulation will be seven years of torment visited upon those who have rejected Christ, and it's going to happen real soon. There are fields," Solomon got closer still and whispered, "there are fields full of warplanes – fighter jets, bombers, you name it, a million of them – just outside the city, ready to go. The Lord only has to give the command and they're on their way."

"Let's hope he doesn't tell them to go today then, eh?"

"You can take the piss, but they're there all right."

"Have you seen them, personally, with your own eyes?"

"No, but I have friends who have, and they wouldn't lie."

Jerry hesitated. What if Uriel had been wrong about Tribulation being a game? It certainly wasn't beyond the bounds of possibility. Furthermore, Solomon had been right about Hell, contrary to Jerry's own expectations, so he might be right about this too. The idea that Rachael could be in even more imminent danger, over and above the fact that she was already damned to Hell, was something Jerry couldn't even begin to contemplate.

A cold draft of air played on their faces and the crowd turned towards the lift entrance. A faint, sulphurous odour became apparent and people looked at one another, distaste registering on their faces. The draft became a rush, and the sound of a fierce wind hurled itself into the waiting hall. With an exhausted hiss, the Hellevator, suddenly, had arrived.

It took thirty minutes to board. As they entered, Jerry read a notice informing him that no more than six hundred people could safely travel on the lift at any one time. Needless to say, neither he nor Solomon had ever been inside a multi-storey lift before, never mind one that had airplane-type seats in it.

Instead of a traditional bell-boy, several stern-looking angels were present. One of them told the passengers in no uncertain terms that they had to stick with the authorised tour guides in Hell and never wander off alone. There had been occasions when visitors had been set upon and robbed of their clothes by packs of the Damned who had then tried to sneak one of their own onto the Hellevator undetected. "As if entering Paradise simply required a change of garments, rather than a change of heart," the angel had said, much to most people's amusement. Finally, the angel advised them all to buckle up as the journey could be a little unsettling, and he and his colleagues moved between the rows of seats to ensure their instructions were being carried out.

"I do hope we get a decent meal on this flight," said Jerry to Solomon, in an attempt to lighten the mood between the two of them. Solomon had his eyes closed and didn't answer. He was praying. "Don't you like flying?" Jerry enquired and received a faint shake of the head in response. "Well, don't worry. If your time's up, then your time's up – no point in getting stressed about it! Besides, this is a lift, not an aeroplane. Whoever heard of a lift falling out of the sky and killing all the passengers?"

Solomon didn't laugh.

The doors closed, an alarm honked three times, and the giant glass-walled box began its descent.

The passengers experienced the signature flip in their stomachs associated with sudden downward movement and many of them cheered and laughed with delight.

To his disappointment, Jerry couldn't see anything outside as they appeared to be travelling through very dense cloud. Water droplets ran from the bottom of the glass sides to the top, but such was the speed of the lift that none of them settled. The cloud changed from opaque white to black, so that the illuminated inside of the compartment reflected back in on itself. This deadened the atmosphere, and the holiday mood was replaced by one of mild anxiety as the lift hurtled blindly on its way.

Then the screaming started.

This was not caused by panic, but by pain. Jerry felt it himself, first of all in his knees where yesterday, being startled by Nathaniel, he had hit them on the underside of the desk. Other sharp sensations pinched him, predominantly in his fingers and toes until, worst of all, the skin on the back of his left hand rose in a swollen blister, unbearable to the touch. He was lucky. To his left a woman writhed in agony, clutching her forehead, and elsewhere he was sure he could hear the sound of bones breaking.

"What's happening?" Jerry asked Solomon through gritted teeth.

"You're feeling all the pain you would have had in Heaven if the Holy Spirit hadn't been protecting you."

"Aren't you hurting anywhere?"

"No. I have a special dispensation because I'm here on angel business."

"Lucky bloody you. Why can't we all have it?"

"Same reason not everyone has faith. You know, m*any are called but few are chosen*. Some are predestined to receive God's blessing and others are not."

"Christ, Solomon, what sort of an answer is that?" Jerry tried to ease the throbbing in his hand by massaging his wrist. "Did you know this was going to happen?"

"Yes. Nat told me. That's why I was praying for you when we first sat down."

"Why didn't you say anything?"

"I couldn't. It's policy. Nat made that very clear to me. You won't be allowed to say anything about it when you get back either; no-one will."

"What? Why not?"

"Because it's better shock value if the pain comes as a surprise. People appreciate Heaven even more when they get back and no longer suffer."

Jerry was unable to find a way through his discomfort to articulate a meaningful response, so he sat quietly, nursing his hand.

The deceleration, when it happened moments later, was rapid, but the shrieking continued. The doors opened and a cold stink filled the air. Paramedics rushed into the lift and immediately started to identify those most badly hurt. Jerry unbuckled his seatbelt with his good hand and, together with Solomon started to head for the exit. He looked around as he left. Several people had lost consciousness and were being urgently attended to.

"You two OK?" an American nurse with chewing gum and attitude asked them as soon as they were outside.

"I don't need any help, but his hand hurts," said Solomon.

The nurse looked quickly at Jerry's injury. "It looks like a burn," she said. "Any idea how you did it?"

"No. I was just sitting there. I didn't do anything."

"It wouldn't have happened in the elevator, honey. Before, when you were in Heaven, what did you do to it?"

Jerry remembered the pain experiment in his mother's kitchen. "I poured boiling water on it," he said, feeling stupid.

"That'll be it then. It won't kill you, as I'm sure you realise. Behind me, on the right, you can go and get it treated. Don't do such a dumb thing again, now, you hear?"

Jerry promised that he wouldn't and followed her directions, in something of a daze.

He and Solomon found themselves a few moments later sitting in a grubby, open-plan waiting area with a number of others carrying minor injuries, watching the chaotic scenes around them. "It looks like the aftermath of a terrible sky-lift accident," Jerry said to Solomon, who failed to respond. "Why don't you carry on? I'll be here a little while, I expect."

"Yeah, I think I will. I never was much good in hospitals," Solomon replied, before sloping off.

"Is it always like this?" Jerry asked the tall, fair-haired doctor who attended him ten minutes later.

"I'd say it is, yes," the medic replied. He wore a plastic name-badge with *Dr Doyle* printed upon it.

"Does anyone ever come back a second time?"

"There are some regulars, so there are, but most don't like the pain of the journey."

All the while Dr Doyle had been examining Jerry's hand. "This isn't too bad. I'll dress it and give you some pain killers. You'll be able to stay and go on your tour."

"Some of the others in the lift looked to be in a bad way. What's going to happen to them?"

"The worst cases just get sent straight back, but mostly we can patch them up so they can enjoy the day out. All part of the service."

"Who pays you?" said Jerry, suddenly aware that his six apples might not be quite enough.

"Tax-payers. You don't need to worry. All health-care in Hell is free at the point of delivery."

"I can't see that system working forever," Jerry replied ruefully.

Once the doctor had finished, Jerry was free to go. He made his way to the green *Exit* sign at the end of the long, grimy ward with its low ceiling of stained and broken polystyrene tiles and temperamental fluorescent strip lighting. Somebody, or some being, who looked very much like one of the angels from back home (*home!*) was standing, dressed all in black, next to the doors that led out of the hospital. He was holding a powerful-looking dog on what Jerry thought was an inadequate leash. Jerry didn't like the dog and suspected, from the half-snarl on the creature's face, that the feeling was mutual. The angel grinned at him, showing two rows of yellowed teeth and, as he went past, growled a throaty greeting. It may have been *have a nice day*, but it was not in a language that Jerry recognised or understood. Already the absence of the Holy Ghost was beginning to tell.

"About time too," said Solomon, grabbing Jerry as soon as he came through the doors into the entrance hall. "The English one is just about to go." He guided Jerry to the far left-hand corner of the hall where a Union Jack placard was being held aloft by a tall, spindly man wearing tortoiseshell glasses and a colonial safari suit. Other national flags were dotted around the room, presumably, Jerry surmised, identifying the different languages provided by the tour guides.

"Before we go," called out Major Blighty in the clipped tones of a clichéd British army officer, "is there anything in particular that any of you would like to see?"

"The lake of fire," shouted someone near Jerry and Solomon at the back of the group of a hundred or so that was gathered round the guide.

"Yes, of course. That's standard. Anything else?"

Something was called out but Jerry didn't catch it.

"Moloch, was that?" enquired the Major. "The child-eater? Yes? Always popular. Let me just see if he's on today." He consulted a clipboard he was carrying. "Yes, he's scheduled to be here so you should be able to see him. Just a word of warning though, he's not always hungry, so don't be too disappointed if he's not actually feeding."

The Major tilted his head back and took one last nose-in-the-air look at his group, turned round and called over his shoulder, "Off we go then; keep up," and led them from the hall.

The party limped and shuffled along. Some were in wheelchairs being pushed by red-shirted individuals wearing badges depicting them as *Hell's Helpers*. Jerry stayed at the back, reluctant to move forward. He might not have done so at all if it hadn't been for the presence of another of those dirty angels – a demon, he now realised – standing behind him with his fearsome, non-muzzled dog.

"They don't really have a lake of fire, do they?" he asked Solomon.

"It's in the Bible."

"And a child-eater?"

Solomon shrugged. Jerry, as so often, could hardly believe what he was seeing and hearing. However, he had seen so many impossibilities since the Rapture that he knew already that the fear inside him was unlikely to be misplaced. He dragged his feet slowly towards the horrors of Hell and the crushing of his hope.

The floor beneath them sloped gently downwards. They were in a wide corridor, curving to the right. It was dark, lit only by small red fairy-lights housed in plastic tubing placed at the bottom of the walls on either side. From far below came the sound of throbbing rock music. Unpleasant whiffs of sulphur hung in the stale, rancid air.

Just as Jerry's eyes had become accustomed to the dinginess, he saw that round the bend a brighter red light was illuminating the tunnel. He could hear muffled shouting. The group, which had not exactly been hurrying, had slowed even further, gawping like visitors to an art gallery.

When he arrived at the exhibit, and he had the sensation that that was exactly what it was, Jerry looked through a glass wall into a cave the size of a squash court. In the middle stood a ragged man, chained to the ground and with his arms tied behind his back. Three imp-like creatures, all in black, poked at him with tridents and spears. He was covered in blood and would repeatedly fall to the ground in his attempts to avoid the thrusting stabbing of his tormentors. It was his shouting that Jerry had been able to hear, and it was the light from the red spotlights in the cave that was flooding onto the path outside.

From time to time one of the little devils would turn to the audience and grin, or poke out a tongue. They looked like children in fancy dress, complete with tails and absurd horns on their heads. A fourth child-devil sat on a stool at the back of the cave absent-mindedly tapping his spear on the ground, looking bored.

The Union Jack had disappeared further down the tunnel and Jerry and Solomon trooped after it, past more torture caves, on both sides now, offering similar fare to the first one. They saw whipping, beating, kicking, and plenty of blood. The smothered anguish of the tormented seeped out to the audience who, seemingly in a trance, continued on their way.

By the time they had gone another hundred metres, the music had become louder and the air noticeably warmer. The activity in the caves was changing too. It was becoming sexy or, more precisely, pornographic. In rapacious scenes that would certainly have earned them a restricted viewing certificate in London's West End theatres, darkly-dressed devils were forcibly copulating with barely-dressed men and women. That is to say, apparently copulating: shadows, judiciously positioned boulders and, in one case, a puzzled-looking donkey, prevented anyone on the outside getting a really clear view.

One woman was pressed up hard against the glass, her bare breasts squashed flat, while a demonic figure rhythmically pushed himself onto her from behind. In an incongruous nod to her need for modesty she was wearing a long, soiled skirt so that, even here, the presumed act could not actually be verified. Not that this stopped a group of a dozen male tourists from observing as closely as they could. The renewed ability of their bodies to feel pain was not the only physiological sensation that had been reignited, and the stirrings of their most basic desire of all was not disguised by the flimsy trousers they were wearing. Embarrassed, Jerry went to move on, although he too could not resist stealing one last look. As he did so, he thought he saw the woman laugh. He watched a moment longer. The woman's agony seemed real enough once more and her face was contorted in agony. Jerry walked away, confused.

By the time they reached Moloch's cave the heat was almost unbearable and the Major could not possibly make himself heard over the thick, soupy throb of the music. He mouthed the words *Moloch* and *feeding*, and pointed repeatedly to the demon's lair. Jerry had never been a great enthusiast of wildlife programmes that graphically showed the tearing apart of living creatures by their hungry predators, but what he saw now was way off the end of horror scale. A woman was chained to a wall, screaming. The object of her terror was plain to see: beyond her reach a blood-soaked crib stood at the mercy of a monstrous demon. He was black, heavy and ugly. His huge, fat feet were planted either side of the crib. Blood dribbled from his mouth and was spattered on his face and chest. He was chewing.

A new smell was mixing with the sulphur; it was vomit.

Moloch swallowed, sneered at the woman and plunged his head into the crib. A baby's hand appeared from within the cot, clenching and unclenching. The infant was still alive.

Jerry turned and ran back up the slope. He would have gone all the way out had it not been for the demon and his dog barring the way. So, he sat with his back to the wall, consumed at least half his bottle of water, then held his head in his hands and waited for his own nausea to pass.

The rest of the Major's party left and there was nobody else in the vicinity when the demon ran out of patience and moved Jerry along. It meant he had to walk past Moloch's recess once more and he intended to do so with his eyes closed. When he got there, however, he felt light-headed and put his hand against the glass to steady himself. He couldn't help but see in. The woman had stopped screaming and was simply standing, casually inspecting the ends of her hair. Moloch put his head into the crib once more, but at an odd angle. The top of his head went in first and he shook it from side to side. Jerry saw both the infant's hands appear before Moloch withdrew his head, grinned at the child, and repeated the procedure again. When he next took his head out he opened his mouth wide. He had not ripped away any flesh and the baby's hands still wriggled and waved.

Jerry just about detected, above the music, a sharp bang on the glass right behind him. The sudden noise seemed to startle Moloch, who immediately started chewing again. But chewing what? The woman began screaming again; hysteria switched on in an instant. *What the hell?*

The demon's dog sniffed at Jerry's legs; it was sufficient motivation to get him going again.

The floor had become level and the tunnel narrowed before opening out again into a huge arena. Terraced rows of backless wooden benches rose up on the left-hand side and, on the right, was the lake of fire. This cavernous room was the source of the music and Jerry's chest vibrated with the unrelenting bass notes as he scurried across to join the rest of his group.

Sweating profusely, he sat on a bench, shielding his face from the heat with one hand and squinting at the scene in front of him. Running from one side of the hall to another, a bed of hot coals separated the spectators from a vast, simmering pool of orange liquid. Flames danced in front of the lake and vapour was rising from it, but there were no flames coming from the lake itself, Jerry noticed, not actual, licking flames. Outcrops of dark rock penetrated the lake from the sides and creatures moved upon them. Creatures and humans. The creatures were demons and the humans were doomed. There was a good deal of poking with spears. One poor man had the shaft of one protruding from his rectum. He staggered and fell into the lake and disappeared from view. Others, too, were being pushed and prodded ever closer to the edges of the rocks and, inexorably, fell into the burnished liquid.

Jerry saw a woman who had been toppled by a blow to the head struggling and screaming in the orange lake. She flailed around without, as might have been expected, turning excruciatingly into a blackened carcass.

Suddenly, the music stopped and every light went out. The band of embers and the flames just behind them were the only sources of light in the whole place. A shiver went through the people gathered there and, distant screaming apart, an uneasy silence descended. The flames died down until they were extinguished and the hot coals faded from view, leaving the nervous visitors in complete darkness.

Something was happening. A form was taking shape, sensed not seen, and very close. The hall seemed suddenly cold and full of danger.

The spotlights, dazzlingly bright, burst into life and shone onto a ferocious, scarlet beast, right in front of them. Those closest to it ran from its presence, tripping over the benches and each other in their panic to get away.

The heavy, dense music with its aggressive, growling lyrics started again. Strobe lighting flickered onto the powerful animal with its seven heads, ten horns and single, female rider. The beast's heads moved menacingly and its huge jaws opened and closed. Even in his fear, Jerry thought he recognised something about the monster but couldn't put his finger on it. His memory was finally awakened when he managed to pick out some of the English words in the mangle of sounds accompanying the music: *Babylon the Great; Mother of Prostitutes.* This was none other than the *Whore of Babylon*, the woman and her mount that the long-forgotten JW leaflet had described and which he had read about and contemptuously dismissed on his final journey into work on Rapture Day.

Now fascinated, as well as terrified, he turned his attention to the woman rider. The flashing lights made it difficult to see but he managed to discern that she was wearing not very much – a skimpy purple and red outfit – and that she held in her hand a golden chalice from which she was drinking. She looked surprisingly familiar; the JW's cartoonist had obviously done his research and come up with a good likeness to the real thing.

The music was building to a crescendo and the frequency of the strobe flickering was increasing until, at last, the soundtrack finished and for a brief moment a single, uninterrupted light blazed down on Babylon's whore. In that instant Jerry looked straight at her and, it seemed, she stared right back. His stomach knotted and he gasped.

It was Rachael.

17

Jerry was up on his feet and shouting her name, but she was already enfolded in blackness while his voice was lost in the resurgent blast of insistent heavy-metal music. He had been sitting on the very end of a bench and he now started to feel his way cautiously down the steps to the front. He didn't have far to go before he was on flat ground.

The recorded music thundered out from powerful loudspeakers, the singer's high-pitched voice striking a frenzied refrain: "Beelzebub, Beelzebub, Beelzebub…"

Jerry crept forward in the darkness, sure that he must be approaching the place that Rachael and the beast had so recently occupied. If he had ever been a praying Christian this would have been the moment to pray for a light to guide him. He didn't pray, but he did get a light, courtesy of the Devil himself. Beelzebub was making his own appearance, rising slowly from the flames that had been re-ignited just a few metres from where Jerry crouched. It was the light from these flames that allowed Jerry to pick out the outline of one of the beast's heads as it was disappearing beneath the floor. The heat was starting to scorch his face.

Beelzebub, Beelzebub, Beelzebub.

He moved to the edge of the pit that had swallowed Rachael and the beast, and peered down into the blackness. He could see just enough to roughly estimate the creature's position and gambled that he really had understood its true nature. Realising that he would only have the cover of darkness for a few moments, he dived into the hole and managed to wrap his arms around the fierce head that he had seen descending a few seconds earlier. He clung on, feeling as he did so the mechanical parts that moved the jaw, and acknowledging a brief moment of admiration for the quality of engineering that had gone into the design and manufacture of the creature. He slid his body underneath the giant, lifeless head and dropped silently to the floor.

Beelzebub, Beelzebub, Beelzebub.

The beast stopped its downward movement with a jolt, and a trap door slid into place above it, shutting out some of the noise from the arena. A gloomy light was switched on and Jerry heard the voice of an elderly man say, "Mind yer step, my love."

"Thank you," replied Rachael in her own, real, sweet voice. Jerry felt the hotness of tears in his eyes but remained where he was, hidden behind one of the beast's legs. He stole a quick look and saw the base of a ladder on the other side of the animal. Rachael was obviously using it to climb down from her place on top of the beast. A short while later he heard a door open and close. His heart hammered inside his chest as he waited a few moments longer and then eased his way out of his hiding place. The old man was facing the opposite direction, putting away the ladder, so Jerry hurried to the exit Rachael had just used. He was reaching for the handle when the end of the ladder slammed into the door, pinning it shut.

"What's your game?"

Jerry turned. "I need to see Rachael," he said.

The face of the man looking at him put him inexplicably in mind of a newt.

"Oh, you know our Rachael, do you? Nice girl. Hoping to get to know her a bit better myself, if you know what I mean."

The two men stared at each other. Jerry knew that if it came to it, he would easily get the better of the older man, especially given the high level of adrenalin currently pumping around his body, but suspected that a physical fight might not be the best way to get what he desperately wanted. The Newt obviously thought the same and was sizing up the situation while keeping the door closed with the ladder. "What you got in there?" he asked, nodding his head towards the canvas bag that Jerry was still clutching.

"Apples."

"How many?"

"Two," lied Jerry.

"Gives us them and you can have two minutes with the girl."

Jerry took out an apple and laid it carefully on the floor. "You'll get the other one when I've finished – in *five* minutes."

"Three minutes," said the Newt. "Any longer than that and I'll call one of the demons."

"OK. Deal," said Jerry, realising as he did so that his ability to negotiate effectively was being seriously undermined by both his desperation to see Rachael and the nervousness invoked in him by the threat of the demons and their dogs.

The Newt lowered the ladder and pulled it away from the door. "She's second on the right. Three minutes, and that's your lot."

A single bare bulb hung from a dusty electric cord, illuminating the short corridor the other side of the door with a languid, yellow light. The smell of stale sweat hung in the cold, damp air. Jerry stood outside her door and knocked on the frosted glass pane.

"Yeah, come in," she said.

Inside the tiny room Rachael had just removed her brunette wig and was placing it on the mannequin stand in front of the mirror. When she turned around Jerry was standing in front of her. She drew a sharp intake of breath, put one hand to her mouth and whispered, "My God." A silence followed, then, "Is it really you?"

Jerry held out his arms and pulled her to his chest. "It *is* me, Rache, at long last."

They embraced for a whole minute, Jerry stroking her hair while Rachael cried. She pulled away, dragged a tissue out of a box on the little dressing table, wiped the make-up from under her eyes and blew her nose. Looking at his white tee-shirt and trousers she said, "You've come from Heaven. I guessed you must be there; I've been so worried about you."

"Likewise. I thought you would be somewhere in Heaven too;

it's been hell not being able to find you. I've only just found out that you were here, but I didn't expect to see you. Not like this anyway."

"What are you doing here?"

"I've been a bit of a bad boy I'm afraid; I got sent here by an angel to teach me a lesson."

"What happened?"

Quickly Jerry explained how he'd been caught searching the Book of Life and how Nathaniel had required him to see Hell for himself.

"This isn't the real thing, you know; this is just for the tourists."

"Yes, I thought it was all a show when I saw Moloch pulling faces at the baby and trying to make it laugh instead of eating it."

Rachael rolled her eyes. "He's always doing that. I'm surprised they haven't sacked him yet."

"I don't think anyone else noticed."

"No. People see exactly what they expect to see."

They kissed each other on their lips and briefly entwined their tongues. Conscious that they were running out of time, Jerry asked, "So what is it really like here, in Hell?"

"Horrible. Cold, wet, miserable. Overcrowded. Nothing like the common conception."

"It doesn't sound great."

"Huh. No, but at least for me it's nice to be back on stage again, even if, well, it's not exactly Shakespeare, is it?"

The muffled music stopped and they heard the sound of distant screams from above. "That'll be Billy," said Rachael. "He always scares the shit out of the punters."

"Billy is Beelzebub. The Devil," she added in answer to Jerry's puzzled look. "Don't worry," she continued as he looked even more astonished, "He's a pussy cat. Terribly vain, of course, but harmless."

"Do you actually *know* him?"

"Not well, but everyone who works here knows him to say hello to; he is the director, after all, as well as the star of the show. Haven't you met Jesus in Heaven yet?"

"Not directly. Sort of felt his presence, I suppose, during worship."

The couple looked at each other and held one another close once more. "What's it like? Heaven, I mean?" Rachael asked as she pressed into Jerry.

"Well, the weather's good, but you're not allowed to have sex."

Rachael stiffened slightly. "So is that why you're in my dressing room?"

"No, of course not. Besides, I'm not sure I could afford the Whore of Babylon's rates."

Rachael moved back a pace and for a moment Jerry wasn't sure if he'd got away with his joke. Then she chuckled and said, "A girl's gotta eat. Anyway, just exactly how did you get this far backstage?"

"I hitched a ride on your pet as you were making your exit and bribed my way past Mr Newt."

Rachael smiled. "How very resourceful of you, but you can't stay here for long."

"I know, he only let me have three minutes and I must have been in here almost that long already. I'll come back another time and we'll figure out how we can…"

"Time's up," called the Newt from outside the door, right on cue.

"Coming," shouted Jerry. Then, to Rachael, "When can I see you?"

"I heard that it hurts you when you come down in the lift," said Rachael. "What happened to your hand?"

"Honey, it really doesn't matter. Tell me, when can we get together?"

"OK. The day after tomorrow. I'm only working the morning shows then and I can meet you afterwards at the hospital."

"Great." They embraced one more time. "I've missed you," he whispered.

"I've missed you too."

The door opened and the reptilian face appeared. "Out of it," he said, gesturing behind him with his thumb. "And don't forget me fee," he added, holding out his hand. Jerry planted a final kiss on Rachael's forehead and an apple in the Newt's hand. The old man led Jerry back through the beast's lair and showed him a different way out. "This'll take you back to your friends, but be quick about it and don't go telling any of 'em about your little parley down here."

Jerry said nothing, pushed past him and ran up a staircase, emerging back into the auditorium just as the last stragglers from the Major's party were leaving.

In the gift shop Jerry found Joe just as Bob had said and successfully completed the cigarette transaction. With his purchase safely stored between Exodus and the third epistle of John, Jerry perused the shop, taking a half-hearted interest in the merchandise while his mind raced with the repercussions of his extraordinary encounter with Rachael and how he was going to rescue her from this hell-hole. Then, to his surprise, he found himself looking at her likeness once again. An entire display unit was given over to painted resin models of *The Mother of Prostitutes and of the Abominations of the Earth*. *His* Mother of Prostitutes and of the Abominations of the Earth; *his* Rachael. They had made her breasts unfeasibly large, although that was not necessarily a bad thing, and the faces on the beast were more comical than fierce, but in all other respects it was a pretty good representation.

"Would you like the Whore, sir?" a shop assistant with crooked teeth and a drooping eyelid asked.

Jerry hesitated. He did, indeed, want the Whore, but not in the manner the woman meant. She must have picked up something of this from his expression because, a moment later, she said quietly, "I know a young lady who would be very pleased to see a gentleman such as yourself, not five minutes away."

"Thank you," said Jerry, "but not this time." He left the shop wondering at the tenacity of the oldest profession and the implications for those tourists who would doubtless avail themselves of the charms of the working girls, confident that as a result of Heaven's freedom from disease, they would not be waking up the next day in Paradise with a nasty little itch as a souvenir of their indulgence.

Jerry met Solomon queuing to get back into the Hellevator. The angels guarding the lift asked them a couple of simple security questions about their worship group and where they lived in order to establish they were bone fide residents of Heaven, and let them in. They sat down together and Solomon showed Jerry a Moloch doll that he had bought as a reminder of God's blessing. "There but for the grace of Jesus..." he explained.

"There but for the grace of Jesus, what?" asked Jerry. "We all get eaten alive?"

"Yeah, except I don't think the baby actually died. I mean, you can't die in Hell any more than you can in Heaven."

"Just a few bites, then. Nothing fatal."

"Yeah, I think so. More of a torture for the mother than the kid, really."

"Poor mother."

"Yeah, but it's what we all deserve, Jerry. I hope it's taught you a lesson. I mean, you know, that was the whole point of this: to make you realise how merciful God has been to you in saving you from Hell."

"Oh yes, I've learnt a lot today. I have a much better understanding of God's mercy now that I've seen with my own eyes how he punishes the unsaved. Thank you."

"Everyone's there because they chose to be. They all wanted to run their own lives instead of putting Jesus at the centre, and now they have to live with the consequences."

Jerry closed his eyes and felt the vibration of the Hellevator as it powered its way upward. A thought occurred to him. "So what did you get out of today, Sol, apart from the satisfaction of seeing me learn my lesson?"

Solomon leaned a little closer. "Accompanying you wasn't the only reason I was sent here, Jerry. It was a test, to see if I could handle what I saw."

"And could you?"

"Yeah. Well, you know, it's not nice but it is what we all…"

"Yes, I know, it's what we all deserve," Jerry interrupted.

"And they chose it."

"Of course." Jerry resisted the temptation to tell Solomon that what they had seen had just been pure theatre. "Why were you being tested?"

"To see if I'd make a good judge."

Solomon saw the questioning look on Jerry's face and continued. "Paul says in one Corinthians chapter six, verse two, that the saints – that's us, Jerry – will judge the world. Now, all the people who were sent to Hell after the Rapture weren't judged by the saints at all, they just went straight there. That's not really fair because we didn't get to judge them, so there's going to be some new trials and they'll need more judges. Nat says I've got what it takes to be a judge but first I needed to see Hell for myself to make sure I'd be prepared to send people there when they fail their appeals."

Jerry was suddenly animated. "People in Hell can appeal their sentences?"

"Yes, because the Scripture needs to be fulfilled. There was supposed to be a gap between the Rapture and the Second Coming when some more people might have got, you know, saved, and when all this judging was going to start. Now the trials have to be reorganised because for some reason it didn't quite happen as everyone had expected."

"It's because the *Book of Life* was closed by mistake. That's why there was no second chance for anyone – they couldn't have had their names written into the database even if they had been, *you know*, saved. Oh God, that's what that other file was – it was for the trials. It was even called T*rials*; I saw it in St Isidore's"

"What are you talking about, man?"

"Oh, it doesn't matter. Tell me about these trials, Sol. If someone is found to be innocent can they really come and live in Heaven?"

"No-one is innocent; how many times do I have to tell you?"

"OK, OK, whatever. I mean, might the judgement be reversed? Do they have a chance of coming to Heaven, even though their name's not in the *Book of Life*?"

Solomon shrugged. "Maybe, if they truly repent and believe."

Jerry was almost beside himself with excitement. "How do people get a trial, Sol?"

"I dunno. You'll have to ask Bob. He used to have something to do with organising trials when he first came here."

"Praise the Lord," somebody shouted nearby and, for the first time in his life, Jerry felt it was a phrase he might even use himself. "Amen," came another. "I'm healed; thank you, Jesus." Jerry looked at his blistered hand and saw that the bandage had disappeared and the skin was totally restored. Throughout the Hellevator people were miraculously returning to perfect health and a great surge of praise filled the lift.

The journey finished, but before they could disembark they were given a stern lecture by one of the angel-guards telling them not to discuss the painful entry process to Hell with anyone, exactly as Solomon had suggested. Not even this outlandish censorship, or the uncritical fashion in which it was accepted by his fellow-travellers, could dampen Jerry's mood, however. Rachael was innocent, no matter what Solomon or the Gospels might say. He could get her a trial and prove it. Hallelujah! Jerry stepped back out into Heaven's light, feeling as never before full of the most wonderful hope.

18

"One of my favourite verses is in this book," said Worthy.

Before retiring to bed after his return from Hell the previous evening, Jerry had checked the chapter and verse that Solomon had quoted to him from Saint Paul's first letter to the Corinthians. He had never been so pleased to discover that Solomon had been right: *Do you not know that the saints will judge the Earth?* To Jerry's delight, the apostle had gone on to suggest that the saints would also be judging the angels. He'd made a note to mention that to Nathaniel next time he needed to ruffle the big guy's feathers.

He'd left the Bible open on his desk and Worthy had seen it when delivering his fresh set of clothes in the morning.

"*Love doth not behave itself unseemly, seeketh not her own, is not easily provoked, thinketh no evil,*" Worthy had said, carrying the book over to where Jerry still lay. "Chapter thirteen, verse five."

"Oh, thanks; Bible in bed," said Jerry, cheerfully taking the proffered book. "Actually, it just says, '*Love keeps no record of wrongs*' here," he added, after reading the verse indicated.

"We Mormons only read the King James' Version. Yours is a modern translation. I think the old one's better."

"Yes, I'm sure. Mind you, the new one is nice and simple, isn't it, and a bit easier to understand? I like the idea of not recording wrongs."

It was only after Worthy had left that Jerry realised quite what not keeping a record of wrongs might mean for Rachael. Indeed, if God loved her according to this biblical gold standard, there could be no evidence available to find her guilty since there would be no records, and, if she was not guilty, she could be released from Hell. Either he was missing something or overturning Rachael's sentence was going to be even easier than he'd expected.

Within minutes he had skipped happily down to breakfast. Mindful of the need to successfully complete his first mission as a tobacco-laden, fag-trafficking mule, he brought the cigarettes with him, still secreted away inside their sacred hideaway. He spotted Bob soon after entering the canteen and quickly joined him on a table that was relatively sparsely populated for that time of the morning. He put the Bible down in front of him and started to slide it across the table.

"Not here," said Bob, tersely. "Put it away."

Jerry laid the book on his lap. Another couple of men sat down near them. They all greeted each other.

Bob, more conversationally, said, "So, Jerry, how was Hell?"

"Fabulous," Jerry replied, drawing disbelieving looks from the newcomers. "That is to say, it was fabulous to see what God – Jesus – has saved us from. Amazing. Amazing grace," he added, hoping that a reference to a revered hymn would distract from his errant enthusiasm for the Underworld.

"Grace indeed. Praise him," said the taller of the two men who had just joined them, while the other nodded sagely.

Lowering his voice so that only Bob could hear him, Jerry asked, "How do people in Hell get trials?"

"What do you know about that?" Bob replied stiffly.

"Solomon told me, and I read it in the Bible."

"Uh-huh," said Bob.

"Solomon also said that you'd know how to fix up a trial for Rachael."

"I know how to fix up a lot of things, son."

"Great. I want to get her tried and then, when she's cleared, there's my dad, my friends and, oh, loads of other people."

Bob kept his eyes on his porridge and didn't look up. "You're jumping the gun a bit, ain't you?"

"Probably. We need to get Rachael a trial first. How do we do that?"

"That bit's simple enough; you just have to ask Jesus."

"Jesus?"

"Yeah, Jesus."

"But I haven't even met him. I've no idea how to find him, let alone ask him for something."

Jerry had become louder in his excited state. His tall neighbour had caught the tail-end of the conversation and interrupted piously. "We have all met Jesus, Jerry, otherwise none of us would be here. And, besides, didn't our Lord himself promise that he would give us whatever we ask for?"

Jerry fantasised about poking him in the eye with a fork and telling him to mind his own bloody business. Instead he said, "Thank you, Keith, I was forgetting." And before he could change his mind about where to put his cutlery, he went off to get himself a pot of tea. He'd calmed down sufficiently by the time he returned to quietly ask Bob, "So, how do I get to Jesus?"

"You can see him tonight if you like."

"What?"

"He'll be at the Crown."

Jerry thought the Crown was a pub and said so.

"Yeah, that's right. It's the one on Redemption Road. There's a quiz there this evening. Come along, and bring the gear with you." Bob motioned to the faux-Bible when he said this.

"And he will *really* be there?"

"I said so, didn't I? But keep it to yourself; we don't want everyone knowing or we'll never get a seat."

Jerry looked unconvinced so Bob continued, "Look, from time to time he comes and runs the quiz. He likes to get close to the people, you know, back to his roots. It's like one of them famous singers doing a gig in a tiny club to prove they've still got what it takes."

"But surely Jesus will always have what it takes, seeing as how he's God?"

"You'd think so, wouldn't you? But he still likes to do it, and he'll be doing it tonight. Trust me."

"You must be very well connected to know he's coming."

"Yeah, well, let's just say I've been around the block a few times. I know people who know people, if you know what I mean."

"Including lawyers?" asked Jerry, whose mind was working quickly.

"Them too, for sure."

"Can we get a really good one for Rachael? I mean the best. She has to have the best lawyer."

Bob finished his last mouthful of porridge and put down his spoon. "There ain't so many of those up here: most of the best briefs ended up in the *Other Place*. Not that a lawyer will do you much good anyway. It's theologians what you need. One decent vicar could make mincemeat of all them flashy barristers. Teach them a thing or two, I can tell you."

"Like Canon John? He's a decent vicar, isn't he?"

Bob looked directly at Jerry. "The best I ever knew."

"Thanks Bob. I'll see you at the Crown."

Jerry scrambled away from the table and left. He was a man on a mission with no time to lose.

There was singing on the bus and Jerry joined in with gusto, expressing his new-found optimism; the nightmare of Heaven without Rachael would soon be coming to an end. He sang for another reason too: the noise stopped him from paying too much attention to his doubt. His first Dark Thought – the one that had postulated the possibility of Hell – was giving birth to a bastard child: *if it was so easy, why wasn't everybody doing it?* He sang louder.

He walked *Old Stony*, beginning with the last hole first, having ascertained from the club house when Canon John had started his round. He eventually found the clergyman on the fifteenth tee, where he relieved his caddy of his duties. "I'll carry the bag from here," he said, "you go and put your feet up."

"I could get used to this servile obedience," Jerry said to Canon John as Marcus started back to the clubhouse.

The Canon took his tee shot and as they walked up the fairway together Jerry thanked him for arranging to get him into St Isidore's.

"You're welcome. All the posts are talking sense now, so I assumed you'd succeeded."

"Yes. I looked into the *Book of Life*, too, John."

The Canon slowed his pace. "And?"

"Her name's not there."

"You're sure? She's not listed somewhere else under a slightly different spelling? Mistakes do happen you know."

"I'm certain. Anyway, there's something else."

"What?"

"I got caught."

The Canon stopped walking and looked anxiously at Jerry. "Who by?"

"Nathaniel. I thought everyone had left, but that slime-ball Zamaleki must have been watching out for me. He got hold of Nathaniel and my favourite angel caught me red-handed."

"You didn't tell him it was my idea, did you?" asked the Canon with genuine alarm.

"No, don't worry; I didn't shop you," Jerry replied and was surprised at just how relieved his companion seemed by this reassurance. It was a while before the Canon thought to ask what happened next.

Walking slowly over an arched bridge which crossed a talkative little stream, Jerry told Canon John about his educational day-trip to Hell. "It's exactly what you'd expect: screaming, torture, pain, fire. They even have a child-eating demon. It's your own worst nightmare."

The Canon said nothing and nibbled the quick of his thumb.

"Rachael's there, John, amidst all that suffering. I saw her."

The ruddy colour of exertion drained from the Canon's face. They had reached his ball, lying subdued on the silent grass. He bent down, picked it up, and handed it to Jerry. "I don't have the stomach for this right now," he said.

Jerry put the ball in a zipped compartment of the golf bag and the two men went and sat on a curved stone bench above the green.

"I need your help getting her out."

The Canon sat up and put his hands on his thighs. "What?"

"I know about the trials. Bob told me that vicars make the best lawyers, and as a Canon you have more firepower than most."

The Canon didn't laugh. He must have heard that line before.

"I'm seeing Jesus tonight – *the* Jesus – and I'm going to get permission for Rachael to have her trial. Will you put her case before the court?"

"Well, I'm not sure. I really don't know if…"

"Nathaniel doesn't know it was you who suggested I hack into the *Book of Life*. That can change."

"Are you threatening me?"

"Whatever it takes." Jerry stared hard at the Canon, not quite believing his own bravado. Neither man said a word for a while until Jerry could no longer stand the tension. "Come on, John. You know that it's not right she's there. She was born Jewish; she never had the chance to hear about Jesus dying for her sin and all that bollocks."

"Ignorance of the law is no defence."

"Well it bloody well should be. How can anyone be punished for not believing a particular religion, even if it did turn out to be the only true one?"

Canon John said nothing. It was his way of expressing agreement, Jerry understood. "I found out something else today," Jerry continued and went on to explain his theory about God not having access to Rachael's *File of Wrong-doing* because he must love her as the Bible says.

"Then why is there *anyone* in Hell?" the Canon asked, deflating Jerry's enthusiasm as he did so. "The problem is that you can use the Bible to support almost any argument; your proof text being a case in point. Paul does say that love keeps no record of wrongs, but if you read the story of Moses receiving the second set of stone tablets on Mount Sinai – it's in Exodus chapter thirty-four, I recall – you will see that Yahweh promises to punish people for the sins of their great, great grandfathers. It isn't possible to do that without remembering the wrong, and remembering it for a mighty long time."

"Does that mean that God's love fails his own test?"

The Canon sighed and took his time to answer. "Perhaps it does; I don't know. He does remember our sins, and punishes us for them, unless we're Christians – in which case he still remembers them but punishes Jesus instead. Either way, any sentimental feelings he may have about ignoring our wrong-doing are trumped by his need to judge us. I told you he was a judge when we first met."

"You also told me he had no moral authority to judge because he was so – what word did you use? – *nasty*. If we could prove that from the Bible then the case against Rachael would collapse, wouldn't it?"

"I can't imagine any court in Heaven finding against God in that way, can you? It would be seen as blasphemy and if they agreed with the argument then all hell would break loose, literally."

Jerry was getting horribly confused. With the exception of the Canon, everybody he'd met in Heaven spoke passionately of God's love for people, yet Jerry kept coming across incontrovertible evidence to the contrary. The existence of Hell, the merciless Flood, even the little Jerry had read of the Bible all pointed to a sociopathic Divinity hungry to punish rather than to forgive: more Sadist than Saviour. "We can't be the only two people who have noticed how unfair all this is, John."

"People see what they want to see. If they're comfortable in their beliefs then they don't want to hear opinions that will unsettle them. That was always true on Earth, how much more will it be the case in Paradise. They have no reason to change."

"Angels!" said Jerry suddenly, as if he hadn't been listening. "What if we got one of them to plead on Rachael's behalf? I'm sure I could get Uriel to speak up."

"Nobody would take *him* seriously. Besides, I called in to St Isidore's to see him this morning to tell him how well the speaker posts were working, and I discovered he was no longer there. They couldn't tell me where he'd gone either."

"Nathaniel!"

"Yes, people would certainly listen to him, but you won't get him to testify in court."

"No, I meant that he would have been responsible for kicking Uriel out of his job," said Jerry, but the seed of an idea had been planted in his head.

The two men discussed the conundrum a little further until Jerry realised he needed to leave in order to get back in time for the quiz. Before he left he had to get a firm commitment from the Canon. "Look John," he said, "I need those Bible references – the ones that show God isn't morally perfect. I know it's a long shot, but I have to try, and you're the only person I know who can do this for me. For Rachael."

The clergyman sighed and then nodded briefly. "Come and see me again once you have a date for the trial," he said.

Jerry embraced the clergyman and, on stepping away, was struck by how the Canon looked suddenly older, such was the effect of the light and how it fell on his face. "Thanks, John," he said as they parted.

Jerry had only gone a few feet when the Canon called after him. "Be careful," he said, echoing Nathaniel's own words from the con-tretemps in St Isidore's, "be very careful."

19

Bob was waiting anxiously for Jerry on the corner of Redemption Road outside the door of the Crown. Like many pubs, the red-brick building had a grandeur about it somewhat out of character with its rather base function. It was three storeys high with a large gabled roof and would not have looked out of place in almost any London high street. Even the name was consistent with the public houses Jerry frequented back home, although the choice of a crown of thorns on the sign swinging from a yardarm above the pavement was certainly unique.

"Just in time," said Bob as Jerry arrived, out of breath.

They went inside and it took Jerry's eyes a moment to adjust to the dinginess of the interior with its low ceiling and exposed, dark wooden beams. A dozen round, wooden tables, each seating eight or nine people, had been crowded into the floor space between the bar and a small, raised stage. A microphone stand had been placed in the centre of the stage, and behind it hung a curtain of shiny streamers concealing an entrance, out of which, in another universe, the singer, or stripper, would have appeared to a raucous welcome.

Bob led Jerry to the far side of the room where two empty seats had been saved for them on a table nearest to the back door. To Jerry's delight, Catherine was part of his group and she smiled as she passed him a bottle of Paradise beer. "You look like you need this," she said.

"We're the non-conformists," she added after Jerry had taken a long draught of the refreshing liquid. "Our team, I mean."

"Oh, yes; sounds ideal," Jerry replied, acknowledging the one or two team members who looked his way. He had no idea what it was they were not conforming to but, given the difficulty he had had in finding like-minded people since he had arrived, thought that maybe some independent thinking might not go amiss.

The evening's compère stepped onto the stage and spoke into the microphone. "Good evening, everybody," he said, his voice amplified over the hubbub of loud voices and catching a squeak of acoustic feedback in the process. "Let's begin with a word of prayer." The noise died down immediately and the majority of people bowed their heads. "Dear Lord Jesus, we want to thank you for the opportunity to gather here in your name and to praise you through our quiz. Please help us to get the answers right, and to give you the glory. Thank you, Jesus. Amen"

"Amen," responded the contestants, heartily.

"Ladies and gentlemen," continued the man on the stage, "I can honestly say that tonight's Quiz Master needs no introduction. Please put your hands together and welcome… our Saviour!" So saying, the MC stepped down from the stage and a spotlight illuminated the shimmering ribbons through which emerged, not the singer, not the stripper, but the Son of God himself. A tumultuous round of applause greeted his appearance; a reception which he acknowledged with one hand raised in thanks and the other shielding his eyes from the glare of light. Once the crowd had quietened down, he said in a voice as smooth and Jewish as a spoonful of kosher honey, "I can't see so well with this light in my eyes. Let there be darkness." Immediately the whole room was blacked out. "OK, not so much darkness; let there be just enough light." The room returned to a comfortable, ambient light without the blinding spot centred on the stage.

Once again, the audience erupted in applause and, this time, laughter as well. Jesus waved them into silence, a big smile on his face. "Ah, it's an old trick, I know, but what am I to do? No new material now for two thousand years."

More laughter from the crowd. Someone shouted out, "What about the Rapture?"

"Yes, it's true, that was new. I didn't know I had it in me. You liked that one, huh?"

The audience's response told him that they did. "I love you, Jesus," a woman called out, to which he replied, "Yeah, I love you too, babe." This earned him yet more applause and cheering.

Jerry leaned over to Bob and shared an observation: "He's much shorter than I thought he would be."

"Everyone says that. There have been too many Hollywood films where he was played by tall guys with blond hair. He don't have no beard neither."

"Oh, no; I hadn't even noticed."

"Look at his wrists," said Bob, tapping his own with an index finger as if Jerry's knowledge of anatomy was such that it would be difficult for him to locate those particular joints on Jesus' body.

Jerry half stood in order to get a good enough view and managed to catch a glimpse of what it was that Bob had intended him to see: ugly brown knots like burn marks on the Saviour's olive skin. The beautification process that had brought perfection to most of Heaven's ordinary immortals had clearly not been granted to its king, thereby ensuring, Jerry surmised, that his scars would act as a permanent physical reminder of the suffering he had undergone at the end of his life on earth. Nevertheless, Jerry thought, Jesus was a handsome devil with his slicked-back hair and easy smile. He knew how to work a crowd too; the Crown's punters responded enthusiastically to his silver tongue, like wedding guests enjoying the best man's speech, wanting to like him, wanting him to be funny.

Notwithstanding his damaged wrists, Jesus obviously enjoyed some privileges in Heaven; he was the first person Jerry had seen since his arrival who wasn't wearing a uniform of some kind. Instead, he was dressed in a simple combination of blue denim jeans and a white tee-shirt. Unlike all the other white shirts in Heaven, Jesus' one carried a logo. The letters *WWID* were spelled out in royal blue, just above his heart.

In response to his question as to the acronym's meaning,

Catherine told Jerry that it stood for *What Would I Do?* "I used to wear a wrist-band that said WWJD – *What Would Jesus Do?* – so that I could always think about how to make decisions that would please him. I think it's really cool that his shirt says that," she added admiringly.

"All right, enough now already," Jesus was saying. "Let's start the quiz. I'll give you the answers as we go along and each team can score themselves. We'll keep an eye on you to make sure you don't cheat!"

People laughed but something in his tone of voice made Jerry wonder if his last point had actually been serious. For the first time Jerry noticed how many angels were standing around the edges of the room, looking like bouncers at a city-centre nightclub. The one nearest to his own table stood with his arms folded, watching the crowd carefully. On a belt around his waist was clipped a small canister, near the top of which the letters CE were clearly visible, preceded by half the letter A. Jerry hadn't seen any angels carrying such an accessory before but, now that he looked, they all seemed to have these cans on their belts. He dismissed the first thought that came into his head as simply not credible. *Why, in Heaven's name, would angels need mace spray?*

Further consideration was cut short as the *Messiah with the mike* declared that theology would be the initial subject in the quiz, and then boomed out the first question. "Is the doctrine of original sin true? In other words, are all men born sinful?"

There was an excited babble in the room as people conferred and then, a few moments later, Jesus called out, "Everybody got that? Good. The answer is *yes*, it is true."

Cheers broke out throughout the pub. Everyone, it seemed had got that one right.

"Next one," continued Jesus. "What's the name of the Nephite Moroni's best-selling fantasy novel?"

Howls of laughter erupted from the crowd. Someone from the

Anglican table stood up and, pointing to the non-conformists, called out, "Don't tell them it's made up; they think it's true!"

This was greeted with more laughter, although not by Bob and his team-mates.

"I'm sure you've all got that one," said Jesus. "It's the *Book of Mormon*. An entertaining little tale but, as you all know, reports of my post-Ascension visit to the Americas have been grossly exaggerated!"

More cheers, followed by a brief round of applause. Catherine touched Jerry's arm and nodded in the direction of the bar where the crestfallen bar-tender was wiping a beer glass very slowly. Like Worthy, his belief-system had been proven to be wrong, and the crowd's laughter rubbed salt in his wound.

"The third question is a bit more difficult. Is the sacrament of baptism necessary for salvation?"

Something of an argument broke out on the non-conformist table but the weight of opinion eventually favoured the view that the rite was a *nice to have* and was not strictly necessary.

"Have to hurry you," Jesus was saying, looking at their table. "OK? Well the answer is, *yes*."

Yet more cheering broke out, but there was considerable consternation amongst the non-conformists. A freckle-faced man shouted out from the Roman Catholic table, "Do you want to come and join us? We can help you with the theology and you can help us with…" Here he broke off and asked the rest of his team, "What can they help with? There must be something!" Gleefully his friends pleaded ignorance, leaving him with nothing to offer. They pulled him back down with lots of back-slapping and finger pointing.

A little bruised by the taunting, Catherine muttered to Jerry, "I'm not sure about that. It's not what my parents taught me."

She immediately regretted her indiscretion as, to her chagrin, Jesus addressed his next comment directly to her. "No, Catherine, it is true. The original sin has to be washed away."

More applause greeted this intervention, particularly from the Catholics, who fancied they were on something of a roll. Catherine, however, folded her hands in her lap and kept her eyes downcast.

"The next question is also a bit of a challenge. Does the Eucharist transubstantiate?"

Jerry put his hand on Catherine's shoulder and massaged it gently. He tried to see into her eyes but her hair had tumbled down and was obscuring her face.

"Eucharist is Holy Communion, right?" he overheard someone say from the next table. "Does it trans-what?"

"Yes, what *does* that mean?" he asked Catherine, hoping that he might be able to get her to focus on something other than her public humiliation at the hands of the very person she had spent her life worshipping.

Bob answered on her behalf. "The Catholics believe the bread and wine become Jesus' body and blood, but it ain't true, is it, Cath?"

Cath shook her head very slightly at the same time as Jesus' voice once more commanded their attention. "The answer is, *no*."

A huge roar of approval broke out from the loose affiliation of Protestants in the pub, contrasting with abject silence from the Catholic and Orthodox tables. Some of the celebration that followed seemed, at least to Jerry, to be a little too exuberant. A number of people were standing on their chairs pointing to the hapless Catholics. One delighted Ulsterman from the Presbyterian team, a square-jawed, thick-set man with closely-cropped orange hair and piggy eyes walked towards them, held up his pint of beer, pointed to it, and asked in a loud voice, "Won't you transubstantiate that, now? Won't you do that, Father?" He was dragged back by two of his team-mates, both equally jubilant and full of piggy-mischief. Their sneering continued from the safety of their team table, but was no less caustic for that.

"Much more of this and things could get a bit tasty, if you know what I mean," murmured Bob to Jerry. Having spent his whole life in parts of London that experienced more than their fair share of *tasty* times, Bob's opinion on these matters was not to be taken lightly.

Jesus was addressing them once more. "OK, calm down, now. Last one in the theology section: does the priesthood have to be celibate?"

The non-Catholics were scenting victory and greeted this question with derisive cheers and a good deal of smirking and gesturing towards their Catholic rivals who did their best to remain dignified and composed. A moment later the answer was given in the negative and laughter showered the Catholic table. Pandemonium broke out: people were pointing towards the Catholics, some helpless with laughter, holding their stomachs, eyes streaming with tears.

The Ulsterman was back on his feet. Although his words could not be heard above the din, their intent was not lost on those he was baiting, and one of them responded with a well-aimed bottle which caught him smack on the forehead, covering him with foamy beer. "We're outta here," said Bob, grabbing Jerry by the arm and forcing him away from the table. Instinctively Jerry reached for Catherine but the nearby angel's muscular bulk had come between the two of them and he found that Bob, with surprising speed, had bundled him out of the back door.

Bob hurried him across the small paved courtyard towards the external toilet block, then around the little building until they were hidden from the view of the pub. Jerry protested, "What about Catherine? We can't leave her in there with a riot going on."

"There's no riot, son. Everything's under control."

"But I saw…"

"Trust me. There's nothing to worry about. Listen. You hear anything?"

Bob was still holding Jerry's arm and the two men stood together listening for the sounds of violence and conflict. There were none.

"I'll explain later. We just have to wait here for a minute."

Bob let go of Jerry and handed him the Bible that contained the smuggled cigarettes. Jerry had brought it with him as instructed, but hadn't noticed Bob pick it up from the table in the rush to exit from the pub.

The toilet block had been built at the foot of a steep, grassy bank. There was a narrow, flat strip between the base of the bank and the wall against which Jerry leant, in a state of some confusion. The smell coming from the toilets was not entirely pleasant and, because his mind was not following any linear trajectory, Jerry wondered what Heaven would have been like if Canon John's demoralised faith had been correct after all and the afterlife had been spiritual rather than physical. Less fetid for one thing; souls don't shit.

It was while Jerry was entertaining such uplifting notions that he heard a cistern flush and a few moments later the Lord Jesus Christ strolled round the corner to scrounge some fags.

"Hello, Jerry," he said.

"Hello, um…"

"Jesus," said Jesus.

"Jesus," said Jerry, who found himself hoping that Jesus had washed his hands.

"I gather you have an offering for me."

Jerry glanced at Bob who motioned with his head to the Bible in Jerry's hand. Jerry passed the book to Jesus who took it and opened it up. He smiled when he saw the contents and said, "Ah, *when a Bible's well used, the Devil's not amused.* Isn't that right, Bob?"

Bob smiled back.

Since leaving the pub Jesus had donned a leather jacket, even though the temperature didn't warrant it. The Son of God found space in the jacket for three packets and, after returning the Bible to Jerry, removed the cellophane wrapping from the fourth. He screwed up the wrapper and dropped it to the floor, opened the packet and offered cigarettes to his two companions. Jerry declined but Bob took one and waited for Jesus to extract one for himself. Once the unlit cigarette was in his mouth Jesus simply touched the end and it burned red, a simple little miracle deployed for the sake of a quick drag behind the bogs.

Bob lit his cigarette from the heat of Jesus' own, in the manner of smoker-buddies everywhere.

Jesus placed the palm of his hand against the wall, a few inches from Jerry's head. The two men were very close and for an insane moment Jerry realised that he would have no trouble in head-butting Jesus and breaking his divine nose. He thought better of it.

Jesus looked up into Jerry's eyes, sucked on his cigarette and exhaled the smoke from the corner of his mouth. The grey smoke curled and coalesced, darkening into a brown cylinder which seemed to move of its own accord and with a will of its own. Jerry looked properly and saw that the cylinder was now a large hornet, buzzing malevolently just above Jesus' head, where his halo ought to have been.

"Best not to tell anybody about this little encounter, Jerry," said Jesus, "especially not my mother."

"I've never met your mother," replied Jerry. The hornet buzzed more loudly and moved a fraction closer.

"Eventually you'll meet everybody, as you may have already realised. As luck would have it, you just happen to have bumped into me fairly early in your stay, and sooner or later you'll run into her as well. She disapproves of this little vice that our friend Bob has introduced me to, so I need you to promise that you won't tell her, or anybody else, about it. Ever."

In spite of his growing sense of anxiety, Jerry replied, "Well, may I ask for something in return?"

Jesus took another drag of his cigarette and this time exhaled directly into Jerry's face. "He bites," he said, indicating the hornet by momentarily raising his eyebrows. "And so do his friends." The second cloud of smoke had turned into a swarm of wasps, many of whom were settling on Jerry's body, twitching with intent to cause actual bodily harm. "And in case you think you can't be hurt, you should know that, if I consider it necessary, I am able to override the normal state of anaesthesia which you have been enjoying since you arrived here."

Jerry didn't feel that *the Lord* was bluffing. "OK. I won't tell."

"Good. Nobody would have believed you of, course, but you know what mothers are like: they worry so. Be gone."

Contrary to Jerry's immediate impression, the imperative had not been addressed to him, but to the bitter stingers who were now transformed into just so much smoke, drifting away in the breeze. Jesus straightened up and with his cigarette-free hand brushed some residual ash from Jerry's shoulder. "Now, what did you want me to do for you? *Ask and it shall be given*: Matthew chapter seven, verse seven. One of my more reckless promises, but there we are."

"I have a friend who's in Hell and I was wondering…" Jerry felt his mouth turn dry as he approached the momentous question, "…if she could have a trial."

"Oh, is that all?" Jesus turned and walked slowly to the grass bank, lay down on his back, and closed his eyes. "This friend of yours is a woman, I imagine."

"Yes. Her name's Rachael. Rachael Bennett."

"Ah, the indomitable human capacity for sexual love and the heroism it elicits. How marvellous. Do you think she would like to worship me, this Rachael Bennett of yours? Could she be happy here doing that forever and ever, world without end, Amen?"

Jerry didn't know how to answer the question and looked across to Bob for guidance, but his friend avoided eye contact, lifting his pinched cigarette to his lips, staring at his feet. Jerry repeated the question, "Can she have a trial? Only it says in the Bible something about the saints being judges."

"I'm aware of what it says, Jerry, and that if it's written in the Bible then it must be true." Jerry thought he heard Jesus mumble something about *bloody Saint Paul*, but he couldn't quite pick it up. "Go on then, have your trial. Bob, you can see to it, can't you?"

Bob nodded his assent. Jerry felt a frisson of both excitement and fear. "So there is a chance that she will be allowed to come here after all?"

"I doubt that it will come down to chance."

Jerry searched for a question that was forming in his mind, but before he could get to it Jesus found it for him. "I know what you're thinking," said the little Lord, sitting up and taking another long drag. "As I'm omniscient, why can't I just tell you what will happen? But actually, when I'm in human form I have to accept some of the limitations of being fully human, such as *not* knowing absolutely everything. You may remember that the gospels recall me telling people that I didn't know when I would be returning to earth, for example. Not that that stopped them all trying to second-guess the Second Coming and convincing themselves that my return was imminent; each generation just as certain as the previous one that they had at last got it right, poor fools.

"I prefer it this way, to be honest. Have you any idea how excruciatingly, nauseatingly, inexpressibly *dull* it is to know *absolutely everything*?" Jesus looked at Jerry, who obviously didn't know what this felt like and returned an expression that he hoped would convey the fact that even a relatively ignorant all-knowing person should have known that he, Jerry, could not possibly have experienced the paradoxical dullness of an omniscient mind.

"God, I don't know how my Father manages it. He must be bored out of his senses."

The end of Jesus' cigarette glowed again as he inhaled through it one final time before flicking it away. It became a firefly, dancing its crimson way through the air before landing on the ground and disintegrating into ashy oblivion.

Jesus got to his feet and announced he had to be leaving. "The Right Hand calls and needs to be sat at," he said and turned, walking up the grass bank and away. The two men watched him go and then made their way back to the pub.

Just before they reached the back door, Bob stopped. "This lot inside won't remember anything about what happened earlier."

"Eh? Why not?"

Bob frowned and squeezed his chin between his forefinger and thumb. "Things ain't always…" he hesitated, then tried again. "People can get a bit carried away sometimes and do things that they probably shouldn't. Things that spoil it for everyone else."

"Things like fighting?"

"Yes, exactly. And when that happens," he continued, "it's best if they can forget all about it, as if, you know, it never really took place. People shouldn't be having a scrap, even if it doesn't hurt them. It destroys the harmony." Bob looked at Jerry awkwardly, like someone confessing an embarrassing personal misdemeanour.

"Go on," said Jerry.

"Well, the angels have a special spray that they use."

"Shit, I thought so. I saw the canisters."

"Yeah, well, it's called Grace spray. It don't do no harm, just makes people forget what went wrong, that's all. Anyway, when things got out of hand in here earlier they, you know…"

"Sprayed them," said Jerry, completing Bob's sentence for him.

"Yeah, but they're alright. Really. They just won't remember the fighting and all that, so best you don't say nothing about it either. OK?"

Jerry nodded his assent to the second request that evening for his acquiescence in a conspiracy of silence. "What if some of them didn't get sprayed?"

"The angels don't miss. Even if they did, it would be that person's word against everyone else's, wouldn't it? They'll probably just forget about it in the end and think they got confused; they ain't going to be able to prove nothing anyway."

"So much for truth and integrity," said Jerry. Then another thought occurred to him. "Why didn't Jesus spray *us*, so that we would forget about the cigarettes? Wouldn't that have been safer?"

"Perhaps, but there was no need: no-one would believe your word against his. Besides, he prefers people to obey him out of their own free will."

"Free will and the threat of being stung half to death," added Jerry. They were about to go through the door when he asked Bob, "Have you ever been sprayed?"

"How the bloody hell would I know that?"

"Oh, yeah. Good point. Have I?"

"Not that I know of, son. Now come on, we're nearly late again."

"Where have you two been – outside for a crafty fag?" asked Catherine as the two men reappeared. "Only teasing. You're only just back in time; the quiz is about to start. Oh, and you'll never guess who the Quiz Master is."

"Who?" asked Jerry, playing along.

"John the Baptist."

"No, I wouldn't have guessed that," admitted Jerry, with candour.

"Imagine! The real John the Baptist, the one from the gospels, doing a pub quiz for us. I'm so excited. Oh, look, here he is now."

Sure enough, a bony, bearded, bedraggled man with fly-away hair and an expression somewhere between suicidal despair and pathological hatred, was holding the microphone on the stage so recently occupied by his more illustrious predecessor. Once the cheering and applause had died down he announced in a mournful voice that the quiz would begin with a section on theology.

"Oh, bad luck," Catherine mocked Jerry, her eyes shining. "I don't think you'll be much good at this bit."

"On the contrary," he replied, like a man in the know. "I think this might be right up my street."

20

"You again," said Dr Doyle. "Didn't see enough suffering last time, then? It's not a bloody circus, you know."

"Actually, that's exactly what it is," Jerry replied. He'd sought out the same medic who had treated him on his previous visit to Hell, hoping that he would be on duty. The first Hellevator ride of the day hadn't been full and finding him had been easy. "I know it's not real; it's just a show."

The doctor took Jerry's blistered hand and started to treat it. "There's plenty of real pain here, so there is," he said. "It doesn't just last for a day, either. Imagine that; hurting for a thousand years and knowing that you've barely started. A million years even, and no end in sight."

"It's impossible to imagine anything lasting forever," replied Jerry quietly. "Even though we know it's true."

The doctor murmured an agreement and after a while asked, "So have you come back for a girl then, is that it?"

Jerry was taken aback. "Yes, how did you know?"

The doctor gave him a knowing, disapproving look. "I see a lot of men like you."

Suddenly Jerry remembered the proposition he had received in the gift shop on his last visit. "It's not like that," he said and went on to describe meeting Rachael, although he was careful not to mention the circumstances under which they had been re-united. "I have to see her again," he concluded, and watched the doctor's face carefully to see if he had been believed.

"You must think a lot of her to put up with this discomfort," said the medic when the bandaging was finished.

"I do," said Jerry, before saying, "Dr Doyle?"

"Michael. My friends call me Mickey."

"I'm Jerry," said Jerry, holding out his un-injured right hand. "I need a favour from you, Mickey. I need to borrow your clothes."

Dr Doyle raised a questioning eyebrow.

"Not your hospital scrubs; your ordinary ones. I guess you changed when you got here."

"I did."

"I can't go wandering around here in my heavenly garb; I'll draw too much attention to myself and, from what I've heard, that can be dangerous." The doctor assented to this point with a nod of his head. Jerry picked up his canvas bag which was full of the produce he'd brought with him. "I can pay you," he said.

Mickey thought for a moment. "Wait," he said, and pulled the green screen around the bed for privacy.

Jerry upended the bag on the bed and out tumbled fruit, toiletries, Bob's smugglers' Bible and six bottles of beer that Jerry had snaffled from the Crown.

"Stay here," said the doctor and disappeared through the gap in the curtain.

Jerry did as he was told, hoping that his trust had not been misplaced and that Mickey would not be too greedy in his demands. He couldn't afford to pay too much.

He didn't have to wait long.

"I think they should fit," said Mickey, tossing trousers, shirt, jumper and coat onto the bed.

"Thank you," replied Jerry with obvious relief. He began changing.

Mickey sat down and picked up one of the bottles of beer. He turned it thoughtfully in his fingers and said, "This is quite a cache you have here." He rummaged about amongst the other items and found the Bible. "What's with the hole in the holy book?" He was peering at Jerry through the gap cut out of the pages.

Jerry explained, missing out the crucial identity of the end customer.

"I hope you're not involving me in anything illegal now, Jerry," Mickey said with a wry smile.

Jerry assured him that he had nothing to worry about and went on to describe his plans for Rachael while Mickey listened attentively.

"Dr Doyle, can I have a word?" A female voice came from the other side of the screen.

Michael popped his head out for a few seconds, then said to Jerry, "I've more patients to see; you'll have to go."

"Of course. What do I owe you for the loan of the clothes? You can choose," said Jerry, indicating the goods sprawled on the bedclothes.

"Well, I'm very tempted by the shower cap," replied Mickey. "But no, I don't need anything. At least, nothing that's in your power to give. Drop my things off before you return home. I'll still be here."

"Thank you. You're very kind."

Mickey whipped back the curtain and Jerry returned his trading currency to the bag. The two men shook hands once more and as Jerry made to leave Mickey held him back. "Tell me," he said, "what is it like living in Paradise knowing that there are billions of people suffering down here?"

"It's hell," Jerry answered without hesitation. "Absolute fucking hell."

"I thought as much," said Mickey. "Good luck with your mission. Let me know how it goes."

"I will. Oh, one last request. Where is the nearest shop that sells electronic goods?"

Mickey gave him the directions and sent him on his way.

Even though the walk to the shop was only a little more than ten minutes, Jerry arrived there soaking wet and very cold. He found what he needed, but the Chinese owner drove a hard bargain and Jerry had to pay with all that he had, bar the Bible, of course. Only very recently had he heard the New Testament parable of the pearl of great price, so he reasoned that his bartering performance – swapping many items, each of low value, for what he prized most highly – would have God's blessing. *This is what Jesus would do*, he thought ironically. *Perhaps I should get myself a wrist-band!*

Jerry spent a miserable couple of hours hanging around in the foyer of the hospital entrance watching the hurt and the sick make their desultory way in and out of the building. He blended into the background with his bandaged hand and no-one gave him a second glance. Mickey Doyle had been right; there was pain in Hell that was real enough, and Jerry felt his spirits sag as he saw its manifestation in the grimacing, exhausted faces of the endless stream of patients seeking some temporary relief from their suffering.

For the first time in his life, Jerry saw people whose blackened flesh gave witness to the effects of frostbite. He realised that, like most of his peer group, he had been shielded from the worst extremes of human suffering during his time on Earth. Sure, he'd responded to disaster appeals when he'd seen the horrors of flood or famine on his TV screen but, once his donation had been made, he'd always been able to remove himself from the tugging emotional undertow that the pictures had created in his mind. But this was different. Unless they were able to have their sentences rescinded, these poor unfortunates would know no end to their suffering; a punishment visited upon them by a God whom he was required to worship for all of time. He knew for certain that such inhumanity, such callous indifference, was beyond him, and marvelled that it was not also beyond Jesus or those who dwelt with *the Lord* in Paradise.

"Boy, am I in for a happy date," said Rachael, who had managed to slip into the cracked plastic seat next to him undetected.

"Oh, sorry. I was miles away."

They stood up and embraced. When they broke apart Rachael studied Jerry's face. "What is it?" she asked.

"I don't know. All this, I suppose, and you here, mixed up in it all."

Rachael put her hand on his cheek. "Don't worry. It's OK," she said, and kissed him. "Come, let me show you my flat. I think you're going to love what I've done with it," she giggled, and led Jerry away.

They held hands on the bus while Rachael re-introduced Jerry to his home town; a place he had last seen on a sublimely beautiful spring morning. The redevelopment it had undergone since then had not, in Jerry's opinion, improved it. Instead, the thrashing rain, the gloom, the griminess of the Underworld architecture, all con-tributed to create a landscape which seemed to him to have a permanent scowl. If an environment could be created to perfectly represent a gnawing migraine, this was it.

Once inside Rachael's flat, it took only a few minutes before the two of them were engaged in that act of devouring passion and furious lust, of sweaty intimacy and noble love that they both knew would be an inevitable consequence of their happy re-acquain-tance. Needless to say, a few months of enforced abstinence had done nothing to improve Jerry's staying power, and he ended the dance in gasping, spurting anti-climax shortly after it had begun. Although this was a disappointment to Rachael it was none too soon for Jerry as immediate post-coital relief coincided with the bursting open of the bedroom door.

"Oh, no! I am so sorry, I didn't realise."

Rachael covered her eyes with her hand and called out, "Hello Bea. This is Jerry. Jerry, this is Bea."

"Um, hello," said Jerry, opting to pull the duvet over his naked buttocks rather than offering to shake hands in the more tradi-tional manner of greeting.

"Jerry, yes, of course; I've heard a lot about you," said Beatrix, before adding matter-of-factly, "Rachael, your parents are here."

"Oh great! What perfect timing. Ask them to come in, will you?"

"What? In *here*?" cried Beatrix and Jerry in unison.

Rachael shook her head and laughed, both hands now hiding her face as the farcical nature of the moment overwhelmed her.

"I'll tell them you'll be out shortly, shall I?" asked Beatrix.

Rachael nodded and released one hand to wave her flat-mate away, her body shaking with hilarity as she did so. Beatrix left the room and Jerry rolled off his lover. He lay on his back while Rachael gradually regained control of herself. Eventually she sat up and felt her flushed cheeks. "Oh dear," she said, "you must come more often," a double-entendre which only served to submerge them both into prolonged laughter from which, if they had been able to choose, they would never have wanted to surface.

After a few minutes they had pulled themselves together sufficiently to enter the lounge where Rachael's parents were sitting together cosily on the sofa. Beatrix sat on the window sill, facing side-on to the room, looking at them with the languid ease of a cat, provoking in Rachael's mind exactly the image of a feline familiar that had been used by the witch's psychotic accusers to such devastating effect five centuries earlier. A battered wooden chair had been brought in from the kitchen, which Jerry parked himself on while Rachael sat on the floor, under Beatrix's window, her back against the ineffective radiator. Her mother and father were smiling indulgently which, in her experience, meant they were about to say something she would regret.

Her mother did the honours. "It's lovely to see you with a smile on your face, darling. Your father and I were always at it when we were your age."

"*Mum*. Thank you. I don't want to know! *Ugh*."

"Come now, Rachael, don't be embarrassed. We're all family," added her father.

"Exactly! Stop talking about it."

"About what?"

"You know what! Enough!"

"Young people today, I don't understand you, never wanting to talk about intercourse. Your mother and I…"

"Oh, for God's sake," said Rachael, flouncing out of the room. Her protest march was cut short by the fact that she had walked straight into the adjoining kitchen and there was then nowhere else to go. Her parents laughed. Jerry didn't know where to look.

Rachael started to make a pot of tea, noisily. "I'm not talking to you until you behave yourselves," she called out.

"Who are you shouting at?" said her father playfully. "Your poor mother and father, harmless and frail in their old age, huh? Just here to see their youthful daughter and her energetic young lover."

"I'll give you frail and old… They never used to be as bad as this," she muttered to herself.

"The damp plays havoc with my arthritis," said Rachael's mother, hijacking the conversation and directing her complaints to Jerry, who was grateful for the change in focus. Her monologue lasted until Rachael had returned and given everyone a mug of tea, by which time her father had grown bored with his wife's self-absorbed lament.

"Yes, Esther. Later," he said interrupting her. "We have an important visitor; he doesn't need to hear your moaning. Jerry, we thought you must have been living in much more exalted company, so what brings you here, apart from the obvious charms of my beautiful daughter?"

Jerry took a deep breath. This was a conversation he had been planning to have with Rachael alone but he could hardly explain his reappearance in her flat as a routine social visit and, besides, his intuition told him he might need some support.

"You're right," he began. "When the Rapture came I inexplicably found myself going to Heaven. I had no idea about any of it; I seem to be the least religious person in the whole place."

"But we understood you have to be a Christian to be let in," said Rachael's mother, pronouncing the word *Christian* with some distaste. "Were you a secret believer?"

"In a way, I suppose I was. But it was such a well-kept secret even I didn't know about it." Jerry went on to explain his childhood conversion and how his mother had revealed it to him.

It was Rachael's mum who gave voice to a thought, the like of which they were all considering in one form or another. "Poor Rabi Bernstein; faithful to his God all his life and has nothing. You barely know yours and you get everything. I am happy for you, of course, and your mother, but still, it hardly seems right."

"It isn't right. There's no justice in it at all, but I think I might be able to do something about it. You see, I've made a discovery: not everything in Paradise is perfect. The timing of the Rapture was a mistake and no-one was really ready for it. Christians were supposed to have some involvement in judging the rest of the world, but that hasn't really happened yet, at least not for the people who were alive on Earth at close of play. So that means there have to be some more trials because if it's predicted in the Bible it must come true. In other words, you may have another chance."

Four pairs of eyes were fixed upon him, but their faces told him they did not fully understand. He tried again, starting with the revelation that an error in software-testing protocol had forced God's hand with the Second Coming; his own spying into the *Book of Life* and his consequent punishment; and discovery of the re-trial process. Esther tutted when she heard that her daughter's name was not in the Book and, at the same time, Beatrix gracefully lowered her arm to gently stroke Rachael's hair with the back of her hand. It was an intimate gesture and, momentarily, Jerry wondered at the nature of the friendship between his girlfriend and the witch.

He had omitted some details, naturally, but Jerry had reached the moment of truth. He was suddenly nervous and, with everyone still watching him, he couldn't return their gaze. "So, the thing is, Rachael," he said to the floor before forcing himself to look at her, "I've actually arranged for you to have a trial."

No-one spoke, although Jerry fancied he heard Esther gasp. Beatrix stopped stroking and Rachael reached up and held her friend's fingers in her own hand. She looked at Jerry in such a way that he couldn't tell if she was angry or glad.

"I… I don't think I can do that," she said at last and Jerry felt his stomach tighten.

"Nonsense! You must go," said her mother, suddenly animated. "Harold, tell her."

"Your mother is right, Rachael. It is the chance of a lifetime," agreed her father, before adding as an afterthought, "more than a lifetime. It's one chance in all eternity."

"You see, if we can prove you're innocent," began Jerry, encouraged by the parental response.

"How will that happen?" said Rachael. "They can't admit they've made a mistake, surely?"

"I've a friend who was a Canon in the Church of England. He's working on some theological arguments. There's a possibility your sentence can be over-turned," replied Jerry, with as much conviction as his doubting mind could muster.

"Even if that were to happen, I couldn't leave my family and friends here. You've no right to expect me to do that, Jerry."

She didn't add, *even if that did mean I could be with you*, but Jerry sensed the message in her tone. Harold and Esther were both talking at once, arguing against their daughter's objections. Rachael folded her arms and looked down, and her parents turned to appeal to Jerry. "You don't have to leave them behind," he said.

He had her attention again. "It'll be a test case," he continued. "Once you are proven innocent we can use the same arguments for your mum and dad, for Beatrix, for all our other friends. My dad, even."

"I like the way this boy's mind works," said Harold. "What do the lawyers call it? A class action, I think. If it works, then there is hope for all of us."

"Exactly," said Jerry. "But one step at a time. What do you think, Rachael? It has to be worth a try, doesn't it?"

Rachael was thoughtful for a moment. "How were you able to arrange this trial for me?" she asked.

"I asked Jesus."

"Really?" said Rachael, astonished. "I thought you'd told me you'd never even met him."

"I hadn't, until yesterday."

"You meet Jesus Christ for the first time and you ask him to help our Rachael?" said Harold, clearly impressed.

"Yes."

"What is he like?" said Beatrix, breaking her silence.

Jerry gathered his thoughts for a moment. "Enigmatic, I'd say. Witty, sharp, charming even, but quite difficult to read. He's a little distant; a bit up himself, too, in my opinion. Maybe all that worship has gone to his head."

They sat quietly absorbing all that Jerry had said.

Harold caught his daughter's eye and raised a questioning eyebrow. "No. I'm not ready," she said. Her parents looked imploringly at Jerry again and he decided he had to take a gamble.

"We don't have time to wait, Rache," he said.

Rachael scoffed. "I should have thought time was the one thing we do have."

"Have you heard of the Tribulation?" he said.

"Yes. Why?"

"Because it's going to start any day. That's why time is short."

Rachael twisted around to face Beatrix, still sitting above and behind her on the window sill. "He said it wasn't true."

"Who did?" asked Jerry.

"Lucifer," answered Beatrix. "The Father of Lies."

"A friend of mine," said Jerry, stretching the truth, "told me there are a million warplanes in Heaven just waiting for the order to strike. Imagine: all those bombs and bullets and God knows what else. There's going to be a whole lot more pain and suffering when the battle starts. We have to move quickly, before it's too late."

The appalling news caused a wave of distress to ripple through the room. "Well that settles it, then," said Rachael. "If there's going to be a war, I can't possibly leave."

Harold thumped the arm of the sofa with his fist and shouted, "Rachael, you *have* to go." At the same time Esther stood up and wrung her hands. Words seemed beyond her but her eyes, her face, her whole body was begging her daughter to change her mind.

"No, Dad. I'm not running away. I can't abandon you now, especially not now. I'm sorry."

Jerry had played his trump card and still lost the hand. Rachael's emotional reaction was the very one he had feared. He went to speak again, but now Rachael was on her feet. "I know what you're trying to do, Jerry, and believe me, I appreciate it, but I have to stay." Esther moved towards her, but Rachael evaded her reach and made her way to the bedroom. Beatrix followed and shut the door behind her.

The three remaining adults looked at each other. Harold went to his wife and held her as she rested her sobbing head on his shoulder. He waited until she had calmed a little and, speaking past her, he said to Jerry, "If we can persuade her to go, do you think she has a chance?"

"It will take something extraordinary but, yes, there is a chance. A slim one, probably, but it's more than zero."

"And this Tribulation of yours. We have heard rumours; is it really going to happen?"

"I don't honestly know. I hope not, but I have heard whispers too."

"Could it be that Yahweh would do such a thing?" asked Esther, looking up from her husband's embrace in bewilderment.

Jerry knew the answer, but didn't want to tell her. "Look, maybe I should try again with Rachael…"

"No," said Harold. "Leave her now. She is upset. You have done all you can. Esther and I will speak with her later."

Jerry felt he was being dismissed and, the truth was, he needed to get back to Heaven where, if he was away too long, his absence would be noticed. So, he hugged Rachael's parents farewell, picked up his bag, and left, his mood as heavy and bleak as the bitterly cold rain.

21

Anxiety had a crippling effect on Jerry's ability to concentrate. He knew he should be working on Rachael's case, but the terrifying possibility that it might not take place at all disabled him and, whenever he thought about it, he quickly descended into a spiral of foreboding. The morning worship encounters still temporarily lifted his spirits a little, as he felt the intoxicating life-force of the Holy Ghost, but the muted exuberance lasted only as long as it took his mind to remember those suffering in Hell those whose bones would never cease to ache in the relentless, suffocating cold; those whose bodies would become wracked by pain and whose minds would surely break under the strain of a life without either hope or end.

It was three days after Jerry's return from his second visit to the Underworld that Bob came to his room to speak with him. "You look like somebody's died," he said, a remark which he, at least, thought was funny. "Your girl hasn't failed her appeal yet, you know."

"She may not even get that far," said Jerry, unhappily.

"Oh yes she will. The Lord has decreed it, so it has to happen," said Bob confidently.

"What if she doesn't want a trial?"

"She ain't got no choice. If Jesus calls you to judgement, to judgement you shall go!"

"He can do that?"

"He can command anything, you dopey so-and-so, what with him being God and all."

"So why can't he command everyone to come to Heaven?"

Bob sighed. "Not this again, Jerry. You know people are free to make their own choices…"

"Except when he tells them to do something *he* wants; like come to a trial."

"Don't get clever with me, son. Rachael's going to have her chance, sooner than you realise, as it happens."

"What? When?"

"Tomorrow."

"But that's far too soon. We're not ready."

"Well that can't be helped; it's all set now and these things can't be changed. It's what I came round to tell you; I knew you'd want to know."

Jerry didn't know what to say, so Bob continued. "They'll be sending a squad of angels to collect her today."

"A squad? What, like storm troopers?"

"Not exactly. Probably just three or four of them."

"I shouldn't think that will be enough," muttered Jerry, conscious of the reception the angels would get once Rachael realised she was being forced to do something against her will.

"Don't worry, she'll be safe enough. I told them to take special care," said Bob.

"*You* told them?"

"Yeah. It's one of my jobs; one of the things I fix. I ain't just some rough old lad from the East End what don't know nothing," grinned Bob.

"So, it's really going to happen, and it has to be tomorrow?"

"Blimey, son, you ain't so quick on the uptake right now are you? I told you, didn't I? I should've thought you might wanna get your brief sorted or your Rachael ain't gonna have a very happy time of it, is she?"

"No. Right. I will. God. So soon. OK, thanks Bob. I really need to get moving."

Jerry pulled on his trainers and was out of the door before Bob had left his seat. His mission was back on, and he needed to make every second count.

The bus journey out to St Stephen's was excruciatingly slow and made all the worse by the jollity of the other passengers on board. Their happiness seemed so superficial to Jerry, given the gravitas of his own mind-set, and he felt annoyed with them as a consequence. By the time he reached the golf course he was ready to pick a fight with somebody, and that somebody would be Canon John if he hadn't done his homework.

"Haven't seen him," said the man at Reception.

"But he plays here every day," said Jerry, trying to deny what he had just been told.

"Not for the last couple of days he hasn't, Jerry."

"Where can I find him? I mean, where does he live?" Jerry was kicking himself for not getting this information from the Canon himself when he last saw him. He was hoping that his friend's unprecedented absence from the golf course meant that he was dedicating himself to preparing Rachael's case. He allowed himself a moment of optimism.

"I don't know. Ask one of the angels."

"No thanks. Doesn't anyone else know? What about Marcus?"

"Sure. Maybe. If he's not still out on the course, you'll find him with the other caddies on the veranda at the back of the club-house."

There were three of them there, just where he had been told, lazing around on comfortable chairs overlooking the wide expanse of the golf course below them. Graciously, Jerry decided the guys were relaxing which, Solomon had once told him, was OK because even God rested after he had made the world and everything, whereas laziness was definitely a sin. Jerry wasn't sure how to tell the difference, but hadn't been bothered to argue the point.

One of the three men stood up. "Hello Jerry," he said, and came sauntering over. "Marcus told me you might come round. He said if you turned up when he was out, just wait here and he'll see you when he gets back."

"Do you know how long he'll be?" Jerry asked.

"Well, he went off a while ago, so he should be back any minute," the man replied airily. "Would you like a drink while you wait?"

"Yes, thank you," said Jerry, resigning himself to hanging around even longer on a day when time was precious once more. When the friendly caddy brought him his revitalising fruit juice, he asked if any of them knew where the Canon might be, but he just had confirmed what he had been told already: Canon John hadn't been seen and none of them knew where he lived.

Jerry removed himself to a more isolated spot with a commanding view of the final hole and scanned the fairway for any sign of golfers. It was a painful wait, not helped by the carefree laughter that occasionally drifted over from the where the caddies were sitting, enjoying their own lack of activity.

It must have been an hour, although it felt longer, before Jerry finally saw a man appear at the far end of the fairway, accompanied by Marcus who was carrying his bag. The golfer was hopeless and his first tee shot squirted out almost at right angles to the intended direction. Jerry heard the man laugh at his own ineptitude and he knew that, in spite of the fact that this guy was playing to the best of his God-given ability, it would take him a long time to complete the hole.

He sat on his hands until the pair eventually made it to the green, whereupon Jerry moved closer so that Marcus could see him. The caddy acknowledged his presence and when the final putt was sunk at last, he declined the player's invitation for a drink and instead came straight over to Jerry. "I've got something for you; come with me," he said as soon as they had met.

Jerry followed him to the caddies' locker room. Marcus opened the grey metal cupboard with his name on it – it hadn't been locked, of course – and from underneath a towel and a pair of shoes he pulled out a plain white envelope. "The Canon told me to give this to you when you showed up. He said you should only open it when you're on your own."

"Thank you," said Jerry and tucked the envelope into the top of his trousers, under his tee-shirt. "Where is he, do you know?"

"Exodus," said Marcus. "You know, the Wilderness Experience; the one where you wander around the desert for forty years, like the Jews did."

Jerry was speechless and his expression must have conveyed the shock he felt.

"I was surprised, too," continued Marcus. "He'd never talked about doing it before. Then the other day he turned up really early and said he'd decided it would be a good experience for him so he was going straight away. He gave me that envelope for you, said it contained everything you'd need, then left before I could ask him anything. He seemed really flustered," Marcus added as an afterthought.

"Can he be contacted while he's there?" asked Jerry, although he thought he already knew the answer.

Marcus laughed. "No, it's one of the rules. The experience has to be as authentic as possible; no-one leaves until they've completed the full term, and they don't allow visitors. It probably goes quite quickly once you get used to it, although, to be honest, I'll miss him."

"You and me both," said Jerry, dryly. He thanked Marcus again and made his way back to the bus stop. There was nobody else in sight so he peeked inside the envelope. There were several sheets of paper containing hand-written Bible references, but no explanatory note on the Canon's last-minute desertion. Jerry put the sheets back and hid the envelope on his person again. He thought about what had happened and realised that the churchman was probably never going to be able to argue effectively against the heavenly system in court. Defending Rachael in person would have dragged him into a position of questioning too much of what he needed to ignore in order to maintain his own sanity. He had made his decision and it had been to suppress his doubts and enjoy as best he could the freedom that ignorance provides. Jerry just hoped that he had done a good enough job on the theology to give Rachael a fighting chance; her defence now rested on precisely that, plus any evidence his own desperate plan might be able to conjure.

Jerry didn't dare look at the papers during the long journey home. There were too many people on the bus and nobody ever read anything in public other than the Bible; to be seen doing so would risk provoking unwanted attention. Instead, he spent the time oscillating between scheming and worrying. It was a horrid trip.

To make matters worse, as soon as he had alighted from the bus and was hurrying into Messiah Mansions, Jerry ran straight into Solomon, the last person he wanted to see, or so he thought.

"Hey, what's the hurry, man?"

"Solomon, yes; that's right. I am in a hurry. I'm just hurrying, that's all."

"I have something to tell you. Something about tomorrow."

Jerry stopped in his tracks. "Rachael's trial is tomorrow."

"I know." For a terrible moment Jerry thought that Solomon was going to tell him that not only had Rachael refused to come but she had also attacked the squad of angels and had consequently been refused her right to ever appeal again. "I'm judging the case," said Solomon with barely disguised pride.

Jerry was flabbergasted. Without thinking, he threw himself at Solomon and hugged his perennial antagonist. "Sol, that's fantastic news," he said with genuine enthusiasm.

Solomon pulled away after the briefest of embraces, and a concern entered Jerry's mind. "Won't there be a conflict of interests, as you're my friend?" he asked, conscious that he was perhaps over-stating their relationship once more.

"No," replied Solomon. "I'll be guided by the Holy Spirit, so I'll be completely fair with her, just as I will be with anyone else. Firm but fair."

Bollocks to firmness and fairness, thought Jerry, *just let her off, you bastard*. Fortunately he didn't have time to express this inflammatory view as Solomon had a question for him. "Who's going to be, you know, defending her?"

"That'll be me," replied Jerry quietly.

A smile flickered across Solomon's lips. "Then I'll see you in court," he said.

Jerry asked where the court was located and what time he needed to be there. Solomon told him and added, "You're allowed to meet with the prisoner thirty minutes before proceedings begin. Don't be late."

Solomon marched off and Jerry stood watching him for a moment, the word *prisoner* hanging in his head like a gutted cow in an abattoir. "Prick," he said, and made his way to his room.

Once there, he sat at his desk and took out his Gideon's Bible from the drawer. He looked at the button on the wall in front of him marked *Service*; the one Worthy had once told him to use if he ever needed anything. He pressed it now for the first time, hoping it would work.

In contrast to his painstakingly slow day up until that time, he didn't have to wait long. He had only spent a few minutes pacing around his room before his faithful butler appeared at the door, sweating lightly and a little out of breath. Jerry quickly gave him the precise instructions he knew would be needed to overcome the likely weak point in his plan. Worthy seemed a little confused but, like a good servant, asked no questions and promised to do as he was told.

Jerry spent some time carefully preparing his room. Everything had to be exact if his audacious plan was to work. As soon as he was satisfied he set about reviewing the material provided by the Canon. There were five sheets and at the top of the first one was written, *God's Immoral Teachings, Actions etc.* There were lists of Bible references under a number of sub-headings which included *Genocide, Infanticide, Misogyny, Slavery, Homophobia, Vengeance,* and *Jealousy.* Against one of the references, in the section on M*iscellaneous Hatred,* the Canon had scrawled a little note that read, *God hates cross-dressers – hopefully doesn't apply to churchmen wearing cassocks!* Intrigued, Jerry looked up the verse in the book of Deuteronomy. It said, *A man must not wear women's clothing, nor a woman wear men's clothing, for the Lord your God detests anyone who does this.* Jerry smiled at his friend's ironic humour.

Jerry scanned the long list, conscious that he had urgent tasks to attend to and that familiarising himself with the biblical detail would have to wait until later. He contented himself with looking up just one more reference, chosen at random. It was from Deuteronomy once more, a book which Jerry thought must have been written when God was in a very bad mood because it was well represented on the Canon's pages. He found chapter twenty-one, verse eighteen.

If a man has a stubborn and rebellious son who does not obey his father and mother and will not listen to them when they discipline him, his father and mother shall take hold of him and bring him to the elders at the gate of his town. They shall say to the elders, 'This son of ours is stubborn and rebellious. He will not obey us. He is a profligate and a drunkard.' Then all the men of his town shall stone him to death. You must purge the evil from among you. All Israel will hear of it and be afraid.

"Sweet fucking Jesus," said Jerry. He marked the passage with a pencil and placed the bookmark ribbon down the page. He wondered how it was possible for anybody to justify the killing of a child, let alone command the parents to oversee such a heinous act, particularly on grounds that were so hopelessly ill-defined.

He read the passage again. It didn't say how old the child had to be in order to receive the ordained punishment but he remembered how he had personally experimented with rather too much lager a few times in his early teenage years and had paid the far less drastic penalty of a thumping headache in the mornings after the nights before. He, and most of his friends, had gradually learned their lessons. God's way of handling such naive intemperance brought a whole new meaning to the concept of being stoned. He wondered again at the severity of the Almighty's treatment of the young, and then recalled Catherine's tearful encounter with the drowned baby at Flooded. He had to see Catherine, and he had to do so straight away. He slid the papers back into their envelope, which he then hid under his mattress; checked the room one final time and set off nervously to find her.

She was in the canteen, sitting with three other friends, chatting happily. The eating area was less than a quarter full, with more people leaving than arriving. Most residents liked an early bed and the day was already well advanced. Jerry collected a coffee and sat down at a table a few rows from Catherine where he knew she would see him. The smell of cooked food made him realise how hungry he was, but he didn't have time to eat.

She smiled fondly at him when he caught her eye, but Jerry looked back seriously and stayed where he was. He had been dabbling in a few white lies recently and he wondered anxiously how easily he would be able to graduate to wholesale falsification, and worse.

Catherine, and those who had been eating with her, got up and returned their trays to the collection point. Some people never did that, Jerry had noticed; the lazy sinners! Catherine kissed her friends goodnight and came and sat opposite Jerry.

"You're so weird," she said. "Why didn't you come over and be with us?"

"I have something to tell you," he said.

"Is it about Solomon? He's got his first trial tomorrow. We were all praying for him this morning in the worship group, where your absence was noted once again, young man! He says you know the person he's judging, but he couldn't tell us who it is. Anyway, we're all planning to be there to support him. Will you come too?"

"I've found out about Caroline, your sister."

Catherine lost her playfulness instantly. "What? What have you discovered?"

"I can't tell you here; there are too many listeners. You have to come to my room."

"But what about the rules?"

"Follow me in a couple of minutes," he said uncompromisingly and pushed his mug of half-finished coffee over to her side of the table. "Finish this and make your departure look unhurried and natural."

Catherine looked uncertain, but Jerry said, "Trust me. You'll want to hear what I have to say." He got up and left, hoping that he had said enough for her to take the bait.

He had; she was in his room in a few moments. She appeared to be a little nervous and held her left hand in front of her stomach, massaging it with the fingers of her right hand. She glanced at the television. Jerry had selected a channel which showed an endless loop of beautiful heavenly vistas accompanied by praise music, although he had muted the sound, not least because he found the songs so irritating.

He was sitting on the bed and indicated that she should join him. Catherine came and sat with him, not exactly touching, but near enough. In a timid voice she asked, "Where is she? Where's my sister?"

Jerry knew that it wouldn't matter what he told her, but if he was going to lie he may as well do so kindly. It wouldn't be for long and she wouldn't remember it in any case. "She's here, Cath. In Heaven."

Catherine's hands flew to her face. "Oh, my God," she whispered. "Are you sure?"

"Yes. I saw her name in the *Book of Life*, next to yours."

Jerry was halfway through a description of how he had hacked into the database at St Isidore's, all of which happened to be true, when Catherine, her eyes moist with emotion, reached out and put her finger on his lips. "I love you, Jerry," she said.

"Well, I'm not sure…" he began to say, but she moved her hand to the back of his head, pulled him towards her and kissed him. He could taste the remnants of his coffee in her mouth.

This was not at all what he had anticipated. "Look, Catherine," he started as soon as the kiss was over, but without any clear idea of what to say next.

"I know," said Catherine. "I've felt it too. I'm so happy with you, Jerry. Now I know Caroline's in Heaven, everything is perfect."

To his relief, she stood up. To his amazement, she did so only in order to remove her tee-shirt and bra. "I've never been with a man before. It feels so right doing it with you now; so right it can't be wrong!" Her shoes, trousers and pants came off in what seemed to Jerry no time at all and he felt a powerful involuntary response to the sight of a beautiful young virgin standing before him, offering herself to him. The offer became a demand as she threw herself on top of him, working her hands through his hair, over his shoulders and then pulling off his tee-shirt. The recent re-awakening of his libido meant that his excitement was starting to make its presence felt in Catherine's most sensitive erogenous zone, and she was responding with furious enthusiasm. *Any minute now*, thought Jerry, *any minute,* as he felt Catherine's breasts on his torso while she kissed his chest, then his stomach, working her way down and pulling off what remained of his clothes as she did so. Seconds later she was looking deeply into his eyes, her hair falling around her face which was alive with newly-discovered pleasure. He felt her legs move apart and she slowly started lowering herself onto him until he could feel her wetness. *Jesus*, he wondered, *surely I'm not going to have to penetrate before I get a response?*

His answer came immediately as Catherine arched her back and let out an involuntary cry; half-moan, half-scream.

The angel had grabbed her shoulders and pulled her away from her thwarted, but mightily relieved, lover, then heaved her onto the floor where she now stood, naked and terrified. "I'm sorry, I'm sorry, I'm sorry," she said, covering herself as best as she could with her trembling hands and shuffling into the corner of the room to get as far away from Jerry and the angel as possible.

"You took your bloody time," Jerry said to the angel. He had known that, as Bob had told him on his first full day in Heaven, being alone with a woman would lure angels to his room. What he obviously hadn't bargained for was that it would take so long before one of them arrived, or that during that time Catherine's advances would become, well, so advanced.

The angel made no response, other than to say, "Clothe your-selves," in a flat, contemptuous voice. Jerry picked up Catherine's clothes and placed them close to her at the foot of his bed. She whimpered and began to dress, desperately fumbling and getting her clothes tangled, in her hurry to cover her nakedness. Jerry turned away to afford her some privacy while he, too, got dressed. The angel was not so accommodating, watching them both, al-though his mind seemed to be intensely focused elsewhere.

"Look, all this was my fault," Jerry said to him, but the angel held up his hand for silence. Jerry sighed and said quietly to Catherine, "It'll be over soon. You won't remember anything about it; it'll mean nothing." The angel looked at him, but didn't speak.

Catherine perched on the end of the bed, her head in her hands, still shaking. Jerry sat at the other end, watching and waiting.

Given the history between himself and Nathaniel, Jerry was ex-pecting his nemesis to turn up and, sure enough, his hunch was correct. Nathaniel appeared a few moments later carrying with him two canisters of Grace spray. He placed one on the desk and gave one to the other angel, saying, "Take her. Make sure no-one sees you do it."

Catherine was escorted away and a moment later, to his relief, Jerry heard the hiss of the spray being administered. She was safe, which was probably more, he thought, than could be said for him. His anxiety was heightened when Nathaniel said, "Suffering has always been one of God's most favoured ways of disciplining his subjects and sometimes we still have to use it even here, in Heaven. So, the Higher Beings have the power to temporarily re-introduce you humans to the sensation of pain."

Jerry decided against telling Nathaniel that he had already received exactly the same threat from the very highest of the Higher Beings.

The angel swivelled the desk chair around and sat on it, his right forearm resting on his right thigh, his left hand squarely on the other. He leaned forward, facing Jerry, and said, "You and the rest of mankind really are beneath contempt. Created from dirt and behaving like it too. You're no better than the beasts of the fields or the birds of the air. There's barely a shred of spirituality in any of you, especially you, Jerry. I told you I would be keeping an eye on you; I tried to show you what you really deserved; I had one of our best men look after you; and yet here you are, the night before you're due in court to try to defend your wretched little Jew, putting your filthy base desires above all else instead of praying and meditating on God. You must have known we would have prevented you from completing your sordid mating act, even if we did only just get here in time."

Jerry said nothing. The truth was he didn't really know quite what to do next, other than to let the angel continue talking and to keep his own wits about him. He got up, walked around Nathaniel and sat on his desk, next to the television. The angel turned in the chair, tracking his movement.

"You know, I sometimes think we've become too soft on disobedience," he said, changing his position and clasping his hands behind his head. "I miss the old days," he continued, wistfully. "The Flood; Sodom and Gomorrah; the slaughter of the Canaanites. And, of course, the Passover. I was there that night, Jerry. I remember it like it was just yesterday."

Jerry remained silent as the blinds outside his window were automatically lowered, dimming the light in the room which was now illuminated only by the brightness from the TV screen.

"There is no feeling quite as exquisite as knowing that you are executing God's justice and carrying out his commands to the letter."

Nathaniel stood up and moved uncomfortably close to Jerry. "I'll never forget my first one. He was eight years old. A handsome little chap too, for an Egyptian."

Jerry sensed the blur of movement but had no time to react. Nathaniel's hand had gripped his throat and lifted him into the air. He was being held at arm's length by the angel, his feet kicking wildly. He couldn't reach Nathaniel's face so the best he could do was to claw at his arm, but he made no impression and the angel's hold on him didn't waver. Breathing had become impossible.

"This is how I killed him, right there in front of his parents and siblings. I held him just like this, in the middle of their house. Naturally, I could have throttled him while he slept in his bed, but they needed to know he wasn't dying a normal death; they had to understand it was divinely ordained that he should die because of the disobedience of their Pharaoh. They couldn't see me; they just saw their boy suspended in mid-air, clutching his throat, his eyes popping out of his head. They were desperate to save him but I kept him out of their reach. I almost felt sorry for them, but you can't let your emotions get in the way of obedience to God, now, can you?"

Jerry, clearly, was in no position to comment.

"I don't know how long it took him to go," continued Nathaniel. "I remember that I held his lifeless body in my grip for longer than was necessary. I didn't want there to be any room for doubt. Imagine how terrible it would have been if one of the firstborn had survived? None of us could have risked the prophecy being unfulfilled. There were many people and animals to kill that night, and the angels made sure they were all dead by morning. That's the thing about Yahweh; he always insisted on attention to detail."

Nathaniel suddenly released him and Jerry crashed to the floor. It took a while for his throat to open up sufficiently to allow him to breathe again. The noise he made sounded like a child with a terrible case of whooping cough. The angel left him gasping on the ground and turned to face the television. "Look at all this beauty," he said, with exaggerated awe, then gently helped Jerry to his feet and positioned him in front of the screen. The two of them watched the landscapes, one perfect scene merging into another. "You see what I mean about attention to detail? Such magnificent handiwork," Nathaniel continued. "All he wants is your worship in return, and your unquestioning obedience."

Nathaniel's hand grasped Jerry on the back of his neck and forced his head down with terrifying speed, smashing his face onto the top of the desk. He felt his nose shatter and, at the same time, a searing pain shot through his mouth. Nathaniel jerked his head back up and Jerry spat out two broken teeth. The angel held his hair and jaw and forced him to continue looking at the television.

"I think most of Yahweh's best work was done in the first six days. It has an enduring quality about it, wouldn't you say?" Jerry groaned and had his face smashed onto the desk again. He groaned louder. "Of course, it was during this period that he decided to make humans in his own image, thereby ensuring that the whole universe got fucked up, but I suppose nobody's perfect. In any case, he tried for hundreds of years afterwards to whip you miserable shits into line, sending you prophets and priests and punishments. Not that it did much good; you are a stiff-necked species, that's for sure." Jerry received another couple of blows to the face from the desk, although whether this was as a consequence of his failures in particular, or those of *homo-sapiens* in general, he couldn't tell.

Nathaniel sighed. "Yahweh is the same, yesterday, today and forever, Jerry, but times change. The traditional ways fell out of fashion and there were murmurings that the Old Man couldn't keep up with the modern world. So, he was made Lifelong President, moved upstairs and the son took over as Chief Executive. Now, I'm not saying that Jesus didn't deserve his chance, or that he hasn't made some good changes. Dying on the cross was a great start and no-one can deny the resurrection was very impressive. He made it absolutely clear that those who didn't believe in him would go to Hell, too, so they've no-one to blame but themselves. But all this emphasis on forgiveness has made people weak. They think they can sin as much as they like and get away with it. Don't you, Jerry?"

Jerry felt himself being lifted once more. He was spun around and this time the back of his head was brought crashing down onto the table. Nathaniel was gripping his neck again, his face not six inches away from Jerry's own. "*Don't you, Jerry?!*" he screamed in a voice of unbridled violence.

Jerry's head was full of pain, way beyond any level he had ever experienced before. Nathaniel flung him across the room and he hit the wall above his bed and slumped onto the mattress, his elbow broken. There was no respite as Nathaniel pulled the bed away from underneath him, so that he tumbled to the floor. He looked up to see the angel standing above him, holding the bed frame which he launched at his legs like an improvised javelin. It hit him just below the left knee and cracked his shinbone. He screamed and clutched at the wound, felt warm blood on his fingers, and began to pass out.

But Nathaniel wasn't finished: he brought Jerry round by holding his head underwater in the sink, then threw him back into the bedroom. The angel had found the video camera that Jerry had optimistically propped on the headboard of his bed. "I'm disappointed," said Nathaniel, holding up the little box of electronic wizardry. "I didn't think you would be so stupid as to imagine I wouldn't see this. Building your case on the fact that God cannot be trusted because he does bad things was going to be difficult, to say the least, given that all the members of the jury love their Creator. You're right, of course, he has been very, very wicked by your human standards, and filming a holy angel admitting as much might have got your Jew a reprieve, but without this evidence, I don't think you'll be convincing anyone." Then, in front of Jerry's eyes, Nathaniel simply crumpled the camera with his bare hands.

Worse was to follow: the camera hadn't been Nathaniel's only find. Lying at his feet was the envelope. He picked it up, removed the pages and read them swiftly. "Oh dear. It seems that your man John is something of a loose Canon," he said.

"Ha! Ha!" mumbled Jerry, through his mangled mouth. "Dat's ver fun, Nat."

"We won't be seeing him in court as he seemed more than happy to agree to spend four decades away from home."

Pushed then, not jumped, Jerry thought to himself and smiled inwardly. No doubt Nathaniel had been very persuasive when making the suggestion to his friend.

"No need to confuse the jury with materiel that won't be understood," said Nathaniel, putting the Canon's work back into the envelope. He held it out in front of him and closed his eyes briefly; the paper spontaneously combusted and burnt itself to blackened ash. Floating to the floor, some of the ash landed in the blood that had seeped from Jerry's body and he reached out to touch it, although he didn't know why.

Nathaniel walked to the desk and collected the canister. When he returned, he crouched down beside Jerry on his haunches. "Let us spray," said Jerry, feebly.

Nathaniel whipped the can across Jerry's face and cut him above the eye. "You know why I'm doing this, Jerry?" he said.

"Teach me... uh lesson," came Jerry's barely coherent reply.

"No. How can you learn if you don't remember anything?"

"Oh yeah, good point, Nat." Jerry had forgotten that he would soon be forgetting this beating, but couldn't form the words to say so. The rasping of his own heavy breathing was loud in his ears.

"I am punishing you for your wrong-doing; it's as simple as that." Nathaniel ran his hand gently over Jerry's blood-soaked hair and then continued. "Whether you learn anything or not isn't the point. You have been disobedient and you need to be punished. The law demands it. You must understand that."

Jerry looked at Nathaniel through his one open eye, and the angel asked him, "Do you have anything to say?"

"Yeah," whispered Jerry. He raised himself slightly and Nathaniel bent closer in order to hear him. "Go fuck yourself," he said, and lost consciousness.

22

Rachael awoke from a deep sleep in a room she didn't recognise. She knew that this was an important day, though, and then she recalled exactly why.

Jerry, similarly, had slept very well but, by contrast, he knew as soon as he opened his eyes precisely where he was and why this was the reddest of red letter days. With a nervous jolt he leapt out of bed; he had to prepare Rachael's defence. With his stomach churning he started to berate himself for sleeping so long and leaving the preparation so late. Why he hadn't done it the previous evening he couldn't imagine. In fact, he couldn't remember anything about last night; what, he wondered incredulously, could possibly have prevented him from working on the trial? There was nothing more important and now he had so much to read and so little time in which to do it. Although he was wide awake, his emotions were those of a terrible nightmare.

He washed in a panic and hurried back to the bedroom. Appalled by his own incompetence, he realised he couldn't remember where he had put the Canon's precious package with its life-changing content. He looked everywhere: on the desk, in the drawers, even behind the cushions on the armchair. With no sign of the envelope, he went as far as lifting the mattress to expose the whole underside of the bed but still found nothing. It was while he was in this position that Worthy entered the room.

"No need to change the bedding yourself, sir, that's my job."

"I'm looking for something," said Jerry. "I can't remember where I left the bloody thing."

"I'm sorry to hear that, sir. Perhaps I can assist you in a little while if you tell me what you've misplaced."

"It's an envelope, and please start looking for it now."

"I'm afraid I can't do that, sir."

"Why ever not?" asked Jerry, who was still holding the mattress on its end.

"Because first I have to deliver a message to you of the utmost urgency and importance," replied Worthy, forcefully.

Jerry didn't like the sound of that and immediately dropped the mattress back onto its frame, fearing the worst. "Who's it from?" he asked.

"It's from you, sir. You gave it to me yesterday and told me to tell you first thing this morning."

"I don't recall doing that. Are you sure?"

"Absolutely. You even said that you might not remember and that I was to give you the message no matter what."

"Oh, well, in that case, what did I have to say to myself?"

"*Love keeps no record of wrongs.* One Corinthians thirteen, verse five."

"Yes, what about it?" asked Jerry, none the wiser.

"You have to look it up, in your Bible."

"Even though you've just told me what it says?" said Jerry, walking towards his desk nevertheless.

"I'm not to leave until you've read it," insisted Worthy.

Jerry took out his Bible and, as he was pretty clueless about the sequence of books within it, he simply opened it where the bookmark lay. He read some verses that had been highlighted with a pencil; some startlingly unpleasant verses. He started flicking through the Bible from the back and soon spotted a sheet of writing paper folded into the very page he had been looking for. The paper was addressed to him.

Worthy waited while Jerry read the note that he had written to himself. "Thank you, Worthy. It's clear now. You may go."

"If you're sure, sir."

"I am."

The servant placed Jerry's fresh clothes on the desk and headed towards the door. Before leaving, he turned and said, "I hope all goes well today, sir. May you find truth and justice, for all our sakes."

"Amen to that," replied Jerry, with uncharacteristic religiosity.

"Amen indeed," said Worthy softly, and left.

Jerry read through the note once more then took out Bob's smuggler's Bible from the drawer. He opened it and removed the tightly-wound leads from their hiding place, looked along the side of the plasma screen TV, found the ports and made the connection. The Chinaman had been right; the plugs and sockets really were universal. *Thank God for that*, thought Jerry, wryly.

Next, he un-taped the small camera from underneath the television, where it had had an unencumbered view of the previous night's proceedings; he connected it to the television, pressed *Play*, and began to see what he had been up to.

Quite a lot, it seemed. The early moments with Catherine made difficult viewing; even though the note he had just read had told him something of what to expect, he still felt considerable embarrassment and was hugely relieved when he saw the first angel appear in his room and put a stop to his intimate encounter. Feeling slightly ashamed of himself, he was grateful that Catherine would know nothing of his exploitation of her as he saw her being led away to have her short-term memory obliterated.

Watching the scenes that followed was both a surreal and sobering experience. His palms began to sweat as he witnessed the beating he had taken and he felt himself wince more than once at Nathaniel's merciless savagery. The flickering light from the television that had lit up the room for most of the filming had been good enough to record the details and had even added a slightly more sinister feel to the action, if that were possible. The sound quality was excellent and Jerry allowed himself a self-satisfied smile when he heard his abuser calling him stupid and watched him destroy the sacrificial decoy camera. It wasn't every day, he reflected, that he out-smarted an angel of the Lord. Now all that was needed was for him to do the same to the Lord himself, a task that would be even more difficult, he realised, as he watched with dismay the burning of his priceless document.

The recording played out, showing Nathaniel instantaneously returning his room to normal, plying him with Grace spray, then miraculously healing his shattered body. Incongruously, the angel had carefully, even gently, laid Jerry down in his bed and had stood looking at him thoughtfully for half a minute or more before finally leaving.

There was nothing Jerry could do about the loss of the Canon's work now; there was no time left. He re-set the recording so that it would be played from the moment he had sat himself on his desk with Nathaniel on the chair looking more or less directly at the hidden camera. He didn't think that showing his unplanned almost-sex with Catherine would win any sympathy in court, especially from Rachael. *No need*, he concluded, *to confuse the jury with materiel that won't be understood.*

He took one last look around his room before leaving with two Bibles tucked under his arm; one containing a single highlighted passage with which he hoped to bring about the collapse of the divine judgement that had condemned Rachael to Hell; the other containing the camera with its devastating witness in case he failed.

Jerry was let into a small, airless room and told that his client would be arriving shortly. Two plastic chairs sat either side of a Formica-topped table and, apart from these functional and unimaginative items, the soulless room was bare. He wished he could be meeting Rachael in a more cheerful location.

He heard the click of her heels coming down the corridor, along with the squeaky noise made by the trainers worn by whoever was accompanying her. The door opened and in she came. Jerry felt his stomach lurch as her loveliness overwhelmed him. She wore a simple blue top with jeans tucked into grey, leather boots. He noticed her classy pearl earrings, partly because he was drinking in every aspect of her appearance, and partly because women didn't wear jewellery in Heaven and he was struck by the novelty of seeing them again. Nor, indeed, did the female inhabitants of Paradise paint their nails and use make-up on their faces, which Rachael had done to such elegant effect.

"You look lovely," he said, still unsure of how Rachael would react to being there with him, in these circumstances.

"Thank you," she replied. She slipped the cream-coloured handbag off her shoulder, placed it on the table and stepped forward to embrace him. He breathed in her perfume and the smell of shampoo in her hair. "I'm glad you're here," he whispered, "although I didn't know they were going to force you to come here against your wishes."

Rachael unlocked herself from his hold and the two of them sat down.

"After you'd left the flat," she said, "and when I'd recovered from the shock, I had a long chat with Beatrix and my parents. They persuaded me I had to come and make the most of this opportunity. I suppose I already knew that it made sense; I was just caught off guard really, what with not knowing where you had been all that time – then you turning up out of the blue and coming back to try to rescue me like you did. I agreed with them that I'd stand trial, for their benefit, not just for mine. Then the angels arrived and made it pretty clear that I really had no choice in the matter. Tell me honestly though, Jerry, do we really have a chance?"

"I hope so, Rache. I've done my best and I think we've got a really good case."

Rachael reached over the table and held his hand, giving him a dazzling smile of encouragement as she did so.

"When you look at me like that," he said, "I feel like I've died and gone to Heaven."

"That's not funny," she said, although he knew she thought it was. "I think we need to talk about the trial. The lady that brought me here told me that I was the *appellant* in the case as I'm bringing the appeal."

The legal term was not one Jerry had ever heard before but thought that at least it sounded better than *prisoner*.

"She said I'd meet my lawyer here. Will that be your theology guy?"

"Oh, he's not coming, I'm afraid, as he's been, um, removed. Don't worry, though, I know the arguments better than anyone. Oh, also," he added with a smile on his face, and to Rachael's astonishment, "the judge is a good friend of mine."

Jerry decided to keep to himself the fact that he and Solomon had been at loggerheads with one another ever since they had met and that, as far as he could remember, they had almost never actually agreed on anything. He wasn't at all sure that Solomon would be doing him or Rachael any favours, but nevertheless was holding on to the hope that their shared experience of Heaven, especially their membership of the same worship team, would carry some weight at least.

He quickly went on to outline his thoughts on how to make her appeal, filling in some of the details on the Canon's untimely disappearance at the same time. She grew concerned at this story, although she brightened slightly when he told her that Canon John had summarised the crucial elements of the biblical argument for him before his enforced absence.

"So let me get this straight," she said, interrupting him. "Your first line of attack is that I shouldn't be sent to Hell because I didn't have a chance to hear the gospels."

"The gospel, singular. Yes, that's correct. *The gospel* is Christian short-hand for the doctrine that Jesus died so that your sins could be forgiven and you could be saved from Hell, but you have to believe it to make it work."

"Right, and if they don't buy that argument you'll be saying that God can't send me to Hell anyway because, no matter what I did or didn't believe, he cannot pass judgement on me as he is morally flawed himself."

"Yes."

"And you have lots of verses in the Bible that show this to be the case."

"Mmm."

"Mmm? What do you mean, 'mmm'?"

Jerry picked at a crack in the table top and told her what had happened to the list of references. While he was doing so, they heard a burst of laughter from somewhere close by in the building. "I've managed to remember one of the verses, though," he said, defensively.

"Let's hope that it's a good one, then," replied Rachael.

They sat in silence for a while. He hadn't yet told her about the recording and was considering doing so when she spoke again.

"You must have them a bit rattled, my love."

"You think so?"

"Well, they seem to be going to an awful lot of trouble to make it as difficult as possible for you to defend me: frightening off your theologian, burning your papers. Perhaps you're onto something after all."

"Yes," said Jerry, enthused again. "Look, I'm sure we can find some of those verses if we look now. There was one about transvestites, I remember."

"Oh, that will be useful," said Rachael ironically, but Jerry took no notice. He had already opened his Bible and was desperately searching.

A few seconds later, before he could find anything relevant, the door opened and a messenger entered to tell them they were due in court that very minute. The trial that would settle Rachael's eternal destiny was about to begin.

23

The court smelled of wood polish. Its high walls were panelled with rose-wood, which gave the room a serious and sombre air. At one end, underneath the isosceles triangle of a fine Palladian arch, the words, *In God We Trust,* were painted in gold letters. Below this overt statement of faith, a wholly inappropriate one to Jerry's mind, given the arguments he intended to make that day, was where the judge would sit. The judge's chair, with its straight, high back covered in deep red leather stood upon an elevated platform, behind a grand wooden desk which curved out into the court in a semi-circle. To the left of the judge's commanding position were two pews, one behind the other, providing uncomfortable seating for the members of the jury. A table and several chairs were positioned at the base of the judge's platform where the clerk of the court and other officials were sitting and, a few feet away, similar furniture stood ready for the appellant and the two sets of counsels. A witness box was located in one corner and, at the back of the room, seven or eight rows of chairs were available for the public, most of which were already occupied. It all looked like the scene from one of any number of television courtroom dramas and Jerry was struck, not for the first time, by how similar Heaven was to Earth, almost as if the former was some kind of copy of the latter with most of the nasty bits removed.

One of the nasty bits that hadn't been removed was speaking in a voice loud enough for Rachael to hear as she took her seat. "Tart! Who does the painted strumpet think she is? Has she no respect?" Rachael's status as a mere visitor to the celestial realm had given her exemption from its sartorial restrictions, and the fact that she could wear her own clothes and apply a little make-up had obviously piqued some jealousy. She remained unfazed, however, merely leaning close to Jerry to whisper, "If she's unhappy with this outfit I dread to think what she'd say if she saw me at work."

Jerry smiled as he remembered the rather shocking sight of his girlfriend playing the sexy Whore of Babylon. If all went well today, she would never have to do that again. He looked around him and picked out some friendly faces in the public gallery: Bob, Catherine, Lela and a few others from the worship group were all there, supporting him. Or supporting Solomon, as Catherine had previously suggested. Jerry hoped it would come down to the same thing in the end.

The level of background conversation in the room was low and fell even further when a side door opened and the jury filed in to take their seats. "They're all men," said Rachael to Jerry when the pews were filled. "Why aren't there any women?" Jerry shrugged. He hadn't thought about it until that moment, and now it was too late. Worse still, he recognised one of the men as Conor, the ginger Presbyterian from Northern Ireland whose head had been the target of the bottle of beer thrown at the start of the pub quiz fracas. Jerry guessed that his confrontational style would be unlikely to do Rachael any favours, and he looked at the other jurors for signs of more sympathetic attitudes. He found nothing noteworthy apart from a certain craziness in the countenance of Ephraim, a small man who had something of a first century look about him with his wild hair and bushy beard. He was ill at ease with himself and his surroundings, fidgeting disconcertingly as he stared darkly in Jerry's direction.

Jerry turned away and looked straight ahead. Either side of the motto on the front wall declaring the court's trust in God, the Ten Commandments had been painted. Jerry's eye fell on the one that resonated with his last conversation with Canon John: *You shall not make for yourself an idol in the form of anything above or on Earth below. You shall not bow down to them or worship them; for I, the Lord your God, am a jealous God, punishing the children for the sin of the fathers to the third and fourth generation.*

Further contemplation was interrupted as the side door opened again and the opposing lawyer strode authoritatively into the courtroom. Jerry's confidence was in need of a boost, but the sight of this individual didn't give it to him.

"Oh no, it can't be," he said quietly.

"What is it?" asked Rachael.

"It's Nathaniel, an angel of the Lord, no less."

"I'm guessing that's not so good for us."

Jerry watched Nathaniel take his seat. The angel ignored him, a look of calm determination on his face. "Actually," said Jerry to Rachael, "now I come to think about it, maybe it'll be OK – more than OK, in fact."

The clerk of the court stood and called in a commanding voice, "All rise."

There was a scraping of chairs and the muffled sound of bodies pulling themselves upright. Then, silence. Solomon entered from the same door which the jurors and Nathaniel had used moments earlier and clambered the stairs to his seat. On top of his normal white attire he was wearing a long gown, also in white, edged with small, scarlet, Assyrian crosses. He seemed very pleased with the thick cotton robe and gathered it around himself as he sat down. He nodded to the clerk, who then addressed the court once more. "Let us remain standing to pray," he said, whereupon Solomon stood up again quickly, along with a few others who had wrongfully understood that his sitting down had been a cue for them to have done the same. There was a little murmuring and then the clerk prayed. "Dear Lord Jesus, thank you for the opportunity to play just a small part in the dispensing of your perfect justice. Help us not to shy away from doing our duty to execute your will, however difficult it might appear to us, and please give Judge Solomon wisdom to do right and obey you in all things. Amen."

A loud *Amen* greeted the end of the prayer, although there was no response from the appellant's table where the concepts of dispensing and execution had not gone down well.

"Be seated," said the clerk, and this time everyone sat down. The clerk nodded to the judge: Solomon's big moment had arrived. He cleared his throat, picked up the gavel and banged it hard on the wooden sound block. A bit too hard, as it happened, and the little hammer bounced right out of his hand and cart-wheeled downwards, where it fell with a clatter on the floor. There was some sniggering while the clerk picked up the gavel and handed it back to an embarrassed-looking Solomon. He rapped the block again, successfully this time, and called out, "Order. Order. The case of Bennett versus God is now open."

Happy that he had got the ball rolling, Solomon sat back on the big, throne-like chair. Nobody seemed to know what to do next until the clerk approached the throne and quietly passed on some instructions to Solomon. The sound block got another whack, unnecessarily so as no-one was talking at the time, and Solomon informed the court that the appellant would now be sworn in. Rachael was ushered to the witness box where she placed her hand, naturally enough, on the Bible and promised to tell the truth, the whole truth, etcetera.

Jerry wondered what God Almighty would swear on if he was required to appear in person and undergo the same ritual.

After a few more formalities confirming Rachael's name, date of birth and so on, the clerk indicated to Jerry that he could begin the appeal.

From the moment Jerry had discovered that Rachael was in Hell he had made it his purpose to rescue her. Yet, now that the crucial time had arrived, he suddenly found he had no idea how to begin. The oddness of the court proceedings so far – Solomon's clumsiness as judge; his own tormentor as the opposition barrister – had undermined him and given rise to an unwelcome sense that the trial would be a sham; that no ground-breaking decision would be made; no watershed precedent would be set. Instead of marshalling in his mind a devastating opening statement, his thoughts were awash with self-inflicted accusations of his own naivety. He had a visceral awareness of his powerlessness; an overwhelming pity for the thinness of his arguments. He stood, looking around for a full minute, the silence and expectation crowding in on him. Everybody was watching him and he had nothing to say. He felt almost as if some physical force were closing his mouth and for a moment he suspected a divine conspiracy. The absurdity of the thought was replaced by another: he should pray to Jesus for help, claim the Saviour's outrageous promise that those who ask will receive. But no, whatever case for pardon that could be made would have to come from his own understanding, his own rationality. His opponent might be omniscient, but Jerry knew that he, and not God, was the one with natural justice on his side. All he had to do was prove it to the jury. Rachael, Beatrix, his dad, and countless billions depended upon him doing so. It was time to speak up.

"Rachael," he began. "Can you please tell us about your religious beliefs back on Earth, before the Second Coming?"

His girlfriend frowned thoughtfully and gripped the top of the witness stand. "My family is Jewish," she said, then hesitated as she picked up a murmur of disapproval from somewhere in the court. Jerry caught a whispered accusation: *killed our Lord*. He ignored it and smiled his encouragement.

"I went to the synagogue as a child – we all did – but as I grew up we became much less observant and just stopped attending. I was never very good at Hebrew and I suppose I just got bored with the ritual: it simply seemed irrelevant."

The muttering in court was getting louder. Disconcertingly to Jerry, some of it was coming from the jurors.

Rachael was noticing it too and tried to take the initiative. "I still quite liked the festivals though, and I have started going to our schul again now that I'm," she stopped, then added quietly, "in Hell."

The scoffing that greeted this confession was clearly audible, as was Conor's remark, "A bit late now, love." Jerry looked sharply at Solomon and gestured that the judge should call the court to order once again. But Solomon didn't seem inclined to risk more encounters with the slippery gavel than was strictly necessary, and did nothing.

"What was your exposure to Christianity?" Jerry asked in a voice loud enough to be clearly heard by all.

"Hardly any. I'd been to a couple of church weddings, but not much more than that."

"What about school? Didn't you hear anything about it there?"

"Not really. Jewish children weren't allowed in the Christian assembly; we had to have our own. And I don't remember anything from our Religious Education classes; I'm afraid none of us took them seriously."

"So you never learnt that Jesus had died for your sins?"

"No."

"You never knew that you needed to believe that particular doctrine in order to go to Heaven?"

"No, of course not."

"Why, *of course not?*"

"Because if I had known that I might have tried to believe it."

Rachael recalled that back in Hell, Rabi Bernstein had once told his congregation that adopting this cautious approach – believing because in doing so the believer had nothing to lose and everything to gain, whereas the opposite was the case for the unbeliever – was called Pascal's wager. In hindsight the idea seemed to have some potency. Rachael noticed that Jerry was smiling at the transparent logic of her answer and she hoped that perhaps they were starting to get somewhere now.

"So why did you not believe? Why were you not a Christian?"

Rachael took her time to answer. "Nobody ever told me; no-one ever showed me that all this," here she swept her hand in a small arc in front of her, "was real."

"And you didn't want to take on a new faith without evidence?" suggested Jerry.

"Precisely. Why would I?"

"Because it happens to be true."

"Well, that wasn't obvious to me."

Jerry asked a few more questions just to ram home the point, but he didn't want to fall into the trap of making a simple argument unnecessarily complicated, so he brought matters to a close. "It is quite clear," he said, directly addressing Solomon, "that Rachael" (he still couldn't bring himself to call her *the appellant*) "did not come to faith in Jesus, not because she refused to believe, or because she rejected him in any way, but simply because she never heard the gospel. I daresay that if any of us had been brought up in a Jewish family with no clear opportunity to hear the good news" (Jerry had learned that *the good news* was a term heavily favoured by Christians to describe their belief in salvation by Christ) "then we wouldn't have come to faith either. It is our assertion then, that she cannot be condemned to eternal torture for not believing a religion she did not inherit and that had never been explained to her."

"*Blasphemy!*"

Ephraim, the unkempt juror, screamed the accusation and stood pointing at Jerry. "Blasphemy!" he called again and, with both hands, pulled at the neck of his tee-shirt until the garment ripped. Jerry's heart was racing but he remained where he was, not knowing what to do, although he was certain that it simply had to be against court protocol for a juror to behave in such a way. The authority of the court needed to be re-established and in a moment it was, not by the judge, but by Nathaniel. The fearsome angel got to his feet and walked calmly over to Ephraim. He touched the torn fabric that was hanging limply in front of the juror's chest and instantly it was restored. Ephraim sat down and Nathaniel turned to face the judge. Spurred into action, Solomon at last picked up his little hammer again, rapped it on the block and said, "Your witness, Nathaniel."

"Thank you, your honour," said Nathaniel smoothly.

Jerry returned warily to his seat and watched the angel cross the floor towards the witness box. When he questioned Rachael it was with the assurance of one who was used to being right. "Who, in your understanding, are the *Chosen People?*"

Rachael took a moment, sensing perhaps a trick question, before answering, "The Jews."

"Quite right," said Nathaniel, as if to a troublesome pupil who had managed the rare feat of providing a correct answer. "And by whom are these people – your people – chosen?"

Rachael took even longer before responding this time. "By God," she said, at length.

"By the one, true God, yes. Of all the tribes that God could have chosen, he decided to make the Jews his people. He built his nation from Abraham's seed; he led Moses through the desert; he appeared to Elijah. He sent his prophets to the Jews; made his covenant with the Jews; gave his laws to the Jews; presented the promised land to the Jews. And when the Lord Jesus came to Earth, to whom did he go first? To the Jews, of course: the Chosen People. And as a Jew yourself, Rachael, instead of understanding that you belonged to the most privileged race on Earth, a people who owed their very existence to Yahweh himself, you considered it to be…" Nathaniel paused for effect, a look of incredulity on his face, "…you considered it all to be *irrelevant.*"

"Shame on you," called out Conor, provoking a muttered assent from several others in the court.

Rachael didn't know how to respond but, in any case, was given no time as Nathaniel was addressing her again.

"Far from being the handicap that your counsel suggested, being born a Jew should have given you every incentive to seek after the Messiah, to discard the old covenant and live in the light of God's new promise to all mankind."

"Amen!" called out Ephraim and a round of applause rippled through the court. Jerry looked pleadingly at Solomon, but the Judge was nodding his head in agreement with Nathaniel and made no move to intervene.

"And your excuse for ignoring Jesus, your stated reason for not addressing the single most important question of your life, namely that of how to obtain eternal salvation, is that nobody told you!"

"*Blasphemy!*" shouted Ephraim once more and tore his shirt again. Without even turning his gaze away from Rachael, Nathaniel pointed to the wide-eyed juror and his tee-shirt was renewed for a second time. Ephraim smiled gleefully and sat back down, but Rachael was frowning. She spoke for the first time in a while in answer to Nathaniel's accusation. "Yes, no-one told me," she said.

"May I remind you that you are under oath?" the angel snapped and before she could respond he said in a commanding voice, "My witness, your honour."

"Call the witness," shouted Solomon, and one of the officials scurried to the side door. Nathaniel simply nodded to Rachael for her to return to her seat. Bewildered and unhappy, she went and sat next to Jerry. They exchanged glances. Neither needed to tell the other that this was not going well.

"Oh, no," said Rachael quietly, as she recognised the slim, dark-haired woman who was now making her way to take the witness stand. It was her erstwhile colleague, Fiona, and Rachael knew immediately what was coming. She listened resignedly as she heard Fiona answer Nathaniel's questions, telling the court that, yes, she had invited her friend to her church on numerous occasions; yes, she had told her how important it was; and yes, she had explained that everybody was a sinner and that forgiveness was only through Jesus. And regrettably, no, Rachael had never accepted an invitation to hear the good news for herself.

"Why do you think she never came?" asked Nathaniel.

"Because it would have been too much of a challenge," Fiona replied.

"How so?"

Fiona looked down and fiddled with her hands while she replied softly, "Rachael was sleeping with her boyfriend, even though they weren't married." A groan of *thought as much* disapproval greeted this revelation. "I told her I was keeping myself for my fiancé because that's what the Bible teaches. I think she knew she would have to stop having sex if she became a Christian and she wasn't prepared to do that."

Nathaniel lowered his voice to match Fiona's and asked, "How can you be so sure?"

Everyone in the room strained to hear Fiona's reply. "Because, on the Last Day she made fun of me in front of the whole office for getting engaged. She told them I was pregnant, even though she knew I was keeping myself pure."

Jerry thought he heard the word, *whore*, in the ensuing murmur. He looked at Rachael. Her eyes were brimming with tears.

Nathaniel let the hostility towards Rachael simmer before addressing the jury. "So now we know the real reason that the appellant never allowed herself to hear the gospel of Christ." He stood another moment next to the witness box and then said curtly to Jerry, "Your witness."

Even though Jerry feared the argument might already have been lost, he got to his feet and, for Rachael's sake, began his cross-examination. "Did you pray that Rachael would come to church with you, Fiona?"

"Yes, of course I did."

"Why do you think God didn't answer those prayers?"

"*Blasphemy!*" roared Ephraim yet again. He jumped up and let his shirt feel the full force of his fury, so that it was soon badly torn once more. This time, however, Nathaniel ignored him and, with a look of disappointment, Ephraim sat down with the garment hanging open, exposing his hairy chest.

Jerry repeated his question.

"God can't always give us what we ask for," Fiona said defiantly.

"Really?" said Jerry. "Didn't Jesus himself say that we just had to ask in order to receive?"

"*Blas* – " began Ephraim, but Conor pushed him back into his seat. "It says that in the Bible, you idiot," he added, although not before a little more damage had been inflicted on his fellow juror's disintegrating shirt.

"Yes, but it has to be according to his will, otherwise we could ask for whatever *we* wanted, not for things that *he* wanted," said Fiona.

"Didn't God want Rachael to come to your church? Wasn't that part of his will?"

Fiona stared at Jerry for a while. "Yes, but he couldn't force her to come."

"Couldn't or wouldn't?"

"She has to come to faith of her own free choice."

"She's come to faith of her own free choice now, Fiona. She has no doubts at all that Jesus is God."

"But it's too late." Fiona's face was showing traces of panic and she looked across to Nathaniel for reassurance.

"Why is it too late? If salvation is through faith in Christ, and if Rachael believes that now with all her heart, why is it too late for her?"

"Everybody knows the rules: you can't start believing once you're in Hell just because it's obvious you've got it wrong. That wouldn't be fair."

"Fair for whom?"

"For everyone who had believed while they were on Earth."

Jerry waited a moment. "So, once it becomes irrefutable that *all this is real*," he mimicked Rachael's arcing hand movement when he quoted this phrase, "knowing it's true can't save you any more?"

"Objection," said Nathaniel. "Counsel is trying to argue against God's means of providing salvation for mankind which is based on perfect justice and grace."

"Sustained," said Solomon, banging his gavel with something of a flourish.

Jerry walked slowly back to his table, then turned on his heel. "Is that what you think, that God's justice is perfect?" he said, in Fiona's direction but addressing his question more broadly. "What if I could show you that that's not true?"

"*Blasphemy!*" shouted Ephraim, predictably. His shirt gave up the struggle as he ripped it clean off his body and stood panting, naked from the waist up.

"What if God gives evil commands?"

"*Blasphemy!*"

"What if God isn't always just?" exclaimed Jerry loudly, over and above the growing calls for his silence.

"*Blasphemy!*"

"*Objection!*"

"*Sustained!*"

"What if God's moral standards are worse than Rachael's? Then he couldn't possibly judge her!" Jerry had to shout this final sentence but, even so, he was almost drowned out by the furore that erupted around him. Nathaniel, of course, objected and his protest was forcibly upheld by Solomon. Ephraim lost his mind and dignity to incandescent rage. Having already destroyed his shirt he started on his trousers, and made swift work of them, ripping through them like a man possessed. "*Blasphemy! Blasphemy! Blasphemy!*" he shrieked and then proceeded to remove his underpants, biting them with his teeth and pulling them apart with his hands.

The sight of him standing bollock-naked among the jury benches had the effect of stunning the room into near silence. "Blasphemy," he repeated, but more quietly this time and sat down with his head in his hands.

Jerry saw his opportunity. He picked up his Gideon's Bible and opened it at the bookmarked page. By the time the court had focused back on him he had started to read the passage describing the rules for dealing with *a stubborn and rebellious son.* By the time he had concluded with *All Israel will hear of it and be afraid,* nobody was saying anything.

Jerry had thought Solomon might have some kind of explanation for the barbaric verses, although he personally couldn't think of one. Instead, the judge went for a limp denial. "It doesn't say that," he said half-heartedly. He held out his hand to the clerk of the court who handed him the Bible from the witness stand.

"It's Deuteronomy twenty-one, eighteen to twenty-one," said Jerry, able for the first time to turn the tables on Solomon and quote him a Bible reference.

The judge took a long time to read the passage. When he'd finished he handed the book back to the clerk and simply said, "He's right; that is what's written."

Conor was now on his feet, unable to tolerate this challenge to his belief system any longer. "You can't just pluck versus out of Scripture willy-nilly. You have to understand them in their proper context."

"In what context is it morally justified to kill a child for disobedience?" asked Jerry calmly.

"They were drunk and profligate as well, not just disobedient."

"Are you saying that makes it OK to kill them? Is that how you would treat your own children?"

"No, but that was Old Testament times," objected Conor. "The New Testament has done away with all that; we live under grace now, not under the law. The law was for the Jews." He ended his remark with a nod in Rachael's direction.

"Old Testament or not," said Jerry, "there was a time when God thought the best way of dealing with disobedient children was to stone them to death. He was so certain of it that he wrote it into his book."

"No, no, no, this is nonsense," continued the juror. "The command is there just to make people realise how important obedience is. It would never have been carried out in reality, no way."

"You're saying that God would never sanction the killing of children?"

Conor was smiling now, confident of his ground once more. "Of course he wouldn't; he's a God of love, not hate. Why, didn't our Lord even say, *suffer the little children to come unto me*? Luke, chapter eighteen, I think you'll find."

Several of the jurors nodded and someone in the public gallery called out, "Amen." Jerry waited until all was quiet again. He looked at Solomon and said, "I have a witness."

"Really?" said Solomon, clearly surprised.

"I need a television screen," said Jerry. Out of the corner of his eye he saw Nathaniel turn towards him, but Jerry kept his eyes on the judge who looked uncertainly between the two counsels.

"It's not allowed," said Nathaniel.

"Why not? How can justice be done if all the witnesses are not heard?" said Jerry. Nathaniel had no answer. "Please, Solomon," added Jerry, looking straight at the Judge. "It's your court, not his." Saying this he gestured to Nathaniel who scoffed just loud enough for Solomon to hear and thereby make up his mind for him. The judge bent down to confer with the clerk, then straightened up and tapped his gavel. "Call the television," he announced which, in other circumstances, Jerry would have found absurd and funny. As it was he simply mouthed his thanks and went back to his chair.

Everyone seemed to have forgotten about Fiona, who now asked timidly, "Can I go please?" She was led away by one of the officials, her eyes downcast, avoiding Rachael's gaze.

"Did you really tell the office she was pregnant?" Jerry asked Rachael, as the level of background conversation rose in the court and one or two people got up to stretch their legs.

"Yes, I'm afraid I did. It was a complete misunderstanding on my part. I felt awful afterwards and apologised to her straight away, poor girl." Rachael paused and then added ruefully, "I am surprised she testified against me though; I had thought we were friends."

Jerry said nothing but wondered if Fiona had been persuaded by Nathaniel or one of his cronies to take the stand.

"Anyway," added Rachael, "I felt sorry for her then and I feel sorry for her now."

"Why?"

"She never had sex on Earth and you told me that it's not allowed up here, so that's it for poor old Fi, a virgin forever and ever."

Jerry could think of nothing to say, so the two of them sat together and watched while the television was brought in and placed on a table that had been shifted in front of the witness stand. Once it had been plugged in and switched on, Jerry removed his camera and leads from their hiding place in Bob's Bible and made the connections. He stood in front of the screen and waited for silence to return. He sensed hope within himself once again and the responsibility that accompanied it made him suddenly nervous. He felt his mouth turn dry.

Before the anxiety could overwhelm him he looked straight at the jury in their twin pews and forced himself to start speaking. "You all, I'm sure, understand the meaning of Hell. As Christians you must be familiar with the Lake of Fire, the torture, the agony, the suffering. You can imagine what it's like: the screams; the open sores; the skin blistering in the unbearable heat; the unquenchable thirst. Pain without death. Forever."

He waited while they imagined it.

"Well, I paid a visit to Hell recently and that is exactly what you see when you go there." He knew he could describe it thus as no-one who knew the truth about Hell would admit to it in court. He glanced round at Solomon who nodded his agreement. "If you fail to uphold Rachael's appeal today, if you think she has already been fairly sentenced, then she will return to that abominable place. I want you to think about that."

He waited while they thought about it.

"It has been God's judgement that Rachael should, in fact, be in Hell. God, so we are told, judges perfectly. He would not, it has been asserted, demand the killing of innocent children, for example. If he did that, we could conclude that his judgement would be very far from perfect."

"Blasphemy," squealed Ephraim and, as his clothes were in shreds, pulled at his hair to demonstrate his horror at what Jerry had said.

Jerry let him calm down and, pointing to the television, continued. "What I'm going to show you here demonstrates that God has indeed demanded the killing of the innocent, and that those commands have been carried out by his obedient servants. You can trust the testimony of the individual you will see in the film, for reasons that will become immediately obvious. He was there when the atrocities occurred and will give you a first-hand eye-witness account. Once you have seen the evidence you will, I'm sure, agree with me…" Jerry paused once more, "…that our God has no business condemning Rachael to Hell."

The court stirred restlessly. Jerry guessed they could not quite believe what they were hearing. In a moment he suspected they would have difficulty believing what they were seeing too. He pressed the play button on the camera and sat down.

He kept his eyes on the jurors and on Solomon while the brutal scenes were played out. He was glad his mother wasn't here to see them. As it was, Rachael clung to his arm and buried her head in his shoulder at the worst moments. The smashing of his bones was particularly explicit and the jurors cringed at the merciless treatment he received.

When it was over nobody made a sound and an uneasy silence filled the court. Jerry was about to make his final plea when Nathaniel himself got to his feet and stood close to the clerk of the court, who looked understandably terrified. The angel looked at Jerry and said, "You filmed this secretly, without permission?"

"I would have thought that was obvious," replied Jerry.

"Then it is inadmissible as evidence," Nathaniel said coldly, looking assertively at the clerk as he did so.

The clerk nodded rapidly and said, "Yes, that's quite correct. Not allowed."

"What?" shouted Jerry, springing to his feet. "You're going to let God off on a technicality? You can't do that."

"I think you'll find I can," replied Nathaniel.

The court was in uproar. People were shouting, some were even crying, and Solomon banged his gavel ineffectively, calling for order that did not come. What came instead was a posse of angels through both the side doors and through the entrance at the back, behind the public gallery. To his horror he saw that one of the angels had pulled out a canister of Grace spray and was shaking it in readiness for administering the memory-eradicating chemical. The others, now that he looked, were doing the same. All his efforts to save Rachael were going to end in failure: her case was simply going to be bullied out of court.

"Don't do it, you bastards. Stop them, someone! Stop them!" he screamed.

Two powerful angels grabbed him and Rachael from behind and frog-marched them towards the nearest exit. The last image Jerry had of the court was that of Solomon sitting powerless and ashen-faced in his chair as the aerosols hissed and the spray started to engulf the room.

24

Even though there was no point in doing so, Jerry and Rachael struggled with their angelic guards all the way down the corridor until they were unceremoniously shoved inside a circular, white room. Jerry turned and slammed his fist against the curved door, but all his thumping and shouting was to no avail. The door itself had no handle on the inside and neither did either of the other two exits which Jerry quickly discovered and tried unsuccessfully to prise open. He and Rachael realised that, for the time being at least, they were trapped.

"What just happened in the courtroom, Jerry?"

Jerry sighed heavily and stood with his hands on his hips looking around the room. It possessed a certain minimalist beauty. Every surface was smooth and bright, and marked out on the floor was a golden triangle, its three points touching the base of each of the doors. "Well, it looks like they won't accept the video," he began.

"Yes, I heard that," Rachael interrupted. "But when they dragged us out they were spraying something into the room."

"Oh, that's Grace. It'll make all the people there forget everything that happened during the trial. The angels are immune to it, though, so they'll still remember."

Jerry explained what he knew about the spray and why it was used. "It's what Nathaniel dosed me with last night after our little chat."

"You were incredibly brave. It looked like he'd killed you."

Rachael stroked the side of Jerry's face and kissed his lips.

"No, they can't kill you in Heaven. Normally you can't feel pain either but, as you heard, Nathaniel temporarily suspended that particular privilege, so yes, I suppose you're right, I was very brave!"

"My hero," said Rachael, and kissed him longer.

"Let's hope it was…" began Jerry, but couldn't finish the line.

"Worth it?" said Rachael.

They looked deeply into each other's eyes before Rachael turned and walked slowly round the room, tracing her finger along the surface of the walls. She stopped at one of the doors and sat down with her back to it.

"Very hot in here, isn't it?"

"Yes," replied Jerry, suddenly aware that the ambient temperature, for the first time in his experience of Heaven, was not comfortable. He went and sat next to his love.

They remained silent for a while before Jerry noticed his Bible on the floor the other side of Rachael. "How did that get in here?" he asked.

"I grabbed it when they started pulling us out. Not very useful now, I suppose, is it?"

Jerry held out his hand and she passed him the book. He flicked quickly through it a couple of times and on the third attempt he found what he was looking for. He laid the Bible open on his lap at the book of Ecclesiastes and extracted from between its pages the photograph of Rachael that he had taken a whole world away. He gave her the picture and she smiled. "You had this with you all the time?" she asked.

"Yes. It was strictly against the rules, of course. We weren't supposed to bring any personal items with us at all."

He put his arm around Rachael's shoulder and pulled her in close, feeling the warmth of her body next to his. They talked for a while about inconsequential memories, content for a few moments to occupy themselves with thoughts from happier times.

Jerry's eyes drifted down to the text he had first seen when he had hidden Rachael's picture. "But the dead know nothing," he read aloud.

"What?"

"Well, you and I know plenty of dead people who know a lot more than nothing."

"So?"

"So how can this verse be true?"

"It isn't."

"But I have it on very good authority that if it's in the Bible it must be true."

"Who told you that?"

"Jesus," said Jerry.

"Oh, well I suppose that is quite a good authority. Did he tell you personally?"

"Yes. Behind the toilets when he was having a smoke."

Rachael shifted her body position slightly so that she could look at Jerry's face to see whether or not he was teasing her. He didn't appear to be.

"Where are all these dead people who know nothing?" Jerry wondered aloud.

"Perhaps they're off somewhere being permanently sprayed with Grace. Sounds quite nice to me."

"Sounds like oblivion," said Jerry. He mused on the state of nothingness which he had previously assumed he would have been entering at the moment of his death. It wasn't so difficult to imagine: just falling asleep and never waking up. Of course, it would have meant missing out on the beauty of Paradise and the excitement of worship, but Jerry's enthusiasm for the latter had been waning for a while, increasingly so as he had been learning more about the Divinity upon whom Heaven's praise was lavished. When he factored in the agony of separation from his loved ones, the thought of living for eternity in Paradise was starting to lose its appeal and by contrast death, real death, was beginning to have its attractions. Certainly for those in Hell, oblivion, were it attainable, would mean forfeiting the agony of agony, and that didn't seem too bad a deal at all.

They had been quiet for a while, during which time the room appeared to have been getting even warmer. Rachael's hair was clinging to the back of her sweaty neck and she slid away from Jerry a little to try to cool down.

"What do you think they're going to do with us?" she asked.

"I don't know."

Jerry removed his shoes and Rachael her boots. The heat was beginning to become stifling and the two of them started to feel drowsy.

"We shouldn't fall asleep," said Rachael, awakening moments later with a jolt. "Let's keep talking. Where do you think these doors lead to?"

"I don't know."

"Well guess, then. It'll keep us awake."

"OK. That door obviously takes you back to Heaven," he said, pointing to the one they had earlier been bundled through. "The one behind us goes to Hell, and presumably the other one to the State of Grace: to oblivion."

"Oblivion," repeated Rachael. "At least it'll be peaceful there."

Jerry smiled and closed his eyes.

Neither of them knew how long they had dozed for, but it was the smell of smoke that woke Rachael first. She had fallen asleep resting against Jerry and as soon as she was awake she nudged him in the ribs. He opened his eyes and was instantly alert.

"Christ," he said.

"Yes, but you can call me Jesus."

The Smoking Saviour was leaning nonchalantly, with his back against the wall, opposite them. One arm was crossed over his midriff, the elbow of the other resting upon it while he held his cigarette between two fingers and took a long draw.

Jerry and Rachael clambered to their feet. "This is Rachael," said Jerry, temporarily forgetting that introductions were unnecessary in Heaven, especially to its omniscient master.

"Yes, I know," said Jesus, the smoke billowing out of his mouth as he spoke. He walked towards them, looking at Rachael. "The Jew who wasn't interested in being Jewish. I can't say I blame you; I didn't much care for it myself."

The three of them were standing close together now and both Rachael and Jerry could smell the sourness of Jesus' smoker's breath. The Son of God himself turned his attention to Jerry and became more animated.

"Very good idea, Jerry, filming Nathaniel making a complete arse of himself. Pity it couldn't be used as evidence."

"*He* was the one who said it was inadmissible; the clerk just got scared and agreed with him," said Jerry.

"Yes, I know. It's a bit of a bummer when the same individual is judge, jury and executioner, isn't it? Still, it did take him down a peg or two, and not before time. I've been wanting to give him his come-uppance for ages; a humiliation that the other angels would hear about and use to keep him in his place. They can be wonderfully spiteful, you know. It's why I let your trial go on as long as it did – I'm sure you'll understand. I think I'll give him a new job in the Grace factory by way of punishment. The warehouse needs a new supervisor; that should keep him out of mischief for a century or so. They never seem to have enough staff up there. Demand's going through the roof, they tell me. Someone must be making a packet."

Jesus smiled, but the other two remained stony-faced.

The Messiah inhaled from his cigarette once more. "Anyway, as I was saying," he continued, "I don't think anyone's tried catching an angel's indiscretions on film before, so well done for that. Clever line on salvation by faith too. *Why is it that faith counts when it's difficult to believe, but doesn't count when it's easy?* I've often wondered about that myself. Needless to say, it was one of the rules my Old Man insisted on. He thought it would be a good way of keeping people under control. You know, don't question anything or you might lose your faith and with it your salvation. To be fair to him, it does seem to have worked pretty well for the last two thousand years."

"So was Fiona right? Is it too late for me?" asked Rachael.

Jesus furrowed his brow as he took a moment to think. "The bigger question," he said, "is whether or not you want to spend the rest of eternity worshipping and obeying me."

"Why do you *need* that?" said Jerry. "Why would anyone want it?"

"Like father, like son, I guess. I can't help the way I am, Jerry, any more than you can."

"But I don't want subservience. Nobody does. Not unless they're – " Jerry stopped himself just in time.

"Don't kid yourself," said Jesus. "You'd get to like it soon enough." He turned away sulkily and stood at the other side of the room, puffing on his cigarette.

A moment or two later, Rachael asked, "Wouldn't you rather be loved?"

"I want that too," said Jesus.

"Then why don't you do things that would make us love you, instead of the Passover and the Flood and, I don't know, sending people to Hell?" blurted out Jerry, unable to stop himself this time.

"I died for you, you ungrateful little sod. You should love me for that."

"Yes, I'm sure Jerry's very grateful," said Rachael quickly. "But, gratitude isn't the same as love. People don't just fall in love with rescuers, otherwise women would only want to marry firemen. Oh, actually, bad example, we do mostly want to marry firemen, but love is different. We love someone because of who they are, not just because of what they did, even if it was very noble."

"Ah, the flaw in the master plan," said Jesus.

There was silence again in the hot, hot room while the three of them stood thinking.

Then Jesus spoke again. "Everything that Nathaniel said about my Father is true. The Old Bastard really is an old bastard, but nobody wants a God like that. If we were to take your little film and show it on all the TV channels in Paradise, people wouldn't be grateful for the revelation. If they'd thought about it carefully enough, they would have been able to work out for themselves exactly what he's like; what I'm like. But they don't want the truth. They want happiness and laughter and warm feelings inside. That's what we give them, in return for the things we need: worship and obedience. There are worse ways to spend eternity."

Jerry went to speak, but Rachael held onto his arm and shook her head at him.

Jesus stubbed out the remains of his cigarette on the crucifixion scar on his left wrist. "I expect you want to know what happens now," he said.

"Yes, please," said Rachael, trying to keep her anxiety hidden.

"I'll be leaving you shortly, back through the way I came. Then, after a while, all the doors will open and each of you will make a choice about which one you personally want to leave through. One will take you to Heaven, one to Hell, and the other..."

"To oblivion," said Jerry, "where the dead know nothing."

"Yes, quite. We don't advertise that option quite so much, but it's implied in the Bible so we had to put it in. Besides, lots of people use it and find the thought of its finality very comforting."

The implications that he had been correct in his earlier, idle speculation about what was on the other side of the three doors, were hitting home and Jerry's nerves were starting to fray. He held Rachael's hand; it was moist and trembling.

"What about Rachael?" said Jerry with an unsteady voice. "Can she choose Heaven?"

"I suppose so," said Jesus casually. "She does believe, after all."

"You can do that for her? You can just let her in, even though her name's not in the *Book of Life*?"

"I'm the Lord of the Universe, Jerry. I can do what the fuck I like."

Jerry's body tensed up as he fought to stay in control of his emotions. The frustration and pain and desperate sadness of his lost life, his lost friends, his lost understanding, welled up within him like dark, bitter bile. The ineffable burden of living an endless life crushed his mind, and the cruel indifference of God's injustice broke his heart. Tears and sweat ran down his face and anger burst from the depths of his being as he yelled at the Son of God, "Then let everyone in, you worthless piece of shit. Her parents, my father, the bloody witch, my friends, the fucking Muslims! Why can't they all come, you..." Jerry hammered his fists into his forehead, "... you bastard," he sobbed.

Jesus looked blankly at Jerry and no-one spoke. Jerry turned away and faced the wall and Rachael came and put a hand on his shoulder.

After a while, Jesus spoke again. "Put your shoes back on. You mustn't leave anything behind. You need to make up your minds soon, otherwise I'll send the angels back in and they'll decide for you; not that you'll be able to stand this heat much longer."

Neither Rachael nor Jerry turned around. They heard a door open and shut. Jesus had gone, and in a very little while they had to make the most momentous decision of their lives.

"You OK?" asked Rachael, gently stroking Jerry's back.

"Sure."

"That was quite a speech you made."

"Yeah. I thought it would be good if I buttered him up."

Jerry turned and embraced Rachael. She laid her head on his chest and he held her close.

"Is, *you piece of shit*, a standard part of church liturgy?" Rachael asked.

"*Worthless* piece of shit," corrected Jerry. "Probably not, no."

"There'll be a reason for that."

A few moments went by in silence.

"In a way, I feel sorry for him," said Rachael. "Jesus, I mean."

"Uh-huh."

"What with a father like that and being surrounded by nothing but sycophants, no wonder he's a bit screwed up."

"Yes."

"Maybe it would have been different if he'd known the love of a good woman."

"Maybe."

"Or man."

"Yes, or man."

The discomfort of their shared body heat forced them apart.

"He did say that we could choose any of the doors, didn't he?" said Rachael.

"Yes, he did."

"So I could go to Heaven if I wanted?"

"Yes."

"In a way we won my appeal, then."

"I suppose we did."

Rachael stood on tip-toe and kissed him. "Go us," she said, and smiled.

Without saying why, but knowing just the same, Rachael put on her boots and Jerry his trainers. It was nearly time.

"If I did choose Heaven, I couldn't be happy there without my parents," said Rachael.

"I know. Maybe we could get them a trial, like we planned, and then my dad and all the others," said Jerry. "We've no guarantee that they'd win their appeals, though. Especially my dad; I haven't knowingly met a single gay up here yet. I don't think they'd be very tolerant of the way he is. But Heaven isn't Paradise without the ones you love."

"And Hell isn't Paradise no matter who you're with."

"Maybe if I was there with you," began Jerry.

"Jerry! It's called Hell for a reason. The pain and suffering goes on forever. There's no escape. It's a terrible, terrible place, believe me. And besides, think of the anguish you'd put your mother through if she knew you were there."

"We're damned if we do and damned if we don't. No wonder people take the oblivion door: at least once they've done that they're not aware of the pain they may be causing others."

"Christ, Jerry, what are we going to do?" said Rachael, panic straining her voice.

Then, she screamed. The three doors were opening.

They held onto each other until the doors were fully open. The stink from Hell mixed with the fragrance of Heaven and the mid-winter-cold freshness of oblivion. Jerry made a move but Rachael held him tight.

"It's OK," he said. "It'll be all right."

Rachael let out a long, anguished groan. "I love you," he said, over and over and over again.

Eventually, Rachael released her grip and Jerry kissed the top of her head. They had run out of time and a sudden calm came over them both.

"He gave us a choice," said Jerry. "A free choice."

"I know."

"It's just a few steps."

Rachael nodded. Without a word being said they both knew what they had decided because, in the end, there was no real choice to make.

No choice at all.

Biography

Paul Beaumont became a Christian as a thoughtful, insecure sixteen-year old. In exchange for worship and unquestioning obedience, Jesus gave him purpose, meaning and girlfriends. It seemed a good bargain at the time but, twenty-five years later, having lived all those years as a faithful servant of the Lord, Paul ended his relationship with Jesus and won back full custody of his life. There were no hard feelings on either side.

A Brief Eternity is Paul's debut novel and draws on many of the lessons he learned in the strange and idiosyncratic world of Christian fundamentalism.

Paul's career has been spent in industry. He is currently saving the world by working in the renewable energy sector.

www.paulbeaumont.org

Lightning Source UK Ltd.
Milton Keynes UK
UKHW040628150420
361732UK00001B/55